LUKAS

ASHES & EMBERS BOOK 3

CARIAN COLE

COPYRIGHT

LUKAS
ashes & embers series, book three
Copyright © 2015 by Carian Cole
All Rights Reserved.
Edited by: Loredana Elsberry Schwartz
Front cover photography by Eric David Battershell
Models: Bobby Gerrity & Kendal Barnes

No part of this book may be reproduced in any form or by any electronic or mechanical means, including information storage and retrieval systems, without written permission from the author, except for the use of brief quotations in a book review.

This is a work of fiction. The names, characters, incidents, and places are products of the author's imagination, and are not to be construed as real except where noted and authorized. Any resemblance to persons, living or dead, or actual events are entirely coincidental. Any trademarks, service marks, product names, or names featured are assumed to be the property of their respective owners, and are used only for reference. There is no implied endorsement if any of these terms are used.

The author acknowledges the trademarked status and trademark owners of various products referenced in this work, which have been used without permission. The publication/use of these trademarks is not authorized, associated with, or sponsored by the trademark owners.

This book is intended for mature audiences.

A thirty-six year old mother of two finds out life isn't over after divorce when a sexy twenty-four year old tattoo artist kisses her senseless under a shooting star.

Ivy thought she had it all—married to her highschool sweetheart, two great kids, and a beautiful house. But her world comes crashing down when she catches her husband with another woman.

When her best friend gives her a gift certificate to a local tattoo parlor to cheer her up, Ivy gets a helluva lot more when inked-up Lukas Valentine—renowned tattoo artist, violin player extraordinaire, and extreme hopeless romantic—captures her heart.

Lukas is an old soul with a heart of gold. When Ivy walks into his shop, he's instantly drawn to her shy smile and down to earth personality. Tired of the dating scene, Lukas is ready to settle down, and he's hell-bent on making Ivy believe they can have the happily ever after they both dream about—with each other.

Despite their age difference, the chemistry and love they share is undeniable. Lukas is everything Ivy never knew she wanted, but can she trust her heart with a much younger man, and can they overcome the hurdles that life keeps throwing in their way?

** *Lukas can be read stand-alone*

DEDICATION

To Tyler, for the creative inspiration

CHAPTER 1

IVY

"Baby, I miss you so much," his voice is raspy with strained desire.

I press the phone to my ear, my heart pounding, a thin sheen of sweat spreading over my skin.

"I miss you, too, more than ever." My fingers tighten around the phone.

"Just wait 'til I get my hands on you tomorrow night. You'd better get a lot of rest tonight because you're going to need it. I'm gonna fuck you so hard you're not gonna be able to walk 'til Monday."

My breath catches and I cover my mouth with my hand. *Tomorrow night. Friday night.*

"Oooh . . . let's just forget dinner and spend the night in bed."

"Mmm, baby, I like the way you think," he sighs into the phone. "I better go now. I'll see you tomorrow."

"I love you." My stomach twists into a knot.

"I love you, too, babe," he says back.

The words are so familiar to me; he's said them to me

thousands of times. But this time, he's not saying them to me, and that's not my voice saying it back. I have said them, many times. But not this time.

This time, there's someone else hearing and saying those words with *my* husband.

I wait for him to hang up before I gently press the end button and put the phone back in its charger next to the bed, my hand trembling so violently that I almost drop it. Hot tears burn in my eyes and spill down my cheeks. Grabbing a tissue from the nightstand, I dab my eyes and run for the master bathroom as I hear him coming down the hall toward our bedroom.

I sit on the edge of the bathtub, trembling, my mind racing, trying to somehow make sense of what I just heard. It must be some sort of mistake. Or a joke. I did *not* just hear my husband on our telephone, at midnight, telling another woman he loves her and he's going to see her tomorrow night.

He misses her.

He loves her.

She loves him.

He's going to fuck her hard.

I lurch toward the toilet and vomit up eighteen years of trust, devotion, commitment, and love.

Now all that's left is lies.

"Ivy . . . are you alright?" The doorknob rattles. "Babe, why is the door locked?"

I wipe my face with a cold, damp washcloth and take a deep shaky breath. "I'm not feeling well. Go to bed."

"Can I get you anything? Unlock the door. I don't want you locked in the bathroom while you're sick."

Still sitting on the floor in front of the toilet, I reach over to unlock the door, and he immediately comes in, standing over me.

"What's wrong?" He squints at me in the bright light of the bathroom. "You were fine a little while ago. Did you eat something bad?"

No. I married something bad.

Concern is all over his face, and it looks sincere, causing my stomach to turn again at the thought of how long he's been lying to me. Right to my face. As I kneel on the floor, I vomit again, and he takes a step backward. My head spins round and round. *He loves her. He misses her. She loves him. Friday night. He's supposed to love me. Only me.*

Earlier, he mentioned having to work late tomorrow night. He's been working nights and weekends for a long time, leaving me and the kids here alone.

He was with her.

Of course.

As I continue to wretch, more signs flood through my mind like evil flash cards.

Strange expenses on our credit cards.

Long nights at the office.

A short temper with the children.

Avoiding family outings.

Lack of interest in sex. *Only with me, apparently.*

My stomach heaves again.

"Ivy, you're worrying me. You never get sick." He fills a

small paper bathroom cup with water and hands it to me. "Try to drink a little water."

Taking the cup, I peer up at him and start to sob. I've loved Paul for eighteen years, and never once in all that time have I ever doubted him in any way. *Not once.*

Confusion shrouds his face. "Are you crying? What's wrong?"

"I heard you." My voice is a scratchy whisper, my throat raw from dry heaving. I take a few sips of water, my hand shaking as I hold the tiny cup and wait for him to say something.

"Heard me what?"

"You, while you were downstairs on the phone." I swallow back the acid in my mouth. "With another woman."

His skin pales, and his hand goes to clutch the back of his head like he does when he's mad or upset. "Fuck." He closes his eyes for a moment and then opens them slowly to meet mine. "You were eavesdropping on me?"

I stare at him in disbelief. "Are you serious? That's all you can say? No, I wasn't eavesdropping. I saw the phone light up and thought one of the kids was calling somebody."

He blows out a deep breath. "I'm sorry. I'm so sorry, Ivy." He paces the small room. "We have to talk. I didn't want you to find out like this." *Oh, God. He's not even denying it.*

I stand up and wobble on my legs for a second before pushing past him into the bedroom. The bathroom is suddenly a way too personal space to be sharing with him. I sit on the edge of the bed, stunned that he hasn't denied anything. *Why isn't he denying it? This is the part where I find out it was some kind of misunderstanding.*

"Paul, what's going on?" More tears stream down my face.

"Please tell me I'm hallucinating or something, or that this is some kind of misunderstanding."

He sits on the bed about three feet away from me. "Ivy, I'm so sorry—"

"You're sleeping with another woman? You love her?" I demand, crying harder.

He rubs his forehead. "I don't think we should talk about this when you just got sick."

"I just got sick *because* of this."

He looks at me and then quickly looks down at the floor like he can't stand to see the sight of me. "I'm sorry. I didn't want you to find out this way," he says again, his voice low.

My stomach pitches, and new tears spill from my eyes.

"Did you want me to find out at all? Or were you just going to keep seeing her behind my back?"

Still staring at the floor, he shakes his head. "I really don't know."

"So it's true?" My body trembles uncontrollably as reality starts to edge back in.

The man I've loved since high school looks me in the eyes and nods his head. "Yes, I've been having an affair."

My heart and stomach both sink, and then rage boils up inside me.

"Are you kidding me?" I hiss, trying not to yell. "I've been having a physical relationship with the detachable showerhead for a year now while you've been with another woman?" All this time, I assumed that his lack of sexual interest in me was due to him working too hard and dealing with too much stress. I never once even considered he was having an affair.

"Please don't yell. I don't want the kids to hear this." He glances toward the hallway. "I didn't plan any of this. You know how I feel about infidelity. I hate it . . . but it just happened."

I let out a half-hysterical laugh. "Really? How exactly did it just happen, Paul? Who is she?"

"The hygienist at the dentist office," he admits quietly, not meeting my eyes.

I cannot even fathom how anyone could be attracted to someone while they are scraping plaque and other ickiness from their gum line. The visual of it almost makes me laugh.

"I can't believe this. The hygienist?" Despite the fact that she's had her fingers in his mouth, as well as mine and my children's, I have to admit she's young, thin, gorgeous, and bubbly. She's the kind of woman that all men want and all women hate but secretly want to be.

"She's like twenty-two years old, Paul. What's happened to you? Cheating on me for a year? Leaving me and the kids every weekend while you spend time with her?! Lying to all of us? What the hell is wrong with you?"

He sits there staring at the floor and doesn't say a word. I want him to give me some kind of answer, some kind of explanation. But he gives me nothing.

I grab another tissue and blow my nose, hating that I'm crying in front of him because I am not a pretty crier, and now I suddenly feel ashamed to look like a mess in front of him.

"So now what?" I ask, even though I don't want to hear the answer at all, because I already know what's coming. "What do we do now?"

"We don't have to talk about that right now. I think you've had enough for today. Why don't you—"

I slam my hand on the nightstand, making him jump. "Don't coddle me, Paul! Just say it. I don't want to drag this on.

This is killing me inside. Do you even see that? Do you even care?"

"Of course I care, Ivy. I care about you and the kids more than anything in the world."

"Apparently not, or we wouldn't be sitting here discussing your affair."

He ignores my sarcasm. "You know I care about you and the kids. I always will. But I think we've grown apart over the past few years. You've said it yourself a few times. We barely see each other. We argue-"

"We barely see each other? Paul, you're never home. I'm always here with the kids! You're either working, or I guess, lately, you've been out dating, having wild sex, and having a fun life with someone else while you forget you have a family at home. The only reason we argue is because you're never here! Don't you dare try to blame this on 'us'. I've been a good wife and mother. I've never strayed. I take care of everything around here."

He closes his eyes for a long time and nods. "You're right. You are, and I know that. You've always been a great wife, and you're a terrific mom." He shakes his head slowly, still looking at the floor, which seems to be the only place his eyes can focus on now. "I guess I just started to want something more, or different, than that."

I stare at this stranger who has taken over my husband's body. "More? What does that even mean? We have two beautiful children and a nice house. Both of us have good jobs. We've been in a relationship for twenty years, eighteen of which we've been married! We have everything you've said you always wanted. What more do you want?"

His face contorts with exasperation and confusion. "I don't know, Ivy. This is hard for me, too. I love you and the kids. I'm very torn. I just . . . I don't even know how to explain it. I guess I just want something different. When I met Charlene, it's like everything I thought I wanted…changed. I don't know how to explain it."

"That's just great. I'm glad to hear that Charlene has led you to the path of true happiness and saved you from your boring, torturous life here with your family. I'm sure her sexy body had absolutely nothing to do with any of it." I hurl my tissue into the small garbage pail next to the nightstand.

"That's not true, and I didn't mean it like that. Maybe because I've only ever been with you, I got restless. Don't you ever wonder what it would be like to be with someone else?"

I turn to stare at him. "So you got bored sleeping with me and had to have some twenty year old? Someone you could fuck so hard they couldn't walk? Is that what you said to her? When did you become a pig? And no, I've never thought about being with another man. Unlike you, I've always been more than happy with exactly what I have, even though you've never fucked me so hard I couldn't walk. In fact, most times, you can barely stay awake to finish the job."

He winces at my comment but reaches for my hand. I quickly pull away. "Don't touch me, Paul."

"I'm trying to apologize."

"Don't. That's not even possible. What are you going to do now? What do you want?" I repeat.

He sighs and looks around our bedroom like he's never been here before. "I don't think it's right for me to stay here anymore with all this going on. I'm going to leave and come back tomorrow to pack some things, and if it's okay with you, I'll come back with a truck next weekend for the rest of my stuff. We should probably talk to a lawyer. I promise I'll take care of you and the kids. You don't have to worry." I can tell by the way he's talking that he's thought about all of this before. He's mulled it around in his mind, trying to figure out what to say and what to do, and now he's just reciting it.

Divorce. He's divorcing me. *And I don't have to worry.* He doesn't even want to try to make our marriage work. I am floored that he can throw eighteen years of marriage away over some girl he barely knows, who is only a few years older than his own daughter.

I shake my reeling head slowly. "Just like that? We're over? You don't even want to try to fix this? We could try couples therapy. Lots of people do that. It's nothing to be ashamed of, and they're very discrete—"

"Ivy, I've been sleeping with another woman for a year. How do we fix that?"

The brutality of his words stuns me. I lost a year of my marriage without even knowing it. How did I not know? How did I miss all the signs?

"I thought you loved me." My voice cracks. "I thought we loved each other." I realize I sound pathetic, but I can't stop the words that shoot from my heart to my mouth, no matter how much I don't want to say them right now.

"I *do* love you, but I somehow fell in love with her, too." He walks slowly to the closet that we share and throws some clothes into his gym bag. "This has been a mess for me, too, Ivy. It's been destroying me inside to lie to you for so long. I know you don't deserve it, and I hate hurting you."

"Then why did you? Why couldn't you just stay committed to us? Why would you let someone come between us?"

He approaches me with his overstuffed bag in his hand. "I don't know. I wish I had a better answer, but I don't. I never wanted to hurt you. Ever. One thing just kept leading to another. You're right—I should have stopped it. I'm an asshole. I know that."

"So you want to leave me and the kids? For her?" I demand.

"Not *for* her. But for now, I think I need to leave. And I'm not leaving the kids. I'm still their father."

My heart cracks and shatters into a million little isolated memories of our life together, splattering like blood at a brutal crime scene. This will never be able to be cleaned up or put back together again. He's obliterated it.

His eyes are on me as I fall apart. I know he can't see it, but all my hopes and dreams of growing old together with the man I love are climbing into that bag with him to be given to someone else.

"Is it because I'm not as thin as I was?" I ask him, my voice shaking. "I can join a gym, buy new clothes—"

"Ivy, God . . . no. You're beautiful, and I still love you. It's not that at all."

I shake my head slowly back and forth as I try to grasp what's happening to us. "I just don't understand what I did wrong."

He takes a few steps closer to me. "You didn't do anything wrong, I swear to you. I didn't plan it, and I wasn't looking for it. Actually, she kinda reminds me of you when we were young. She's happy and carefree. I like being with her and not having kids screaming and fighting, or on the other side of the bedroom wall, blasting video games and music. I'm sorry."

"You wanted kids, Paul. They make noise."

"I know that. But come on, Ivy. We had Macy when you were eighteen and I was nineteen. We were way too young to have a baby. We never got to enjoy ourselves or each other. And as soon as she was able to be by herself a little bit and not need one-hundred percent of your attention, Tommy came along. I guess I want to have fun for a little while, while I'm still young."

"You should leave now." My voice is dull, lifeless. I refuse to look at him. I've had enough. His resentment toward his own family is making me hate him, and I want to inflict some sort of bodily harm on him.

He hesitates for a moment and then just turns and leaves. His footsteps pound down the stairs, and the front door squeaks opens, then closes. His car door slams and then backs out of our driveway, the headlights flashing across the bedroom windows.

And he's gone. Just like that.

I sit on the bed, staring at the wall in a daze, until the sun comes up, wondering what the heck just happened.

CHAPTER 2

LUKAS

Insomnia is a bully of the worst kind. Pushing me. Shoving me. Laughing in my face. Waiting 'til I feel safe and then kicking me in the skull. I fight back, but we all know how this story goes—the bully wins.

So I lay awake, staring at my cathedral ceiling and feeling uncomfortable in my own bed. Not just because I can't sleep, but because there's a chick next to me that I know I'm never going to sleep with again. I want to love her. I *should* love her. She's cute with a banging body and long silky black hair with blue highlights. Her eyes are like fucking sapphires, and she has a giggle that sounds like a demented elf. She's a musician, like me, so she gets me. She knows when to stay and when to go away, and she sucks me like I'm a cherry lollipop.

There's just one thing that's wrong.

Rolling over toward me, her lips press against my cheek. "You're so much nicer in bed than Vandal ever was." I feel her lips turn into a smile as she snuggles against my shoulder.

Yup. That's the thing that's wrong—she slept with my older brother a few times. Actually, I'm pretty sure sleeping wasn't involved at all while he had her tied to his bed being *vandal*ized, as he so nicely puts it. Even though I've tried, I just can't get that out of my head. I don't want to be second choice, or get my brother's leftovers. Who would want to always be compared to his brother? I don't want to be with a woman that Vandal has seen naked and violated. I want someone that's just ... mine.

I sit up, slowly untangling myself from her, and try to find my clothes in the dark room.

"Where you going?" Her hand lands on my back, her voice drowsy as she fights off sleep.

I turn toward her, dreading that I'm going to upset her, but I feel like the band-aid ripping approach is probably best.

"Rio, I can't do this anymore," I say softly.

"Do what?"

"This. Us."

Bolting up, she holds the sheet against her naked chest. "Why?" Her bright blue eyes darken.

"I really like you. You're one of my best friends ... it's just not going past that for me. I wish it was."

Her usually pretty face falls into a sad frown. "Lukas ... I love being with you. Maybe we just need some more time. Don't think about it going any further, just let it happen."

I slowly shake my head. "I won't do that to you." Standing, I pull on my jeans. "I'm sorry. The last thing I want to do is hurt you."

"That's what I love most about you," she says wistfully. "You're the only one that actually cares and doesn't treat me like a toy."

I hate that my brother has boned every chick within a hundred mile radius, and I hate myself even more for not being able to move past it.

She crawls across the bed toward me, her long dark hair forming a silk curtain over her tits. "Lukas, it's all right if you don't love me. I can deal with that. Really." Hope and desperation taint her voice, and it upsets me to hear that in her. She's so much better than that; she just doesn't know it yet.

Picking her clothes up off my bedroom floor, I place them next to her so she can get dressed. "It's not all right with me," I say. "And you deserve more. Don't settle, okay? You don't have to. The right guy will come, trust me. And he's going to be lucky as hell."

"I doubt it," she replies, slipping her shirt over her head.

"I'll wait in the living room for you, and I'll take you home."

"Lukas?" Her soft voice stops me before I get to the bedroom door. "There might not be a right one for any of us. Maybe that's just a myth, ya know?"

Maybe so, but I believe in the mythical and have faith in the legends of time. Fantasy drips through my veins. It's what's kept me alive.

CHAPTER 3

IVY

If someone had told me a few months ago that my husband was going to leave me for another woman, I would have laughed in their face. To say I was completely blindsided would be an understatement. While Paul got to move in to a nice new condo, buy new furniture, date a pretty young woman, and start a new exciting life of fun with the bubbly, younger-me clone, my life turned into a mess of stress and confusion. It seems unfair to me, that he's the one who did something wrong here, but I'm the one suffering. Having to tell our seven-year-old son and seventeen-year-old daughter that their father moved out was the worst thing I've ever had to do. How convenient that Paul didn't have to see the shock and devastation on their faces or answer their endless questions.

Having Paul in the house again a few weeks after he officially moved out to pack his things was another slam to my heart. He left almost everything that I mistakenly thought held meaning to us, or might hold some kind of sentimental value to him—wedding pictures, vacation pictures of us with the kids, and souvenirs from trips we took. He left paintings and decor items that we picked out together, even silly things we had from our first dates when we were in high school. I can't understand why he wouldn't want anything from our life together, as if he intends to just forget we were ever a couple.

My best friend Lindsay has been coming over almost every day after work to check on me. I've never been depressed before, or had any reason to worry about my life and my future, but now, I'm consumed with it. Paul totally ripped the rug out from under me, and I'm feeling stuck in a sort of odd hazy limbo, unsure what I'm supposed to do next.

"Sam has this really good looking friend who recently separated from his wife." Lindsay gives me a sly grin while we sip coffee in my kitchen.

I roll my eyes at her. "Lindsay, please. I don't want to be set up on any dates, especially with someone who also just got separated, because he's either been screwed over and is in a slump like me, or he's the evil-doer. I don't want any part of it."

"Live a little. You can't sit in this house forever. You're just getting more depressed and gaining weight. Don't let that asshole win."

Her words hurt, even though I know she doesn't mean them to be offensive. "Thanks, Lin. I gained ten pounds, not fifty. I'll lose it."

"I know you will, hon. I'm just worried about you. I want you to be happy. The best way to get over someone is to get on top of someone else. You're so pretty. Lots of men would love to hook up with you."

"Mommy, what's hook up?" I look down at Tommy, who has quietly materialized next to me.

I shoot daggers at Lindsay and stroke his head. "It means go to dinner, honey. Why don't you go start your homework?"

He makes a face and trudges off to the living room. As soon as he's out of earshot, I turn to Lindsay again. "Please watch what you say around him. He's really confused about what's going on. And I'm not getting on top of someone else!"

"I'm sorry. I didn't even see him come in. Why can't your kids be noisy like mine?"

"Trust me, they make noise. They've both been a little crazy since Paul moved out."

"They'll adjust. That's what kids do."

I rearrange the fruit in the bowl at the center of the table. "They want him to come back. They ask me all the time when he's coming back home."

"And you? Do you want him to come back, too?"

I focus on an apple and shrug. "I don't know . . . maybe. I miss him. I miss our life together, having a partner. Or at least the delusion I had a partner, in my case. I don't want to grow old alone."

"Ivy. No." She pulls my hand away from the apple. "Stop touching the fruit and listen to me. I know you miss him and this whole thing sucks. You're the sweetest, most devoted person I've ever met. Don't you dare let him come back after doing this to you. You have to focus on *you* now. You've never done that." Her wedding rings dig into my fingers as she squeezes my hand. "You always put him first, and the kids first. Hell, you even put me first. You have to put *you* first now. You have to be Ivy without Paul, and I know that's scary, but you *have* to find out who *you* are. Do the things you've always wanted to do. Color your hair, get your nails done, buy some funky clothes, get a puppy, get a tattoo. Get all the things you've always wanted but he didn't like. Go out and let yourself meet new men. Let the real Ivy out."

"You don't think I'm real?"

"Of course you are, but how many things have you not done because he didn't like it, like not coloring your hair because he thought it was a waste of money? I want you to let the real you out now that you don't have to worry about him censoring you."

I smile weakly at her. "I've always wanted to color my hair that pretty red color, or ombre, or whatever it's called. And I've wanted a tattoo forever. And a puppy . . . I always thought the kids should grow up with a dog."

She grabs her purse and starts rifling through it, piling things onto the table as she rummages. "Go to the salon next week and get your hair and nails done. And . . . I have the perfect tattoo artist for you. I won this gift certificate, actually, for a tattoo with him. He's a friend of a friend. His work is amazing. He mostly works on musicians and models and people like that, and I am now giving you my gift certificate." She hands me the gift card and I take it hesitantly. "I want you to do this. For you."

I bite my lip as I stare at the card. "I don't know, Lindsay. A tattoo . . . at my age?"

"For the love of fuck, you're thirty-six, not a hundred. Everyone has a tattoo."

"Who's getting a tattoo?" Macy walks into the room and heads straight for the fridge, a beautiful blur of long light brown hair and big blue innocent eyes.

"I'm trying to tell your mom she's not too old for a tattoo,"

Lindsay replies while stuffing her belongings back into her purse.

Macy stares at me with her mouth open. "Mom! You're getting a tattoo? That's so cool. Can I get one too?"

"Not until you're eighteen."

She rolls her eyes dramatically. "What*ever*. Can I go with you and watch?"

"I'll think about it. Do me a favor and go check on your brother. Make sure he's okay with his homework."

"Don't bring her with you," Lindsay says when Macy leaves the room. "You need to do some things as *you* and not as Mom."

"Anything else? When did you become my life coach?" I tease, knowing she's right. I need to learn to do things on my own as a single woman, and not as a wife or mother, which will be way easier said than done since I've been both since I was eighteen. I don't know how to be anything else.

She stands and comes around the table to give me a hug. "I don't want you in a rut, that's all." She pulls away and smooths my hair. "You're so cute, Ivy. Please do the things we talked about. Now, I better head home and feed my family."

"Okay. I love you. Say hi to Sam and the kids for me."

"I will, and think about getting on top of someone else, too. A good sexy fling could really cheer you up."

"Go." I point to the door, laughing at her.

CHAPTER 4

IVY

You can do this. You can do this. With each step from the parking lot to the sidewalk, I flip-flop back and forth between forcing myself forward to the studio and running back to my car, driving home, and spending the rest of the night eating ice cream while curled up in bed with a book.

Just as Lindsay described, the building is very unique. It appears to have been a chapel or church at one point in its life, with grey stone exterior, stained glass windows, and a steeple on the roof. A stone sign on the front lawn has Hearts & Arrows Tattoo Studio engraved in large flourishy, old English lettering that appears to be made of old wrought iron pieces. My heels click on the slate walkway as I approach a huge red wooden door with metal gothic accents. Taking a deep breath, I push the heavy door open, a cowbell announcing my entrance. I wince at the sound. No turning back now.

"I'll be right there!" The words bellow from another part of the building beyond the foyer.

The interior of the studio is nothing like I expected.

Actually, I'm not sure what I was expecting. I guess I assumed it would be like the cold, dirty looking tattoo places I've seen in movies—large men with long, scraggly beards smoking cigars and hanging around looking sketchy. Hearts & Arrows is a mixture of luxurious Gothic and Victorian decor, with dark hardwood floors, and a red velvet antique couch with matching chairs in the waiting area. Artwork in ornate vintage gold frames hang on the walls. Picking up one of the aged leather bound photo albums from the mahogany coffee table, I realize it's a portfolio of the artist's tattoos and slowly flip the pages, impressed with his designs. The detail and shading are intricate and very realistic, especially the portrait tattoos of people and pets, which look like real photographs. Lindsay was right—this guy is truly gifted. My nervousness starts to ease up a little, knowing that at least the tattoo will be beautiful if I don't pass out and make an idiot of myself.

"Okay . . ." He comes out from behind the large thick curtain divider and stands behind the glass counter in the waiting area. "You must be Ivy, my six-thirty? You're my gift card winner."

"That's me." I put the book down and turn fully toward him, and the moment our eyes meet, an odd sensation comes over me. A warmth sparks deep in my core and seeps to my heart, creating a flutter that spreads throughout my body.

Deep chocolate truffle eyes lock on to mine, while a crooked smile and curious tilt of his head tells me he feels it, too. In fact, I'm pretty sure he feels exactly what I'm feeling, judging by the entranced expression on his face.

He clears his throat nervously and extends his tattoo-covered arm and hand to me. "I'm Lukas. Have we met before?" Slipping my hand into his, that strange feeling buzzes through me, stronger now that we're touching. Grounding myself, I take in the sight of him. He's young, I'd guess early twenties, and he's covered in tattoos. A faded grey t-shirt stretches over his broad chest and toned muscular shoulders, revealing full-sleeved artwork. His hair is long, a bit past his shoulders, and jet black with razored edges. A silver barbell piercing decorates his eyebrow and a hoop hooks through his lower lip. His eyes are dark with amber flecks—what we gals would describe as bedroom eyes. Way too sexy to be looking into for long periods of time. He holds on to my hand for a few moments longer than what would be the norm, then slowly lets go.

"No," I answer softly, unable to pull my eyes from his.

Although something about him *feels* familiar, I know for a fact I've never seen him before. I would definitely remember him. Even though I've never been attracted to someone like him before, he definitely has something going on about him that's warming my insides in a very foreign way and throwing me off my inner axis.

An adorable boyish smile slowly spreads across his lips. "You look so familiar." He shakes his head, sending his shaggy hair flying around like a black halo. "So, you ready?" His voice is raspy, kinda like when you've been at a concert all night screaming.

"I think so," I reply, smiling back. "This is my first . . . I'm a little nervous." I clutch the bag I brought with me that has a pair of shorts and socks for me to change into, which he suggested when we emailed earlier this week.

He gestures with his hand for me to follow him behind the dark heavy curtain. "I love virgins. Don't be nervous. You'll be fine. I'll go nice and gentle. If you want to change into shorts, there's a bathroom right through that curtain there. Just make a left."

. . .

I quickly change my clothes and return to his work area, smiling nervously at him as I climb into the chair. He already has all his tools laid out on his workbench: the gun, itty-bitty cups of ink, and paper towels. Rock music is playing in the background, too, which I don't recall hearing earlier, and incense is burning in the corner. He snaps on a pair of black latex gloves like a gothic surgeon and swivels his stool toward me.

"I have your sketch here," he says, " . . . and I gotta say. I really like it, and I think you're gonna love it."

He holds up a large piece of tracing paper for me to look at. It bears a design that I simply described to him via email a week earlier—a vine that swirls from the very top of my outer thigh down to my ankle, with swirly pieces that have different colored jewel-like flowers, as well as tiny butterflies and hummingbirds scattered about with wispy fillers. His sketch is an amazing work of art in itself. In fact, it's so beautiful that I want to frame it and hang it on the wall at home. Somehow, he has captured exactly what I envisioned in my head.

Speechless, I stare at his drawing for a few moments. "Wow . . . it's perfect." I'm a bit nervous that it's such a big tattoo for my first, but I don't want to get some little tiny meaningless tattoo to 'practice' with before this one. I want something that's worth it, something I'm committed to, that symbolizes the new me.

Grinning, he tapes it up to the wall next to the chair. "I tattoo freehand. That means I don't sketch it out on you first, like an outline, and then fill it in. Instead, I tattoo just like I would draw or paint on paper and canvas."

"Oh . . . so, what if you make a mistake?" I ask.

LUKAS

Laughing a little, he shakes his head. "You're the first person to ever ask me that."

Leave it to me to be the first idiot to offend this amazing artist. "I'm sorry." My eyes glance back to his sketch. "I didn't mean it as an insult. Just curiosity, I guess."

"Hey, I'm not offended at all," he answers. "I admire cautious people who aren't afraid to ask questions, especially about some guy marking their body for life."

I wait for him to continue, but he doesn't. "Well?" I urge, raising my eyebrows up at him. "What happens if you make a mistake? Is there some kind of eraser thing?"

He looks at me sideways and winks. "I don't make mistakes. And if I did? I'd do it so well you wouldn't even realize it happened."

"I see," I grin, admiring his confidence.

"Some things in life, you just can't do over. They're meant to be permanent, whether they're what we expected or not. Doesn't mean they're a mistake."

I blink at him, allowing his words to sink in. "Very wise words, Lukas. Impressive."

"Yeah, I'm like a walking fortune cookie. It's from reading too much."

"You can never read too much. How does that saying go? 'He who reads lives a thousand lives'?"

He nods and gives me his crooked yet very charming and still hauntingly familiar grin.

"So much truth in words, Ivy."

Looking me over, he nods his head to the music and scoots closer. "Okay . . . why don't you lay on your left side . . . the chair reclines back like a bed." He flips a lever, leaning the chair back, then puts his hand on me and guides my leg slightly. "Is that comfortable for you, for now?" he asks.

I nod, a little flustered at his hand on my thigh. "Yes, it should be."

"Alrighty, you let me know if you start to feel uncomfortable or woozy or any stuff like that, okay? I brought you a bottle of water, too, in case you get thirsty."

"Thank you. That's very thoughtful." I rest my head against my bent-up arm and bite my lip nervously, eyeing him and all his apparatus. I feel like I'm at a strange doctor's appointment.

As he brings the gun to my flesh, I clench my teeth, bracing myself for the unknown.

The first few seconds, I want to scream and kick him in the face. It burns. It's noisy. And holy shit, it hurts. How the hell do people do this? *WHY* do people do this? I try not to move my leg, and wonder how safe this is. It feels like he is literally digging a hole straight through my leg.

He stops and looks up at me, peeking out from under the hair that has fallen across his face, and once again, I'm overcome by that bizarre feeling. My heart just seems to freeze . . . and then jumps back to its rhythm again. I blink at him, trying to bring myself back to normalcy.

"Ivy . . . you doing okay there, doll?" Laying the gun down, he hands me the water bottle, eyeing me with concern. I take it from him and drink slowly. He called me doll. I should be offended, but I'm not. In fact, I'm pretty sure I'm blushing. *Jesus.* "You're all tensed up." A gentle squeeze of my leg meant to comfort me sends a jolt of heat straight up my thighs. "You're doing great. I know it feels kinda strange, kinda like a bee is attacking you non-stop, but just try to relax, okay? It's really not as bad as it feels, and it's not as deep as it feels, either."

I laugh nervously and sip the water again. "I guess I wasn't sure what to expect. It does hurt." I look at the first part of the vine that he's started. Even this tiny bit looks really great, and the excitement of seeing it helps distract me from the pain.

"You have to just put your mind elsewhere," he says. "Separate yourself."

"I'm sorry," I reply. "I know you're probably not used to older women in here being all scared and jumpy." I ease my body back down, giving him the 'go-ahead' to continue.

He picks up his gun and starts again, but it feels like he is being gentler and lighter now. "Old?" he repeats with narrowed eyes, wiping at my leg with a paper towel. "You're not old."

"I'm pretty sure I am not your average customer."

"I have no average customers. How old are you, thirty? That's not old."

"Try thirty-six."

He scoffs and re-positions my leg. "Shit, that's not old either, and you look great. I see some young girls in here that look awful from doing drugs, abusing their bodies, baking in the sun. Hell, most of them have fake body parts. I don't know what I'm touching half the time, and what might break off or pop." He smiles up at me. "You have a really sweet natural beauty."

Heat rises to my cheeks again, and I quickly look away from him and focus on the far wall. "Thank you for saying that. I guess I'm just starting to feel old. My daughter is almost eighteen, and I feel like all the women I see around me are young and thin, with these amazing bodies, looking like they just stepped off the runway."

"Eh, trust me. Underneath all the makeup and the clothes, they ain't all that. In fact, they're pretty fuckin' boring, too. Most of them can't even carry a decent conversation, unless it's about themselves."

His soft humming to the music as he works his gun back and forth over my leg distracts and lulls me, putting me more at ease. "So how come you wanted to get a tattoo?"

I decide to just be honest rather than tell a silly lie. "I've always wanted one, but my husband said they were ugly and a waste of money."

He wheels closer to his bench and changes something on his gun. "Ugly, huh?" He pushes his hair out of his eyes, his arm muscles flexing and rippling while he does whatever he's doing, and I have to tear my eyes away before he catches me. "I guess there's a ton of ugly people walking around then. But I don't see you as one of them." He wheels back over to me and places his hand on my thigh, once again sending a slight tingle traveling up between my legs. Good Lord! When was the last time I was touched there? Or the last time I felt butterflies?

His voice interrupts my butterfly moment. "And your body is yours—you can do whatever you want with it. No one should ever tell you what you should think, do, wear, or anything else."

"Easier said than done when you're married."

"So how is he going to feel when he sees this on you?"

"He won't ever be seeing it. We're separated."

His smile doesn't go unnoticed. "Well then, it sounds like he won't be inflicting his opinions on you anymore, so now you can spread your wings. Just like this little butterfly right here . . ."

He taps my leg, and I follow his gaze to see the beautiful little butterfly he's etched onto me forever.

"It's beautiful," I exclaim. "It looks so real. How do you do that?"

"See? That was supposed to be a bird, but I fucked it up and now it's a butterfly."

My mouth falls open until I see the playful grin spread across his lips. "I'm kidding," he says. "I just wanted to see your face. And it was pretty funny."

"Not funny," I reply, laughing.

I lay there for two hours while he works, but it feels like an eternity. We talk a little and then fall into a comfortable silence, just listening to the music while I try not to think about the burning, digging feeling. Finally, he backs away and announces that it's a good place to stop until my next appointment.

Sitting up and stretching out, I look down at my leg and notice its very red and angry looking around the artwork, but the design itself is beautiful. The vines, flowers, and butterflies look so realistic, almost 3D. I have no idea how he can make something look so realistic and pretty with that tattoo gun.

"You like?" he asks, gently laying a large white bandage over it and taping it to me.

"I love it. I can't wait to see it finished."

"Soon enough." He winks at me and stands up. "You feel all right to walk around?"

I swing my legs off the chair and stretch out a bit more. "Yup."

"You have awesome pale skin, my favorite type to work with. The ink always looks so vivid on it."

"Um, thanks . . . I think," I answer, blinking up at him.

"Yes, it's a compliment. . . . you're beautiful."

Is he flirting with me? No, he's just being nice and polite. He hands me my jeans and shoes, a sweet gesture that feels oddly intimate. "You can go change while I clean up, then we can book your next appointment if you still want to?"

"Definitely. I'm not backing out now. I need to see this artistic creation of yours finished."

He gives me a grateful smile. "Good girl, I'm lookin' forward to it, too."

I head to the bathroom to get dressed and fix up my hair a little while I'm there, because I look like I just woke up. Glancing at my watch, I realize it's nine-thirty already. I've been here for almost three hours. Shoving my shorts in my bag, I join him up front, my leg sore as I walk.

He's bent over a large day planner with a lot of scribbling on it, comparing it to his cell phone. I can't help but smile at how determined yet confused he looks.

He notices my sympathetic smile. "I'm trying to use this new app to keep track of my appointments, but I still rely on this paper mess," he tells me. "Old habits die hard."

"I know what you mean. We've just had all new software installed where I work, and I still don't trust it completely."

"What do you do for work?"

"I'm a Human Resources manager."

"Wow. That's really cool. Do you get to fire people?"

I let out a laugh. "Yes, sometimes. I hire them, too. I don't like firing people. It's not fun at all."

He sighs and goes back to studying his calendar. "So how about the Friday after next, at six-thirty again?" he asks. "Then you'll be my last appointment again, and I won't have to rush."

I take out my cell phone and check my calendar. I know I have nothing to do, but want to make sure there isn't anything going on with the kids. There's nothing in that little square of a day on my calendar. *As usual.*

"That works for me. You really shouldn't be working on a Friday night, though. I could come a different night, or over the weekend if that's better?"

He writes my name down on his calendar and then types it into his phone. "I don't usually have any plans at night. The weekends are pretty booked here for months. That's when everyone wants to come in."

"That makes sense. Thank you then, for seeing me on a Friday night."

"No problem." He hands me a piece of paper. "This is the care sheet. Be sure to put lotion on it twice a day. It will feel a little sore for a few days, and then it will scab up and get itchy. Do *not* scratch it or pick at it. Wash it gently. If you have any questions at all, just call me. The shop number and my cell are on there."

"Okay . . . thank you." The scab part sounds concerning and kinda gross to me. Lindsay didn't mention scabs or itching. "How itchy exactly?"

"Like really itchy. Like an itch you can't scratch."

"Is there such a thing?"

He grins wickedly at me. "Oh, you have no idea."

He comes around the counter and walks toward the parlor door with me. "I'm going to walk you to your car. It's late."

My heart jumps a little at his thoughtfulness. "You don't have to do that, Lukas. I'm a big girl." I smile up at him as I walk under his arm that's holding the door open.

"I insist. It's dark in the parking lot, and you never know what kind of psycho could be creeping around out there, wanting to scratch your itch."

"I guess you're right," I agree as we walk together down the parlor's walkway.

"Were you married for a long time?" he asks, glancing down at me.

"Eighteen years."

"Yikes. You got married young."

"Yeah . . . seemed liked a good idea at the time." I look down at my feet as we walk. It's surreal to think that half my life was spent with someone who let me go so easily.

"Can I ask what happened?"

I breathe out a long sigh. "He met someone else, and that was it. He just left."

"Just like that? Really?"

My car and an older Corvette are the only cars parked in the dark lot, and he leads me right to my car. I turn to him before unlocking my door. "Yeah, pretty much just like that," I reply. "It was devastating. I never saw it coming. I thought everything was fine."

"That really sucks. I'm sorry."

I hug myself against the cold chill in the air. "Thanks. I thought we'd be married forever, ya know? I didn't think I'd be dumped at thirty-six for the first younger, gorgeous girl that gave my husband a little bit of attention. I guess our vows and our family meant more to me than to him."

"He's a fool."

"Maybe, or maybe I'm the fool, thinking I'd be living that fairytale of happily ever after."

Lukas opens my car door for me. "Nah, don't give up on that. You know how fairytales go. You gotta kiss some frogs before you find the prince, right?"

I laugh as I climb into my car. "Hey, I didn't think guys knew about fairytales," I tease.

He grins down at me, holding on to the doorframe. "I'm not like most guys, Ivy. See ya in two weeks." He pushes my door shut, and I watch him walk across the parking lot back to his shop, when he turns around about halfway and gives me a little wave. Blushing, I wave back at him as I start my car. Hot damn, he's cute.

CHAPTER 5

LUKAS

I'll be honest, I remember most of my clients by the design I put on them. All their actual names and faces kinda mesh together in my mind. It's the canvas of their flesh I remember forever. But tonight, Ivy's coming back, and I'm actually looking forward to seeing her again, which is unlike me because I don't usually form any attachments to my clients. Of course, I enjoy working with them, but I'm usually so focused on my designs that I'm lucky if I can remember anything else about them at all. Something about Ivy is different, though. From the moment I met her, it was like getting struck by lightning, and I haven't been able to get that chick out of my mind.

Right before Ivy's appointment, I make a last-minute decision to run upstairs to my apartment above the shop to put a clean shirt on and wash my face. Just as I'm coming down the spiral staircase from my place to the back of the shop, the front door cowbell sounds. I find her in the waiting room, looking at some artwork on the wall, her back to me. She's short, petite and curvy, with long wavy auburn hair that I suddenly have an urge to take in my hands and feel it glide through my fingers like silk. It looks like she came directly from work this time, because she's wearing a black pants suit instead of jeans.

"Hey," I say, and when she turns and smiles at me, I get that zappy feeling inside again.

"Hey, yourself. This drawing is beautiful. Did you do this?" She gestures to a charcoal drawing of a dragon perched on a mountain that I drew about five years ago.

"I did."

She looks back at it and then at me again. "It's absolutely beautiful. I wish I could draw."

"Thanks. I've always loved to draw, even as a little kid," I say. "You want to come on back?"

She nods and I lead her back to my work area and take the sketch of her artwork out of a big folder on my table.

"So how's it looking and feeling?" I ask. "Everything okay?"

She beams. "I love it. It's so pretty. I think I spent way too much time looking at it. It was sore for a few days and then got really itchy, just like you said, but I promise I didn't touch it."

I grin at her. "Awesome. Why don't you go get changed, and I'll get ready?"

"Okay. I'll be right back."

When she comes back, I have to smile at how different she looks wearing a faded t-shirt, black cotton shorts, and white socks, compared to the business outfit and high heels she had on a few minutes ago. She's adorable.

"What?" she asks, noticing me eyeing her as she's climbing onto the tattoo chair.

"I love how you went from looking all professional to cute in five minutes flat."

Her cheeks redden at my words. "Well, thanks. I had to work late, so I didn't have time to change first."

I gently run my hand over the design on her outer thigh, visually mapping out what I want to do for this appointment. I should have put gloves on before I touched her, but I didn't, because I wanted to feel her, and just as I imagined, her skin is soft and warm. A quick fantasy of me running my hands up her naked thighs flashes through my mind.

"You could have cancelled if you were having a bad day. I would have understood," I say, reluctantly pulling my hand away from her porcelain skin and swiveling the stool around to grab the gun off my table.

"No, I wanted to come," she lays down on the chair and stretches her legs out. For someone so short, she has some damn sexy legs on her. "I've been looking forward to this. Plus, my son is with his father for the weekend, and my daughter had plans tonight, so I would have just sat home in an empty house anyway."

Leaning carefully over her body with the tattoo gun in my hand, I realize how bummed I would have been if she had cancelled. "I'm glad you came," I admit, glancing up at her. She catches my gaze and then quickly looks away. Her shyness intrigues me even more. "So, how have you been?" I ask, hoping some conversation will help her relax a little. I can feel by how taut her body is that she's wound up like a top.

"Good. Crazy busy at work, as always, but I like it because it makes the time go by and keeps my mind busy so I can't dwell on things. "

"I like that, too. Things have been really busy here the past few weeks, and I love it. I'm never bored."

"Do you work here alone?" she asks.

"No. My brother, Vandal, works here, too, but he's also in a band, so sometimes he's not able to come in for a while if he's practicing or on tour. I may have to hire someone else to help keep up with all the appointments we have."

"That's great. So many small businesses are struggling right now. It's a nice change to hear that someone is doing well."

"So true. I feel very blessed and lucky." I gently turn her to her side a little bit and bend her knee up so I can get a better angle, and the feeling of my arm leaning against her bare thigh sends a rush of heat to my cock. *Fuck me.* I never get turned on when I work on a female client. Ever. I shake my hair out of my eyes and peek up at her, but she seems lost in her own thoughts.

"Speaking of small business, I have to find someone to come and fix the roof on my shed. During the last snow storm, a big icicle pulled a few of the shingles right off," she says, oblivious to my attraction to her. "Paul was still coming by to do little things like that, but I guess, obviously, he's not going to keep doing stuff around the house now that he's shacked up with someone else."

"I take it Paul is your ex-husband?"

"Yes. Now, he's saying we may have to sell the house, too, because he moved into a new expensive condo with his girlfriend. It's really stressing me out."

"Shit," I say, feeling the muscles in her leg tightening as she gets more upset. "That sucks." Her ex-husband sounds like a first-class asshole to me.

She shakes her head. "I'm sorry I'm venting to you. It's just been one of those weeks, ya know? And I guess I'm just stupid because I didn't think this stuff would ever be happening to me." Her voice cracks a little, and I stop working to look up at her. Her eyes are watery and her cheeks are flushed, the sight tugging at my heart.

"Ivy, you're not stupid." I gently squeeze her leg, aching to comfort her but not knowing how without crossing a line. "I'm pretty sure, when people get married, they don't expect that they'll be shafted by that person years later, and have their entire fucking life uprooted."

"No." She sniffles. "I never even imagined it."

I wheel my stool across my small work area, grab the box of tissues on my table, and hand them to her.

"You must think I'm a mess," she says, taking a tissue and wiping at her eyes. "I'm so sorry."

"You're not a mess." Actually, I think she's beautiful, and it's way more than just her looks. I can tell this woman has a heart of gold, and it shines right out of her like a spotlight. "You can vent on me all ya want. I've been through a lot of crap myself, so I understand. Trust me. I'm a good listener."

I pick my gun up and continue my design on her, trying to be as gentle with her as I can be. Knowing that I'm inflicting even the slightest amount of pain on her bothers me.

"Are you married?" she asks suddenly.

"Nope."

"Well, you're young. You have tons of time."

I wipe her leg with a cloth. "True. I think I'm one of the few guys that actually wants to get married. I just can't find the right girl."

"That's hard to believe. You seem like a really nice guy, and you're very talented. I'm surprised women aren't lining up for you."

I laugh. "Not the right ones, that's for sure. I tend to attract the crazies or the wrong ones in general. I just broke up with a girl a few weeks ago that I still feel bad about. She was a great girl, really pretty, and we had a lot of things in common. I think she actually cared about me, too. She was the most normal girl I've dated in a long time."

"That's a shame. What happened?"

"She slept with my brother a few times before I hooked up with her."

Ivy scrunches up her face. "Oh."

"Yeah, exactly. I just couldn't get past it. Do you think that's wrong of me? Do you think I should be able to just forget about that?" I ask, wondering if there's something wrong with me, or if maybe I'm too picky.

She thinks about my question before answering. "No, I completely understand. I think, for a lot of people, it's awkward to be intimate with a person someone else you are close to has also been intimate with. Some things aren't meant to be shared."

"Exactly! I couldn't see myself having dinner with her over at my brother's house, sitting at his table, knowing he screwed her. It would make me crazy thinking about it, and I don't think I could *not* think about. I can't un-see that shit in my head, ya know?"

She laughs. "I totally agree. I'm sorry, I'm not laughing at you. It just sounded funny, the way you said it," she says. "I feel sick every time I think about the fact that Paul was having an affair for a whole year before I found out. Just thinking that he was having sex with another woman, and then coming home to me, pretending he had been at work and acting all normal, is disgusting."

"Fuck yeah it is. Was he sleeping with both of you? Not at the same time, obviously, I mean, while he was married to you?"

"Apparently so. He'd stopped having sex with me for months. Almost a year." She turns her head away from me, her face reddening with embarrassment. "I just thought he was tired from working. I didn't think he was getting it better someplace else."

"Shit. That sucks. I absolutely cannot stand cheaters. I feel really bad for you."

She sighs and faces me again. "Please don't feel sorry for me. I feel lame enough already."

"I don't feel sorry for you. I just feel bad for you because I don't think you deserve it. He's a shithead."

"My thoughts exactly."

I add a few more flowers to her design before I get up the courage to ask her my next question. "Did you eat dinner today?"

"No . . . I didn't have time to."

"When we're done here, we could go to this little cafe down the street. They're open 'til midnight. I haven't eaten yet, either."

Her leg muscles stiffen again beneath my hands, and I silently beg her to say yes.

"I don't know . . . I should probably just go home," she answers nervously, chewing her bottom lip.

"To the big empty house? Forget that and come with me. They have killer soups and sandwiches, and their lattes are awesome. Do you really want me to eat alone like a loser?"

She smiles shyly at me. "No. Of course not."

"Then grab a bite with me. Save me from my impending loser-dom."

She squirms in the chair. "Lukas, I'd love to save you from your loser-dom, but I'm not sure that's a good idea."

I flash her my best chick-melting smile. *What the hell am I doing? Am I really trying to hook up with a chick a decade older than me?* "It's just a sandwich. No strings, I promise."

She sighs and laughs, and I love how pretty her lips look when she smiles. Like a little doll. "Okay. I *am* hungry, actually."

"Cool. Let's try to put in a little more design time, and then we'll go, okay?"

She nods. "That's perfect."

I have a strict no-dating-the-customers-rule that I imposed on myself when my brother and I opened the shop four years ago. And even though this technically isn't a real date, I'm growing more and more attracted to Ivy, and I really have no idea why. I work on all kinds of attractive women every day but remain detached from them, even though a lot of them literally throw themselves at me and offer me everything from blowjobs to threesomes. There's just this *thing* about her. Maybe it's her shyness. Or the ache I feel in her. Or maybe it's the crazy tingling feeling I get every time I touch her or look into her eyes. Either way, I just know I want to spend more time with her without jabbing needles in her.

"How long have you worked here?" she asks me.

"My brother and I opened this place four years ago after we inherited some money from our grandfather."

Her eyebrows rise in surprise. "Oh! I didn't realize you owned it."

I smile as I add delicate shading to the tender spot just above her knee. "Yup. I own the building, too, and I live upstairs."

"Wow, I had no idea. I'm very jealous of your commute," she teases. "What was here before you moved in? I love the uniqueness of the building. I know it was a church or chapel at one time, right?"

"It was quite a while ago. Before we moved in, an older couple lived here that sold antiques. They were cool enough to let us keep some of their antique furniture and artwork. The furniture in the waiting area is all antiques, and a bunch of the furniture in my apartment is, too. I love vintage decor, especially anything Victorian Gothic." I pause working on her design. "I'm fascinated with the history that's attached to certain objects. I feel like antiques have a story to tell, and that they carry with them a little piece of each person who owned it. Like an imprint, I guess. Sometimes, I like to run my hand over the old wood and just try to feel the past seep into me."

She listens with a fascinated expression as I talk. "Lukas . . . that's so beautiful. I'm impressed. Most men have zero interest in things like that, especially someone your age."

I look up from her leg to meet her eyes. "I've never acted my age, Ivy."

"Can I ask how old you are?"

"Twenty-four."

Her eyes widen. "No fair. I'd love to be twenty-four again."

I reposition her, and she turns so she's lying on her side so I can get to the back of her leg. I can't help but notice her shorts creeping up and exposing more of the back of her thigh leading up to her ass. I fight the urge to run my hand up the back of her leg and caress her. I want to hear her sigh under my touch.

I blink and try to refocus on working. "Well, you can't go back, but you can move forward. Try not to think of what's changing in your life as all negative," I encourage her, trying to calm my dick down at the same time. "Try to look at it as an opportunity for new things." *Yes. New things like my lips all over your body.*

"You sound like my friend Lindsay. I guess the two of you must be right."

I wheel away from her and place my gun down on my worktable. "Okay, pretty lady, time for a new thing right now. You're coming to the cafe with me."

CHAPTER 6

IVY

I*t's just coffee. It's not a date. Keep him company while he eats, nibble on something, and then go home. No big deal.*

My reflection in the bathroom mirror is not what I want to see. I look tired. My eyes look a bit puffy and dull. A grey hair is visible. *Shit!* I reach up, carefully grab it, and yank it out.

Ouch!

I'm definitely getting my hair done. Soon.

Rubbing the new sore spot on my head, I wonder why Lukas wants to have dinner with me. Given his age, I'm sure we don't have too much in common. With his looks, he must have tons of pretty young girls he could be spending time with on a Friday night, not wasting time with someone as boring as I am.

He feels sorry for your lonely ass.

I frown in the mirror and tell myself it doesn't matter what a twenty-four-year-old guy thinks of how I look. Grabbing my bag, I unlock the door and meet him in the waiting area.

"How about the Friday after next? Same time?" he asks, scribbling on his calendar again.

I don't even bother to check my calendar app. "That's perfect."

"Awesome. You ready?"

I nod and he comes around the counter. "I know it's freezing out, but do you mind if we walk? It's only two blocks. The cold air wakes me up," he says as we head outside and he turns to lock the door behind us.

"Walking sounds great. And I actually really like the cold," I reply. I love this street; it's quaint with lots of great little unique stores and boutiques, which is one of the many benefits of living in a small, artsy, New England town. Being December, Christmas lights decorate most of the shop windows, making the street look very much like a holiday card scene. I hope I can find an affordable house to live in, if Paul decides we have to sell our house, because it will break my heart to move from this little town I grew up in and love so much. I want my kids to grow up here like I did.

"Does your leg feel okay?" Lukas asks. "I didn't think of how sore it might be when I asked you to walk."

I smile up at him, touched by his sweet concern. "It doesn't really hurt at all."

The cafe is small but cozy, decorated very much like a living room. There are small tables adorned with candles, a few loveseats with oversized pillows, pretty Tiffany-style lamps, and an electric fireplace with a large stone mantle. In one corner is a Christmas tree with wrapped presents beneath it. I immediately fall in love and know I will be coming back here. Only four other customers are here at the moment—two sitting on a love seat reading, and two others are chatting softly at a table.

"Hey, Lukas, you getting the usual?" the girl behind the counter asks, giving him a big toothy grin.

"Yup," he replies then turns to me. "The vanilla brown sugar latte is killer," he hints.

"Okay then, I need that. And I'll have the turkey and cranberry croissant."

Lukas pays, refusing my attempt to pay for my own, then leads us over to a secluded table in the corner where we wait for our food to arrive.

"This place is so cute and cozy," I say, looking around. "I want to just curl up and read."

He nods. "I love it here. I come here almost every night after I close up . . . mornings, too, for my coffee. Sometimes, local musicians play acoustic here at night. I'll walk down here, grab a coffee, and listen to some tunes and unwind before I head home."

"I have a feeling I'll be back on the weekends to get breakfast."

"Cool. Maybe I'll catch you here sometime."

My cell phone rings, and I pull it out of my bag, knowing it's one of the kids.

"I have to take this real quick." Lukas nods while I bring the phone to my ear. "Hi, Honey," I say happily.

"Hi, Mommy."

"How's your night? Are you and Daddy having fun?"

"Yeah, we watched cartoons, and Charlene made me macaroni and cheese."

"That's great. It's your favorite."

I hate Charlene.

"Yours is better, Mommy. Can I come home now?"

My heart cracks. "No, sweetie. Remember, we talked about you having a sleepover at Daddy's new house this weekend? He'll bring you home on Sunday."

Lukas frowns and leans back in his chair, stretching his long legs under the table.

Tommy sighs into the phone. "Okay . . . what are you doing, Mommy?"

"I'm having dinner with a friend right now, sweetheart. You have fun with Daddy and Charlene, all right? You can call me any time you want to talk to me, and I'll see you really soon." I almost choke saying Daddy and Charlene to my own son.

"Okay, Mommy. I miss you." Ah, my sweet little boy.

I smile and hold the phone tighter. "I miss you, too, and I love you a big bunch. Good night, now."

"Night."

I wait for him to end the call and smile at Lukas as I put my phone back into my purse.

"He's having a hard time understanding why things are so different," I explain.

He nods, a warm smile on his face, reaching his eyes. "It's totally understandable. You're a good mom. Your face lit up when you talked to him. You're the kind of mom I wanted when I was his age."

I wait until the waitress bringing our food has gone before I reply. "My kids are my life." I take a sip of my latte. "Wow, you were right. This is delicious!" The vanilla and brown sugar latte is sinful.

He grins. "It's my fave, and I actually start to go through withdrawals if I don't have at least one a day."

I take my knife and fork and cut my sandwich into small one-inch pieces, while Lukas watches me in confused fascination.

"Are you cutting up your sandwich to eat it with a fork?" he finally asks.

"Yes," I reply, taking a bite off my fork.

He laughs as he watches me. "That's . . . different. Can I ask why?"

"Are you laughing at me?" I tease. "If you must know, ever since I was really young, I've just had this aversion to sticking food into my face, or biting into things. So I eat everything with a fork."

"Really? What about, like, ice cream cones, or bananas? Or an apple?"

I shake my head. "Nope. None of that. I put it in a dish and cut it up and eat it with a fork or spoon."

A naughty, crooked grin spreads across his face. "Okay, I'm going to try really hard to refrain from making a sexual comment about all of that."

I feign shock. "Lukas! You shouldn't be thinking about my mouth and sexual things."

He groans and bows his head, his long hair falling into his face. "I'm definitely thinking about it now."

I know I'm blushing five shades of red, but flirting with him feels good and safe because he's not a jerk. I sorta like his naughty playful side, and how he's bringing it out of me, too.

"Let's change the subject from what I do with my mouth," I suggest. "So how about you? Any kids?"

"Nope. I love kids, though. And I'm still kinda thinking about your mouth."

A giggle escapes me before I can stop it. I really shouldn't be doing anything to provoke him into more flirting. I watch him place his napkin on his lap before he starts to eat, a hint that he was raised with manners.

"You mentioned a brother. Any other siblings?" I take another bite of food off my fork, ignoring the impish glint in his eye as he watches me chew.

"No," he answers. "At least I don't think so. I didn't even know I had a brother until about five years ago."

"Really?" I ask, my curiosity piqued. "How did that happen?"

He swallows his food. "According to my grandmother, my father is a famous musician and slept around. A lot. He got a few women pregnant and then just dumped them. He did it to my mother and to my brother's mother. Who knows who else? Anyway, my mom was only eighteen and had a drug problem." He pushes his hair back away from his face. "She gave me up to her grandparents, and they raised me. She never came back, and I've never met my father."

What a horrible way for a child to start their life. I can't even imagine leaving my kids for anything, no matter what. "Lukas, I'm so sorry. That's terrible beyond words. Did you grow up happy?"

He stares across the room for a moment, like he's pulling up memories from an old album in his mind. "At times, I was happy, yes. My great-grandparents were pretty old and not equipped to have a little kid. My great-grandmother homeschooled me and didn't let me out much. They raised my mother, too, and she put them through so much they kinda thought that if they kept me safe inside and away from the outside world, I would turn out better and be easier for them to manage."

"It sounds like they were just really worried about something happening to you, and like you said, just wanted to keep you safe. Were you lonely?" Thinking of Lukas as a beautiful little boy, being kept in a house and not outside having fun with other kids makes me want to cry.

"I didn't have any friends to play with, but I didn't know any better, so I guess, for me, it was all normal. I played in the attic mostly. Even back then, I loved all the old stuff they had stored up there. I drew and painted constantly, and read anything I could get my hands on. They had a lot of old books. I taught myself how to play music on some old instruments they had, too. When I was about ten, they both started to fail mentally and physically, so I took care of them. I cooked, I cleaned, had to remind them to take their meds . . . everything pretty much."

"Oh my God, you were so young to have to do all that! Tommy is only seven, and I can't even *imagine* him having to take on that kind of responsibility."

He shrugs and takes a bite of his sandwich, chewing carefully before he talks again. "I did what I had to do. They were all I had, and I was all they had. I loved them. They were as good to me as they could be. My grandfather got bad first. He developed dementia and had to be put in a home, and passed away a year later. I tried to take care of my grandmother, but she was having a real hard time with her own health and then grief. She fell in the kitchen one day and smacked her head on the counter. She died right there in front of me. I went into shock and sat there for an entire day on the floor next to her. I was afraid to call 911 because I knew they were going to take me away. I spent some time in the hospital for a little while after that." His voice wavers and his eyes brim with the beginning of tears. Instinctively, I reach across the table and touch his inked hand.

"Lukas . . . I'm so sorry. I don't even know what to say," I have to blink back my own tears just thinking about how devastating all of that must have been for him. He was way too young to have to go through all of that.

He wipes his eyes with his other hand, not moving his hand from beneath mine. I'm touched by his emotion and the fact that he doesn't try to hide it or act ashamed of it, like most men would. "It sucked," he says. "After I was let out of the hospital, I was put in a foster home, but I really didn't get along with them. They didn't like how quiet I was, the things I drew, my attraction to antiques, or that I enjoyed sitting in the dark. They wanted me to be social, go to dances, cut my hair, and get involved in sports. I didn't want to do any of those things. It just wasn't me. I didn't feel like I belonged there."

"You sound like you were a good kid. Maybe just a bit of a loner?"

He smiles a sad smile at me. "Yeah, I was. I still am."

"There's nothing wrong with that. I am, too, actually. I've always been really shy."

"I sensed that about you." He turns his hand under mine, so our palms touch, and our eyes shift from our joined hands to slowly meeting each other across the dim table. Warmth spreads throughout my body, from my head to my toes, and settles in my stomach. Lowering my eyes, I gently slide my hand away from his. He strums his fingers on the table for a moment and then picks up his coffee. The candle flame dances on the table, mimicking the waltz slowly starting between us, the tiny steps forward and back. *I'm not ready for this.*

"So, um, how did you find out about your brother?" I ask, trying to recover from whatever the moment was that just happened.

He clears his throat and runs his hand through his hair, and I find myself wanting that hand to be mine touching that dark silky hair. "My father's mother found out that her son had two kids he never told the rest of his family about. When her husband died, she hired a private detective to find us so we could be included in his inheritance and become part of the family."

I swallow my food and gape at him. "That's incredible. And are you, now, part of the family?"

"I am. My grandmother, the one that looked for us, is an amazing woman. She's just . . . so cool. It turns out, most of the family is kinda famous. My uncle, who is my dad's brother, is a retired musician who was really well known many years ago, and his sons, who are my cousins, are in a really popular rock band. My brother is part of that band now, actually. And my aunt is a best-selling author. The money I inherited allowed me to partner up with my brother to buy the building and open the shop. It's always been a dream of mine to have my own business."

"And you're both tattoo artists?"

"Yeah, it's kinda cool. We have a lot in common. He's just a bit fucked up, though. Not exactly the easiest person to get close to. He's got some issues."

"I'm sure that will change in time. I imagine it must be hard to form a family bond with people that you didn't grow up with. Especially for men, I think it's harder for them to form relationships."

"You're right. It's kinda weird to just all-of-a-sudden have a bunch of people in your life that you never even met." He pauses. "I don't give up on people, though. If I want someone in my life, I make sure they are."

My heart flutters as I wonder if that slight infliction at the end of his sentence and that spark in his eye is hinting toward me. *No. No way.*

I'm thrown by the intense attraction I feel toward him, unsure how to react to it. I've never been attracted to a man so much younger than me before, and I definitely have never taken notice of men with tattoos and long hair, but those things mixed with his sensual brown eyes, sweet personality, muscular body, and heart-stopping smile have my insides doing somersaults. When he smiles, I can tell he *feels* it, and means it. He's what I call an old soul. There's a quiet deepness about him, like he knows things that he couldn't possibly know, and he has a therapeutic, yet stimulating effect on me that I'm drawn to like a magnet.

"How 'bout you?" he asks. "Brothers and sisters? Close family?"

"I have a brother who's two years older than me. We're a close family. My parents live here in town, and I grew up here. My brother lives about an hour away, so I get to see them all pretty regularly, and of course on holidays and birthdays." I take a quick sip of my coffee. "My parents are still a little freaked out over the idea that I might be getting divorced. They're old fashioned."

He raises his eyebrows. "*Might* be getting divorced? Is there a chance you and Paul might be getting back together, then?"

Embarrassment heats my face. "No. Not at all. I think I still go into denial at times. Obviously." I smile weakly at him.

"Would you take him back?"

Damn, this guy is direct. "Lukas . . . I'm not sure I want to talk about that."

"Shit. I'm sorry. You're right. It's none of my business." He sits up straighter. "I didn't mean to be rude."

"You're not rude at all. You're a sweetheart, and I appreciate you bringing me here for this delicious latte, and for being so nice. It's still just hard for me to talk about that stuff."

He holds his hand up and smiles. "Say no more. I totally get it. I want you to have a good time, not be uncomfortable."

We talk about lighter things while we finish eating, until finally, I glance at my watch and see the time, which has flown by.

"I didn't realize how late it was getting. I should really get going. I like to be home when Macy gets there, so she's not coming home to a dark empty house."

"Gotcha." He reaches into his pocket and places a few dollars on the table. "I'll walk you to your car."

The street is much quieter on our walk back, as all the stores are closed for the night and hardly any cars are driving by. The air is chilly, and it feels like snow could be on its way. Usually, I hope for a white Christmas because it's my favorite holiday, but this will be my first Christmas without Paul. Years of our own little family traditions have been casually thrown away. I hope I can still make sure the kids have a happy holiday, and they don't have to feel the effects of the separation too badly.

"Do you live alone?" I ask as we near his shop. The stained glass windows on the upper floor are glowing beautifully, and I wonder what his apartment looks like inside.

"Yup. I've had some roommates in the past at other apartments, but this place is sacred to me, so I really don't want any friends living with me and trashing it. It's pretty big inside, three bedrooms. Do you want to come in and see it? It's really pretty. The woodwork and the stained glass are all original. It's actually been in some magazines."

Eek. I can't go into his apartment. That would be totally inappropriate. *Right?*

"No, but thank you," I say politely. "It sounds really

beautiful."

He looks down at me with a hopeful smile. "Maybe next time," he says.

Just like the last time I was here after hours, my car and an older black Corvette are in the dark parking lot.

"Is that your car?" I ask, motioning to the 'Vette.

"Yes. That's my baby. I wish this place had a garage I could keep it in. It's the only thing I don't like about living here."

"Corvettes are such pretty cars. I've always liked them."

Reaching my own boring mom-car, we stop walking and he turns to me. "Me, too," he agrees. "Especially the older models. They have beautifully designed curves, like a woman."

Wow. Very sensual comparison. And true.

I lean against the front fender of my car and peer up at him. He really is extremely good looking—those dark eyes, paired with his chiseled jaw and crooked smile, make me want to just sit and look at him.

"Thank you for dinner," I say, hating to end the first good night I've had in a very long time. "It was really good, especially the latte. That was yummy."

He steps closer to me and pushes his hair out of his face. "I want to see you again," he says softly, a hint of nervousness in his voice.

My insides melt, and I of course reply with something lame. "I have my next appointment in two weeks."

He gently lifts my chin with his finger and holds it there, luring me to look up into his deep, chestnut eyes. "No. Not for that," he replies.

"F-for what?" My voice is shaky, just like the rest of me right now. Having his body so close to mine, his finger still under my chin, and those eyes of his locked on to mine are all shocks to my sheltered little foundation.

"Dinner," he replies. "I can cook for you, or we can go out. Your choice."

"Lukas..." *I can't do this.*

"Don't say no, Ivy." His voice is gentle and hopeful. "I'll give you as many forks as you want, and I'll try not to think about putting things in your mouth," he teases, making me laugh. I'm not sure how he can be so sweet, adorable, and sexual at the same time. It's completely rattling.

"I'm really not ready to date yet," I admit. "My head is still messed up."

He strokes his finger back and forth under my chin, and I want to rub on him like a cat. "Everyone's head is messed up, Ivy. Messed up is the new normal."

"Yes, that's very true."

"So, say yes. Don't think of it as a date. No expectations other than good company and good food. And forks."

I try to stand my ground, even though it's getting harder by the second with his sexy voice and pleading eyes. "It's not a good idea. I'm not ready, and I think I'm just a little bit too old for you. I'm very flattered, though."

He tilts his head. "Really? Or is it that you think I'm too *young* for you? Because your age means nothing to me."

"Well, it *is* a big age difference, no matter how you want to spin it."

He moves a little closer to me, our bodies almost touching, and I put my hand up between us and rest it on his chest. I meant it to be a resisting gesture, but as soon as I touch him, my intention falters. He feels so solid, so real, so warm... *So much like a man.* I feel dwarfed between the car and his tall, fit body. His chest and shoulders are so broad that I cannot even see around him. As I look up at him, I see a shooting star fly by in the sky over his head.

"You have no idea how captivating you are, do you?" he says softly. "Your face and your eyes just now... wow."

"I just saw a shooting star. I haven't seen one of those in years."

Something in the air tonight feels magical. I'm not sure if it's from being with him, or if the stress of the past few months is slowly dissipating, allowing me to enjoy small parts of life again. Whatever it is, it feels damn good.

"You have to make a wish, then," he says knowingly. "Or gift it to me."

"What would you wish for? I need to know if it's worthy before I gift it to you," I murmur, my fingers very slowly rubbing the middle of his chest, as if they have little minds of their own. The fabric of his tight flannel shirt is thin and soft, letting me feel the warmth of his skin through it.

"I'd wish you'd have dinner with me, and I'd wish I could kiss you goodnight."

My stomach does cartwheels, and I can feel his heart beating faster beneath my hand, just as my own is.

"Lukas... that's two wishes..." I whisper, suddenly barely having the ability to speak or breathe.

He leans his head down closer to mine. "You looking at me like that, and saying my name like that, just makes me want to kiss you even more."

I swallow hard, unable to tear my eyes away from his. "You really shouldn't be saying things like that," I breathe, my voice quivering. He's got my nerves in overdrive. Hell, who am I kidding? He's got my entire mind and body in overdrive right now.

He moves his hand to cup the side of my face. "Close your eyes, Ivy. Let's make our wishes at the same time."

Lukas is a wizard, and I've quickly fallen under his spell.

My eyes flutter closed, and his lips touch mine, so softly that we are barely touching at all, but it's enough to make me see even more shooting stars, this time behind closed eyes, in that place where magic happens. His kiss is completely unexpected but way too perfect to not let myself have. I drop my bag to the ground and bring my hands up to rest on his shoulders. He kisses me a little harder, his tongue gently touching my lips, silently asking permission for more. Parting my lips, I let him kiss me deeper, his tongue slowly meeting mine, caressing in enticing circles. The feel of his tongue piercing and lip ring is so strange to me, yet incredibly erotic. I think I like it. His hand goes to my hip, pulling my body possessively but gently against him, as his kisses grow more passionate and urgent. My legs begin to shake with timid desire, my hands squeezing his muscled shoulders, hanging on to him in this sudden dizzying realm he's led me into. Did a first kiss ever feel like this before? Has *any* kiss ever felt like this before?

No. Not for me. Not ever.

He oozes skilled sensuality; every touch, every breath, every kiss is measured in perfect timing and depth. This is not an awkward, clumsy, rushed, and horny boy touching me for kicks. Not by a long shot. He's savoring everything. And I don't want him to stop.

Grasping my waist with both hands, he effortlessly lifts me up onto the hood of my car, bringing me closer to eye level with him. He moves between my parted legs, guides my thighs around his jean-clad hips, and covers my mouth with his again, kissing me long, deep, and tantalizingly slow as he gently holds my face in his hands. It's the kind of kiss that brands complete want and ownership. He leaves no doubt that he wants me. The logical part of me is telling me to stop him, but the lonely, aching part of me takes over, and I slide my hands up his chest and over his shoulders to clasp behind his neck. My fingers tangle in his long silky hair, and I love how new and different it feels. *Everything* about him is so different, like tasting an exotic food for the first time that quickly leads to crazy indulgence. That magnetic pull I felt the first time I laid eyes on him is a force to be reckoned with right now. It's controlling me, taking over every part of me, squashing my fears and reservations, and paving a very clear path that leads directly to this man. I cannot even begin to understand or make the tiniest bit of sense of this attraction. But it's there, and it's stronger than anything I've ever felt in my life.

Suddenly, he stops kissing me, his lips just a whisper away from mine, and stares into my eyes for a few moments, before letting his dark eyes slowly close. He pulls me closer against his body, his hard cock pressing against me through our clothes, sending a hot surge of raw desire through me.

What I glimpsed in his eyes shook me even more than his kiss.

Passion.

Affection.

Desire.

All feelings that carry the ability to give immense pleasure and pain. Neither of which I am ready for.

I slowly try to pull myself away from him, but he holds me close against him.

"Wow," I say breathlessly, leaning my head against his shoulder.

"Come upstairs with me, and let's see if we can upgrade that to a *holy shit*," he whispers, his hand resting on the back of my neck, gently squeezing.

My insides quiver at his words. I am so out of my league right now with him. Could I actually please a man like this, with my lack of experience, not to mention my very not-perfect body? I wonder, if I buy the thigh master and do it for ten hours a day, what kind of results I can achieve in a week, coupled with one of those cabbage soup diets maybe.

"Lukas, I can't. I really have to go home . . ."

He doesn't let go of me. Instead, he takes my hands in his and holds on to them between us while his eyes seek out mine.

"Don't be nervous." He lifts my hand to his lips and presses a kiss to it. "Come upstairs with me. I want to sit on the couch with you and hold you and kiss you for hours. We don't have to do anything else. I just don't want this feeling to end." His eyes are full of hope and want, reflecting my own emotions. I feel so connected to him, like everything we are feeling is the same. Equal. Together.

God, I want him. *So bad.* I cannot think of anything that would be better than being in his arms for hours. His kisses and touches are a slice of heaven I have never even dreamed of, and I want more.

I try to catch my breath and regain my composure. "I can't. It's getting late, and I really don't want my daughter worrying about where I am. She's not used to me not being home."

He nods and takes a long, deep recovering breath. "You're right. I'm sorry."

He lifts me up and places me back on my feet again. "You're beautiful," he says, pushing my hair over my shoulder. "I couldn't wait to see you again today. I've never felt like that about a client before."

"Why are you telling me this?" I reach down to pick up my bag, my hand shaking. I want to believe I'm shaking from standing out in the cold, but I know it has nothing to do with the cold and everything to do with the affect he's having on me.

"Maybe to find out if you felt it, too?"

I can't hide my smile as I look at this insanely gorgeous guy in front of me. *Insanely gorgeous young guy. That I have no business to be making out with in a dark parking lot like a teenager.*

"Lukas . . ." I can't lie to him. He's way too honest to be fed lies. I refuse to not acknowledge the immense good I see in him, even after only a few hours of talking. "You are an amazing guy. Really. In a different time or place . . . I would be jumping all over you. I felt it, too. As much as I was excited about the tattoo, I was equally excited to see you again. There's something very special about you. But . . . I'm a mess." I shrug and his smile slowly fades, as I'm sure mine is, as well. "I just can't have any more complications in my life right now. I have to get my life together and take care of my kids. I'm in no position to be doing *this* with someone like you."

He flinches. "Someone like me?"

I touch his arm and shake my head. "I meant young like you. We're in totally different places in life."

"I was in your place in life a long time ago, Ivy. Way before I should have been. Don't judge me by my age or think I'm some immature kid."

"I know you're not. I can see that. Trust me."

He shoves his hands in his pockets and shakes his head. "I'm not going to keep you here to argue this out. I know you have to go, and I don't want your daughter to be worried." He leans down and kisses my cheek. "Drive safe, and I'll see you at your next appointment."

I breathe in the scent of him before he pulls away. He smells so good—a mix of incense from the shop and his cologne.

"Thank you for dinner," I murmur. "I really enjoyed talking with you and getting to know you."

"Same here, Sunshine. You have no idea how much. My

dinner invitation stands—any time you're ready to accept it."

I get in my car and watch him walk around to the other side of the building, away from the shop entrance, so I assume the door to his apartment must be over there. Squinting in the dark, I see a balcony off the side of the building that I didn't notice before. A new light turns on upstairs, and he walks by the window, pulling his shirt over his head. Even in the shadows, I can see how muscular he is. *Great, Ivy. Don't be a voyeur now, on top of everything else.*

Regret fills me as the light goes out, and I wonder if he's in his bed right now, if he's thinking about me. I wish I could have gone upstairs with him and spent more time with him. Somehow, he makes everything feel better. Even just talking to him, I felt relaxed, happy, more myself. More like the girl I used to be . . . like Charlene is now, as Paul so aptly pointed out.

At least I don't scrape plaque for a living, Charlene.

And guess what else, Charlene. Paul will never kiss you the way Lukas just kissed me. That much I know without a doubt.

I start my car and turn the heat on, giving it a few minutes to warm up. I'm still breathless and reeling from his kisses and feeling his hard body pressed against mine. My panties are wet from wanting him so much. As I stare up at his window, my mind wanders to the feel of his piercings against my soft flesh, and now I know why some women squeal over men with piercings. What that must feel like in other places . . .

My cell phone rings, the noise scaring me out of my daydream. I dig it out of my purse and see it's my home number on the caller I.D.

"Hi, Macy," I answer cheerfully.

"Mom, where are you? It's after ten." Role reversal can happen so unexpectedly.

"I know, honey," I say, flustered. "My appointment lasted longer than I expected. I'm on my way home. I'll be there in less than half an hour." I pull out of the parking lot, hoping Lukas doesn't see I was still sitting in my car watching his windows.

"Well, why did I have to come home if you were staying out late?" my daughter demands. "I could have stayed out with my friends longer."

Jesus. My first night out after dark, and I'm already battling with my teenager.

"Because you're supposed to be home at ten. That's why."

She sighs in exasperation. "Seriously, Mom, I'm almost eighteen. None of my friends have to be home by ten. It's totally lame. Now that Dad is gone, can you just forget that and let me stay out later? I don't drink or anything. We just hang out and talk or get coffee."

"Macy, your father is not gone. We're separated, but he is still your father, and your curfew was his rule."

"Yeah, Dad isn't exactly great at sticking to the rules himself, now is he?"

Grinding my teeth, I try to pay attention to the road as the familiar pounding in my head returns. "We talked about those comments, Macy. I know this is difficult. It is for all of us."

"Not for Dad, just the rest of us."

I silently agree with her. Paul got to move in with Charlene the Great, and meanwhile, the kids and I have been thrown into an unwanted mess.

"Sweetie, I know. Things will get better."

"Tomorrow, I'm supposed to hang out with Shelly. Can I at least stay out 'til midnight? Or can she come here? We're going to do a Vampire Diaries marathon."

Crap. Tomorrow night I'm supposed to have dinner with

LUKAS

Tim, a guy I work with. He cornered me in the break room every day for two weeks until I agreed to go out with him. I refuse, however, to consider it a date. When I agreed to have dinner with him, I figured it would shut him up for a few days, and then I could cancel a few days before, telling him I had to do something with the kids. And of course, I've had such a week from hell that I forgot to do that, so now it would be rude to call him tomorrow morning and cancel at the last minute, especially when I have to see him every day. You would think, with me working in Human Resources, I would know better than to ever agree to engage in any kind of out-of-office interactions, which, oddly enough, the company I work for doesn't have a policy against. I make a mental note to bring that up at the next staff meeting.

"Mom? Hello? Are you even listening to me?"

"Yes, I just remembered I have to go out tomorrow night for work, so why don't you have Shelly over? She can sleep over if she wants."

"Awesomeness! I'm gonna go call her right now. Love ya." She ends the call, done with me.

Later that night, as I'm sitting on the bed applying lotion to my tattoo and admiring how beautiful it is, the memory of Lukas' hands lingering on my leg as he worked on me, how little electric tingles raced up my spine at his touch, come to the forefront of my mind. I haven't felt like that in so very long, if ever at all. I wanted him to keep touching me, and I wanted to get my hands all over him, too. I wonder if tattoos cover his entire body. *What would it feel like to glide my hands over those muscles and twist my fingers in his long hair?*

As I'm getting into bed, I find a tiny black feather on my pillow. Frowning, I pick it up, wondering where it came from. I open my nightstand drawer and tuck it into the corner. It's too pretty to throw away.

Snuggling under the sheets, I'm exhausted but unable to fall asleep because I can't get these thoughts of Lukas out of my head. I can't understand why he's interested in me. Could it be some sort of joke? He really didn't strike me as the game playing type, though. I can't help but wonder why someone like him would be interested in me? I'm old, boring, and I have stretch marks. I have two kids. Clean laundry is the highlight of my weekend, and my life is a mess. Why would a hot young guy want anything to do with any of that? It makes zero sense.

Despite all that, I can't deny that I *really* like him. He's sweet, considerate, talented, and definitely knows how to kiss. I never thought a kiss could make me feel so much, not just within myself, but to actually be able to feel emotion coming from him as he kissed me. It was nothing short of incredible. I would have loved to go upstairs with him to kiss him all night, but I doubt it would have stopped there, and I'm not ready to get naked in front of anyone. I don't think I'll ever be. My own husband didn't even want to have sex with me, so I'm pretty sure Lukas would be repulsed by me.

Rolling over onto my side, I decide all I have to do is get through one, possibly two more appointments, and then I won't have to see him anymore, which is probably for the best. Then this little excursion of random excitement will be over, and I can go back to my boring life as a pending thirty-something divorcee with no life.

CHAPTER 7

IVY

The next day, when I drag my ass out of my bed and go down to the kitchen for coffee, I find Macy staring out the kitchen window like a rabid animal.

"Holy hell, Mom," she says excitedly when she sees me. "That snow guy you hired is so cute!"

Snow guy? Confused, I watch her go to the refrigerator and grab a bottle of water as she continues talking. "I'm going to go bring him some water because he looks hot and dehydrated. But mostly hot."

"What? What snow guy?" I ask, still not following the conversation. "Macy, what are you talking about?" She skips out the back door before I have a chance to stop her and get some answers.

I didn't hire a handyman yet, so I assume that Paul sent someone over here to take care of the shed roof, to let himself off the hook. I grab my coffee cup, hoping Paul is paying this guy so I don't have to, and look out the window to see my daughter talking to a very muscular young man with long black hair just past his shoulders, wearing a black thermal shirt, faded jeans, and workboots, who's standing next to our shed with a shovel. I can see the tattoos on his hands from here.

Oh, damn. It's Lukas!

What the—?

I watch as my beautiful daughter flirts with him, playing with her hair, and standing way too close to him. She's wearing a tight sweater, her favorite jeans, and big fuzzy boots. She tilts her head, giggling at something he's saying. They actually look really cute next to each other.

Oh no. This cannot be happening.

I feel like a squirrel in the middle of the road with an oncoming car, going this way and then that way and then the other way again. Total confusion of epic proportions.

Should I be feeling jealous? No. *But I do.*

Should I be glad that a guy as nice, talented, and caring as Lukas might be interested in my daughter's attention? Yes. He'd definitely treat her a lot better than the last boy she dated, who I caught trying to sneak into her bedroom like a little perv. I kicked his ass right out of here.

But I don't want Lukas interested in my daughter for any reason, because all I can think of is how he kissed *me*, and the passion I saw in his eyes, and how he made my legs weak. I can't even think about him making my daughter feel that way, because I want him for myself, not to mention that I don't want my little girl feeling that way until she's at least thirty.

I watch him from the window for signs of flirting with Macy, but I don't see any, and I'm ashamed to admit I'm glad.

And what is he doing at my house anyway? How does he even know where I live?

I want to go out there and interrupt them, but I can't because Macy will be furious and embarrassed if I do that when she's so obviously flirting with him. A sick feeling creeps over me as I think about what my daughter would say if she knew Lukas and I were friends, and possibly a little bit more. This is definitely not a situation I ever thought I would be in.

Feeling guilty, I watch them talking until she spins around and comes back inside, smiling from ear to ear.

She playfully fans herself with her hand as she comes through the door. "Wow, is he hot. Did you see the body on him, Mom?"

My God. When did my daughter start thinking about men like this? She was five only yesterday. *Wasn't she?*

I smile weakly from behind my coffee cup. "Macy, he's a friend of mine. He's my tattoo artist."

Her jaw falls open in shock. "Oh my God, Mom, are you kidding me right now?"

"Nope."

She pounces into a chair at the breakfast table. "Mom! Can you talk to him for me? Kinda set us up or something? I was hoping he'd ask for my number, but he didn't." Her face turns into a pout, just like it did when she was a little girl. "Is he single? Do you know?"

The awkwardness of this entire conversation makes me queasy. "I think he is, honey, but I think he might be a little too old for you. He's in his twenties." And too young for me, I remind myself.

She rolls her eyes. "The boys my age are lame, Mom. And they don't have bodies like him. And those tats! Not to mention his hair and those eyes. And that lip piercing. He's amazing."

All true, but I simply cannot even contemplate any of this with my daughter. Talking about men, and being attracted to the same man? No. Just no.

I knew that by having her when I was just eighteen I would always be a young mom, but I am definitely not prepared to hear my teen daughter talk about how sexy a man is, especially one that just about kissed me senseless the night before and I'm still swooning over. I blame this new mess on Paul. His lust for Charlene has put us all in awkward positions.

Macy jumps to her feet. "I'm gonna go upstairs to call Shelly and tell her about him. I'm gonna snap a pic of him from my bedroom window to show her."

"Macy, don't do that!" I yell as she bounds for the stairway, but it's too late. She's already gone.

I grab a sweatshirt that's draped over one of the kitchen chairs, step into a pair of boots that are by the back door, and walk out to the back yard to find out what Lukas is up to.

"Hi . . . What are you doing here?" I ask, squinting against the sun as I approach him.

Smiling, he points to the shed, like I didn't know it was there. "I fixed it."

"I can see that, and it's really nice of you to do, but why? You shouldn't be doing things like this for me. You're not a handyman."

He shrugs and wipes his face with a bandanna. "I just wanted to do something for you. Now you don't have to worry about it. It took about ten minutes. No big deal."

Again, he's melting my heart. "That's incredibly sweet but totally not necessary. I could have found someone to do it."

He takes a sip from the bottle of water Macy gave him. "Now you won't have to." He nods toward the house. "You have a really nice house. It's big. Very suburbs."

"I honestly appreciate you doing this, but really, you didn't have to. And as you can see, my teenage daughter has developed an insta-crush on you."

He twists the top back on the water bottle and actually blushes a little. "She's cute but too young for me. I like older women. One in particular." He tilts his head toward me with that adorable crooked smile on his face.

How does he make me feel so wanted with just a few words and a smile?

"Lukas, this cannot happen. I feel really bad that you came over here to do this, and I'm going to pay you."

He scrunches up his face. "No way. You can pay me by going out with me tonight."

I cross my arms. "I have plans tonight."

His eyes narrow at me suspiciously. "Really?"

"Yes, really."

"Okay, then," he says, looking unhappy. "How about Sunday night?"

Damn, he's persistent! "I can't. My son is coming home from his father's."

"Next week then? Any night. You pick."

I laugh and shake my head. "I give you credit for your persistence, but I can't. I like you, I really do. I just can't. My daughter thinks you're hot. I can't even wrap my head around what she would say if she knew I went out with you. It's way too strange for me."

He turns to close the shed door and latches it, giving me a great view of his broad back. I love how his hair falls down past his shoulders and his butt looks amazing in those faded jeans. He turns around to face me again, and I quickly look away.

"Ivy, it doesn't have to be strange. Just tell her the truth. She'll be okay."

"What truth? There is no truth."

He reaches for my hand, holding it in the warmth of his.

"The truth that I'm interested in you, and hopefully, you feel the same way. I mean, you were just checking out my ass, so that must mean something, right?" he teases.

Pulling my hand away, I glance uneasily up at Macy's bedroom window, hoping she's not taking pictures and uploading them for the world to see.

"Lukas, please. I can't do displays of affection from a stranger in front of my kids. They're confused enough already over their father and his new girlfriend. And I was *not* checking out your ass."

"You can't punish yourself for what he did. He's enjoying his life. You're allowed to do the same. Eventually, your kids will see you with another man, just like they're seeing him with another woman. I know it sucks, but unless you plan to stay single for the rest of your life, which would be a total fucking shame, then you have to let your kids see you around other men."

"I know that, but . . ."

He pulls a pack of gum out of his pocket and pops a piece into his mouth. "But what?" he asks "Is it me you don't want them to see you with?"

I stare off for a moment before answering. "They would have a hard time with it." I admit, trying to envision introducing him to my kids.

Leaning his back against the shed, he blows a bubble, pops it, and looks at me. "With *it*? With me? Are you embarrassed to be seen with me?"

I hate making him feel like there's something wrong with him, because there isn't, because he's wonderful just as he is. He's just wrong for *me* in this time and place.

"No! Not at all! It's just them seeing me with another man, and especially one that's younger and looks like a rock star.

They're used to their father. He's clean cut, works in an office . . . I don't want to throw too much crazy at them all at once."

His jaw muscles flex and clench. "Please don't say that. I hate that term: rock star."

"I'm sorry. I'm not trying to offend you," I stammer, knowing that I *am* offending him because I can't find the right words to explain what I'm trying to say.

"Ivy, I don't care what other people think, and you shouldn't, either. I'm not saying you shouldn't care what your kids think, but I don't think it's a big deal to date a man younger than you, or one that looks like me. There are way worse things going on in the world they're going to see." He takes his sunglasses off the top of his head, runs his hand through his hair, and puts the glasses on his face. "If they were my kids, I'd want to show them that we should accept people for who they are, not what they look like or how old they are, or what they do for work."

I stiffen and back away from him. He's right, but I don't need some twenty-four-year-old kid with zero parenting experience lecturing me. Of course, I don't want my children to be judgmental. I want them to accept people of all color, religion, career choice, and sexual orientation, no matter what.

"You're right," I agree. "But you really don't know what it's like. It's just hard, being a parent. I'm trying to do the right thing is all."

"I'm sure it *is* hard. Now, what night are you going to let me take you out?" he asks as we walk across the back yard together toward the house.

"You don't give up, do you?"

"No. Until you outright tell me you will never, ever go out with me, I'm gonna keep asking. You should go out with me just to shut me up."

I shake my head at him and feel my cheeks heating.

"Why? I don't get it. I'm boring. And difficult, as you can see."

He puts his arm around me and leads me to the side of the garage where we're invisible from all the windows of my house.

"I like challenges," he teases.

I wonder if he's going to kiss me back here on the side of the garage, and if he does, I don't think I'll have the power to resist. He looks incredibly hot all sweaty, his hair messy, dark sunglasses covering what I know are sensual hooded eyes looking right through me.

"Seriously, I like you, Ivy. I'm tired of dating all these batshit crazy chicks in the party scene. I'm not into it. I want to be with someone normal and settled down that I can trust." He touches the tip of my nose. "Plus, you're adorable. You even look great in the morning."

Oh, shit. I completely forgot that I came out here to talk to him right from crawling out of bed, with sweats on.

I put my hands over my face. "Oh my God. I totally forgot I didn't have any make up on and I look like a slob."

He grabs my hands and pulls them away to uncover my face. "You're beautiful. Don't hide."

I gently take his sunglasses off his face so I can see his eyes, and just as I expected, they're dancing with sincerity and sensuality.

"Lukas, you're incredibly sweet."

He grins, and my insides melt like butter in a hot pan. "I know that, doll."

Resistance is so damn hard around him.

"I just don't think it's a good idea," I say again, trying to convince both of us. Even I'm getting tired of hearing myself say it.

He takes a few steps away in frustration and then comes back to stand in front of me. "I think it's a great idea, Ivy, but I'm not gonna beg. That's just fuckin' pitiful. But will you do just one little thing for me?"

"That depends..."

"Think it over and give me an answer when I see you at our next appointment. All right? I'm just asking you to have dinner with me. Nothing else. I'd love to kiss you again, but I'll take dinner for now."

He must think I'm a freak. Who acts like this when a guy asks them out for dinner? Me, of course. That's who. Because I'm completely socially inept.

"Okay," I agree. "I'll think about it."

"Finally, some progress." He smiles from ear to ear then backs up and does his little wave thing. "Later, gator."

I know I've got a silly grin on my face as I watch him walk away.

CHAPTER 8

LUKAS

After I leave Ivy's, I drive to Gram's house for a visit. Since I usually work on Saturday, I don't get to visit her on the weekends when the rest of my family does, but I cleared my day today so I could fix Ivy's roof and have a little downtime for myself. Thankfully, all my clients were really cool about rescheduling.

Gram's house is like the hub of the family; everyone comes and goes constantly. Her house has six bedrooms, so some of us sleep there at random times to keep her company or just to hang out.

My brother Vandal's sports car and a tricked-out pickup truck that I think is my cousin Talon's new toy are in the driveway when I get there.

As soon as I walk through the back door, I'm met with the smell of baking, because Gram pretty much cooks non-stop. Cookies, pies, stew, shepherd's pie, lasagna, meat loaf—you name it. She's either cooked it, is cooking it, or is planning on cooking it.

"Uncle Lukas!" Vandal's five-year-old daughter flies across

the room and throws herself into my arms. Holding her high, I spin around with her in my arms as she giggles.

"How's my girl?" I hold her against my chest and plant a big kiss on her cheek.

"Good! We're making brownies!"

I carry her toward the kitchen, where Gram and Vandal are standing over the center island.

"Brownies?" I repeat. "My favorite."

Vandal nudges me with his elbow. "Yeah, not those kinds of brownies, man," he jokes.

I kiss Gram on the cheek as she's stirring batter in a big bowl, and she smiles up at me. "Honey, what a nice surprise. Why aren't you working?"

I lower Katie down to her feet and watch her run to the kitchen table to play with her toys.

"I had something to do this morning, so I rescheduled everyone to take the day off." I grab a cookie from a big plate on the counter and turn to my brother. "You're working next week, right? If you're going to be out a lot with the band, we're going to have to hire another artist."

He nods and runs his hand through his long black hair. "Yeah, I'll be there. Lemme think about hiring someone else. I'd rather not. I wanted it to be just me and you, and not deal with the bullshit of employees."

"Language, Vandal," Gram whispers, nodding over at Katie.

"Me, too," I agree. "But it's getting really busy. I can't do everything myself. I think we need a receptionist at the very least. I can't keep stopping to answer the phone. It makes the customers nervous."

"Fuck that, we don't need someone to answer the phone. Let it go to voicemail and call them back."

LUKAS

Gram smacks Vandal up the side of his head with the spatula. "Go put a quarter in the jar!"

Vandal rubs the side of his head, where he has a smudge of brownie batter now. "What the fuck, Gram?"

"Stop swearing in front of the baby! Now go put a quarter in the jar."

Cracking up, I watch him dig around in his pockets. "I don't have a quarter," he says. "I only have a twenty."

She shrugs. "I don't care. Put it in the jar." Gram is like a dwarf—maybe five feet tall, gray hair, little rimmed glasses, and usually dressed up wearing tons of jewelry. Her personality is a scream, and she keeps all of us guys in line, usually having us in hysterics. We all love her and would kill for her.

The swear jar is stuffed with bills and just a few quarters. "Gram, what are you going to do with all that money you've extracted from all of us?" I ask. I've lost about a hundred bucks in that jar myself.

She puts the baking pan into the oven and sets the timer. "Never mind that. You boys swear way too much in front of Katie. Do you want her to start swearing and sounding like a truck driver?"

"Yes," Vandal replies, grinning at Gram. He loves to get her riled up.

"Don't make me smack you again," she retorts.

I watch Katie color a picture of a rainbow and a unicorn for a few moments, and she suddenly smiles up at me, her two front teeth missing. I ruffle her hair and lean down to kiss the top of her head.

"This one is for you, Uncle Lukas," she tells me in her sweet voice. "When I'm done, you can take it home and put it on your wall, or maybe tattoo it on someone."

"I would love to do that, Princess Katie."

Vandal crosses the room and sits in the chair at the table next to Katie. "Hey, I heard you dumped Rio," he says, grabbing some crayons.

Frowning, I lean against the wall and shake my head. "Yeah, I did. Is there anyone you haven't screwed?"

He tilts his head like he's thinking about it. "Not many, bro. You may have to move to the west coast."

"Very funny."

He chooses a purple crayon and starts to color one of Katie's pictures. "So why'd you dump her? She's fun."

I grind my teeth to keep from swearing. I don't want to lose twenty bucks. "I don't want your leftovers. That's why."

"You're not gonna find a virgin, pal. Suck it up."

"I'm not saying a virgin. Just someone *you* haven't been with."

"Why? I can give you honest reviews. Like a critique service."

"I'm going to fucking punch you in the face in about two seconds," I warn, even though I'm laughing. He's such an asshole sometimes.

Gram pipes up from across the room. "Lukas . . . you know the rules."

Oh, fuck me. I pull out my wallet. "You're killing us, Gram," I tease, shoving a five dollar bill into the jar.

"Someday, you will both thank me."

"Someday, we'll both be here for a loan," Vandal shoots back.

I saunter over to Gram, who's rinsing the dishes in the sink. "Hey, Gram, I was hoping we could talk for a few minutes."

"Of course we can." She grabs a towel and dries off her hands. "Let's go in the other room."

LUKAS

I follow my grandmother to the den, which I know is her favorite room because it's filled with all of my late grandfather's most coveted things. I wish I could have met him before he passed away, and thank him for changing my life. But sadly, without his death, my father wouldn't have had come clean about having two sons, and I wouldn't be here now.

Gram sits on the leather couch and pats the spot next to her. "Come sit by me, Lukas. You have a glint in your eye. Have you met someone?"

I love my grandmother for so many reasons. She's not just the sweetest and most caring person I've ever met; she's amazingly in touch with every single person in her family. She truly knows each of us and what makes us tick. Being the matriarch of a family of mostly male musicians and artists can't be easy, but she keeps us in line and makes all of us feel loved and accepted, even when we've messed up.

I flop onto the worn leather couch and stretch my legs out in front of me. "I did meet someone, Gram. I need some advice."

She clasps her hands on her lap and beams. "I knew it! Okay, let's see if I can help. Tell me all about her."

I sigh, feeling lost about how to explain my feelings. How do I explain that heart-stopping jolt I feel every time I see or touch Ivy? I hardly even know her.

"She's a client."

Gram raises her eyebrows at me.

"I know, I know," I say, holding my hands up. "I broke my own rule, but there's just something about her. Every time I touch her, my stomach does back flips. I can barely tattoo her without my hands shaking. I've never felt like that before."

"Ahhh . . . chemistry is *so* wonderful. I remember that feeling."

"Yeah. *That.* She's really cute, too, and kinda shy. She has a good job, and she's totally normal. She doesn't party. She doesn't have fake tits or gobs of makeup . . . she listens to me when I talk, like she really cares about what I'm saying, ya know?"

A warm smile touches her lips. "She sounds like a lovely girl for you, sweetheart. I like her already."

"Yeah, but here's the problem—she won't go out with me."

"Oh," Gram says, frowning. "Well, why not? Why wouldn't she want to date you?"

"She's thirty-six. Her husband just left her a few months ago, after being married for eighteen years. He had an affair with a younger girl. She's got two kids—a teenage daughter and a son a little older than Katie. Her head still seems kinda messed up over it. She keeps saying she's not ready, and that I'm too young for her."

Gram listens intently, her eyes growing wider the longer I talk, and she finally lets out a low whistle.

"Oh, boy. You have your work cut for you, I'm afraid."

Taking a deep breath, I stare at the old grandfather clock against the wall, which belonged to my great grandfather, and then my grandfather. The cherry wood is gorgeous and perfectly carved, and the ticking lulls me as I stare at it, almost hypnotizing me. Gram knows that I'm in love with this clock and has promised to will it to me when she passes, which is something I don't even want to think about, but I'll cherish that clock forever.

"If you really like her, you're going to have to be patient with her, but also let her know how you feel. She probably feels very confused right now and distrusting of men in general, and I really don't blame her."

"You're right. She's scared. I can see it when I talk to her."

"I'm sure she is. And the age thing, for her, it probably seems like a big deal. I would guess that she *feels* much older than she actually is. You're mature for your age, and eventually, she'll see that, but I'm sure it's going to take some time."

"So what do I do? I kissed her last night, and it was off the charts. I know she felt it, too, but she keeps putting walls up."

"I'm not sure, love. I think you're going to just have to give her time. Let her know that you're willing to wait for her. Are you?"

"Hell, yeah. I'll wait. I don't want to, obviously. But for her, yeah . . . I'll wait."

She puts her small hand on my arm. "She needs to feel like you could be someone stable for her. Her husband just shattered her world, right?"

I nod. "Yeah, she was blindsided. For real."

"Then you have to gain her trust. She has to find out what a wonderful man you are. And you really are, Lukas. You're a gentleman. She doesn't know it right now, but soon she will, and she'll be very lucky to have you in her life."

I don't mind giving Ivy time to figure out that I'm not gonna hurt her, but damn, I want her. Now.

Gram squeezes my arm softly to get my attention. "And what about the children? Are you ready to be involved with a woman who has two children? That's a lot of responsibility, and it won't be easy. She's not going to be able to just get up and go on a whim, or hang out all night at concerts with you. Have you thought about all of that?"

I roll my head back and forth against the back of the couch. "Well . . . sorta, but maybe not in that much detail. I love kids. I have no problem with her having children. I haven't even told her I play in the band sometimes."

She smacks my arm. "Lukas! You have to tell her. No secrets, all right? When will you boys learn? I tell you all over and over. No lies. No secrets. Why is it so hard?" She shakes her head in exasperation.

Laughing, I give in, knowing she's right. "Okay, okay. I'll tell her. I'm going to ask her to come to the next show with me. Maybe she'll actually say yes."

"You have to bring her here when you get this sorted. I want to meet her."

"Definitely. I could love this chick, Gram. I can feel it. She's the one."

A huge smile spreads across her face, and her eyes sparkle.

"You're such a romantic, Lukas. You're just like your grandfather. You remind me so much of him when he was your age."

I straighten up and turn fully toward her, interested to hear more about my grandfather. "Really? What was he like?"

She literally glows as she gazes at his photograph on the wall. "He was a very special man. Smart. Generous. Good looking. Everybody loved him."

"I wish I could have met him."

"I think most of you boys get your romantic side from him. Your Uncle Ronnie is the same way. Unfortunately, your father is not. He's not a lover, but a drifter. He doesn't know what he wants. He never has."

I stare at the clock and chew the inside of my cheek before asking my next question, not sure I want to hear the answer. "Do you ever hear from him? My father?"

She shakes her head and frowns. "No. Not since your grandfather passed." Her voice drops. "But that's okay. He told me about you and Vandal, and that's all that matters. I can't chase your father anymore. He's taken years off my life already."

"I don't understand what his deal is. Why doesn't he care about us?" I'll never understand why my parents didn't want me, and even though I try to tell myself it doesn't matter, and that it's their loss, and all the other bullshit that therapists and shrinks fed me growing up, it still bothers me that I was given away and forgotten like trash.

"Sweetheart, he doesn't even care about himself. He's not capable of caring about anyone else. We all love you and Vandal, no matter what. Don't let his bad choices and shortcomings affect you."

I crack my knuckles and stand up. "I should get going." I take her hand and help her up. "Thanks for listening to me."

"Anytime. You'll be here for Christmas? You can bring your friend and her children. The more the merrier."

I'm not sure Ivy will be ready to have a family Christmas dinner with me in a few weeks. Especially with this crew. "We'll see, Gram."

Vandal and Katie are still at the kitchen table coloring when we return from our talk, and my cousin Talon has joined them. Vandal is grinning like an idiot and I can tell something is up.

"What's so funny?" I ask him.

He nods his head at Talon. "Tell him."

My cousin just shakes his head and says nothing. "Tal, tell me," I say. "What's up?"

"He's getting married!" Katie yells excitedly.

"What? To who?" I don't even remember him having a girlfriend.

"In a month or two, I'm not sure yet."

Vandal nudges him again. "Tell him all of it."

Talon makes a face, and I can tell Vandal is pissing him off. "It's a social experiment that a group of psychologists and relationship experts are running. My mom is friends with the director."

I squint at him. "Social experiment? What's that mean?"

"He's gonna marry a total fucking stranger," Vandal interrupts. "Like a lab rat."

My gaze rivets on Talon, shocked. "Wow, really? A stranger?"

He nods. "Yeah. We don't get to meet or see each other, or know anything about each other at all. We see each other for the first time at the wedding."

"Holy shit." I don't know what else to even say. It's crazy, but also, kinda cool.

"We have to fill out all these quizzes and talk to the shrinks, and they match us up with what they think is our perfect match. So, we get married and have to stay together for six months. After that, we can stay together or split up, and we each get fifty thousand dollars."

"So you're doing this for the money, right?" Vandal asks.

"No, asshole. I don't need money. I have shit luck with chicks. I want to see if this works."

I lean against the wall, captivated with this idea. "I think it's wild," I say. "Is it televised? Like a reality show?"

He shakes his long light brown hair. "No. We just journal everything."

"Well, I think it's cool, and I'm really interested to see how it goes."

"Aren't you supportive?" Vandal teases.

"You're a dick."

"Boys! I cannot even count the amount of money you owe me right now. Do you think I can't hear you just because I'm over here making meringue?"

"Sorry, Gram," we all say in unison.

"And you," she points to Vandal. "Leave your cousin and your brother alone. There's nothing wrong with wanting to find love."

"They're gonna find themselves buying *Divorce for Dummies*, Gram. Don't you care?"

She throws a bowl into the sink. "Of course I care. But I want you to be nice to others."

"I can't, Gram," Vandal replies. "The darkness lives in me."

Gram shakes her head, but I can tell she's laughing. Vandal is going to make her insane. And rich.

"I'm outta here," I say. "Van, I'll see you on Monday?"

He nods without looking up at me because he's coloring a butterfly black in Katie's book. "Yup," he says.

"Talon, good luck, man."

"Thanks."

Katie stands up on her chair and puts her arms around my neck. I hug her back tightly. "Uncle Lukas, do you want to come home with us tonight?"

Kissing her forehead, I gently place her back down on the chair. "Not tonight, baby. But when Daddy needs me to babysit, you can come to my place."

"Yay!" she yells.

"Tonight, we're watching cartoons, Katie-bug," Vandal says, and then glances to me. "Lukas, you can come hang out if you want."

"Thanks, but I've got some stuff to do." I grab another

cookie and give Gram a hug as she hands me a big Tupperware container filled with cookies and brownies.

"Take these, honey."

Well, damn. I'm going to be on a sugar high for the rest of the weekend.

CHAPTER 9

IVY

I stop at Macy's bedroom door and peek inside to see what she's doing. She's laying on her bed, reading with her ear buds in. Her room is actually clean for once, which is a huge difference from a few months ago when she had so many clothes thrown around that I couldn't see the floor. I hope this is going to be a new habit.

She suddenly looks up and pulls the ear buds off. "Hey, Mom. What's up?"

"I'm heading out, but I won't be home late. What time is Shelly coming over?"

"She's on her way here now. Did you talk to that cute guy? Maybe kinda hint around that I like him?"

I get an instant stress headache and a strange feeling in my stomach. "No, sweetie, I really don't talk to him. He's just my tattoo artist. He only stopped by to fix the shed."

"Well, maybe at your next appointment you could sorta say something?" she asks hopefully.

"Macy, I'm not sure I feel comfortable with that. I'm your

mother, and that would be inappropriate. Just behave yourselves while I'm gone, please. There's food in the fridge."

"Whatever. Have fun." She puts her ear buds back in and goes back to her book, dismissing me for now.

Fun. I have no faith that tonight will be fun at all, and I wish I could just stay home. Waiting in the living room, I watch the street from the window until I see Tim's car pull into my driveway. With a heavy sigh, I put my coat on and head outside into the frigid night air, not even giving him the chance to come to my front door. Do men even do that anymore for a date? Not that this is a date, but I'm curious.

"I would have come to your door," is the first thing he says when I get in the passenger seat of his SUV, so I guess some men still do show up at the door

I shrug. "It's all right."

"I thought we'd try that new bar and grill place," he says, backing the car out into the street.

I force a smile at him. "That sounds great."

I'm not even hungry, because my stomach is still in knots over Lukas. I tried to distract myself all day by cleaning the house and doing laundry to get my mind off him, but instead, I found myself daydreaming about him randomly throughout the day. Suddenly, I was having quick flashbacks of how his lips felt on mine, sending warm shivers coursing through my body.

"I'm glad you finally agreed to go out with me. I've thought you were attractive since the day you interviewed me." Tim smiles over at me and then averts his eyes back to the road. "I was disappointed to find out you were married, to be honest."

Ugh. How do I even reply to that? I'm a little disturbed that he was checking me out during the interview process. That seems a bit unprofessional to me. I really shouldn't have agreed to this dinner. I already know that there isn't any chemistry here, and I'm not going to want to go out with him again, so it's going to be really awkward if I ever have to fire him. I'm sure he won't be attracted to me then.

"Well, like I said, Tim, I don't believe in dating co-workers."

"I'm hoping I can change your mind."

Saying nothing, I turn to stare out the window, just as we're driving past Lukas' tattoo parlor. Could the timing be any worse? Red holiday lights shine from around his business sign, and little lights glow amber in the upstairs windows of his apartment. As we drive further away, a sense of sadness creeps up on me. If I had said yes to Lukas earlier, we'd probably be having dinner together right now. I could be smiling at how his hair falls over his face, covering those dark, sexy eyes of his.

The new restaurant is packed. Even with the reservation Tim made, we have to wait thirty minutes to get a table. It's so loud, from the music playing over the speakers and people talking around us, that we really can't talk while we wait, which he takes as an opportunity to play around on his phone.

"The emails never stop," he finally says to me. "It's hard to get away from work."

I smile sympathetically at him. Tim is an electrical engineer, and a good one from what I've heard. His performance reviews have been consistently excellent since he was hired five years ago. He's definitely not a slacker.

"It's okay. I understand," I reply.

Finally, our little pager goes off and we're taken to a table not far away from the bar. There aren't many places to eat in this small town, so it appears that everyone is flocking here to eat and hang out.

"You look great," Tim says after I take my winter coat off and sit down across from him at the tiny table. I notice his eyes lingering at the v of my sweater. I normally don't wear anything that shows off even the tiniest bit of cleavage at the office, but when I go out, I like to look a little more human and less like an office worker. Now, though, I'm afraid I'm sending the wrong message. Not that my boobs are huge or really very visible, but there is a bit of cleavage showing, which he's managed to zone in on.

"Thanks," I say, opening my menu and strategically holding it so he can't look at my chest anymore. I hate this awkwardness. Tim isn't a bad looking guy at all, to be honest. In fact, he's actually pretty good looking. His short brown hair is perfectly styled in the latest men's do, with a little bit messed up at the front. He's tall and lean, with bright sky-blue eyes. He always dresses well, and looks as though he's stepped out of a men's clothing ad. A lot of the women at the office flirt with him and hang out in his office for unnecessarily long periods of time. I peek up at him as he peruses the menu. Maybe I'm being too hard on him and need to drop my defenses a little. He *is* a nice guy—a little annoying sometimes, but still a decent, hard-working guy. Lindsay is right; I need to give people a chance and not run away from everyone just because Paul hurt me.

"What are you going to have?" I ask him while I attempt to narrow down my own choices.

"I think I'm going to get the rib eye. I've been dying for a good steak. How 'bout you? Please don't get a salad," he jokes.

I smile over the menu at him. "I think I'm going to have the vegetable ravioli. That sounds really good."

He nods in agreement. "It does. I've heard everything here is good."

The waitress arrives to takes our order, and I order a white wine with my dinner, hoping it will calm my nerves.

"So, how have you been doing?" Tim asks. "You know, after everything that's happened?"

The way he says it makes me feel like I've been in an accident or something. Like there was an *incident*. I wonder if people in the office have been talking about me, feeling sorry for me. I want to crawl under the table and hide.

"Okay, I suppose. It's been a hard adjustment for me and the kids, but I'm slowly getting used to the perils of being single," I reply, slightly sarcastically.

"How old are your kids?"

"Seventeen and seven."

He bites into a roll. "Seventeen?" he repeats, with his mouth full of bread. "Damn. I didn't realize your daughter was that old."

I nod and sip my wine. "Yes, I had her right out of high school." I'm not sure when seventeen became an age that was considered old.

"I don't have any kids," he says, taking another roll from the basket in the center of our table. "I can't imagine having a teenager right now at my age, though."

"I'm surprised you're not married." I wonder why a man in his mid-thirties isn't married, and to the best of my knowledge, never has been. Maybe that's a red flag that he's a player, or just not a good catch.

He laughs. "Yeah, I've heard the rumors floating around the office that I'm gay." *Yeah, or that.*

"Are you?"

He almost chokes on his bread, throwing his head back laughing. "Ivy, I can assure you, I am not gay. I just haven't met a woman I felt like I could stay committed to for the rest of my life." He takes a sip of his beer. "If it happens, it happens. If not, I'm totally fine just dating and having a good time. The last thing I want is to get married and then end up having an affair because I wasn't ready to give up variety."

I blink at him from across the table. "Yeah, that variety is a bitch."

He nearly spits his drink out. "Shit, Ivy, I'm sorry. I wasn't thinking."

Clearly.

"Don't worry about it." I catch his eyes ogling my chest again.

"You've had my interest for a long time, though, so who knows what could happen. Maybe you'll be the one to catch me."

Um. No. I gaze around the restaurant, hoping the waitress will show up with our food soon, and I do a double take when I see Lukas standing at the bar, laughing with a group of people. A gorgeous girl with long blonde hair is standing next to him, laughing with him, her hand on his arm. *Oh my God.* I gulp half my drink as he turns and his eyes lock on mine, as if he could feel me looking at him. *Dammit.*

I have no right to feel jealous, but I do. *Again.* He didn't waste any time finding someone else to spend time with tonight, now did he? And here I thought he actually really liked *me*.

"I'm starving. I hope our food gets here soon," Tim announces.

"Me, too. I haven't eaten all day," I answer vaguely, smoothing my napkin on my lap.

I look back over at Lukas to find him walking right toward our table. Uh oh. Something tells me this may not be good.

He stops next to our table and smiles down at me. "Hey," he says. "What a surprise to see you here."

I smile back. "Likewise. Tim, this is Lukas. Lukas, this is Tim. We work together."

Lukas shakes Tim's hand. "Nice to meet you, man," he says, but I can see his jaw clenching. He doesn't hide his feelings well at all.

I want to kiss the waitress for showing up with our dinner at that exact moment and saving me from further awkwardness. "Well, I'll let you two eat," Lukas says. "It was nice to see you again."

"You, too. Enjoy your night," I say back. He nods to Tim and walks slowly back to his date at the bar.

"Who was that?" Tim asks.

"Just a friend."

Tim cuts his steak and makes a surprised face at me. "Him? He doesn't look like someone you'd be friends with."

"Why is that?" I inquire, offended by his remark.

"That hair and all those tattoos? And face piercings? What the hell? How does someone like that even get a job? You're in HR, Ivy. Would you hire someone that looks like that?"

I slowly chew my ravioli. "I guess it depends what the job was, Tim. He's a tattoo artist, so the way he looks goes with his career choice. He actually owns his own business and he's very successful. He's not a criminal."

"Well, he looks like one."

And you look like an asshole.

My phone beeps in my purse, and I reach down to pull it out in case it's one of the kids.

It's a text from an unknown number.

Meet me by the restrooms please.

I look up quickly to see Lukas heading to the back of the restaurant.

"Tim, excuse me for just a moment. I have to go call my daughter."

"Is everything okay?"

"Yes, just parenting stuff is all. I'll be right back."

I make my way through the crowded restaurant to the hallway where the restrooms are, and find Lukas standing there, waiting for me.

"What are you doing?" I demand.

"I was going to ask you the same. Who's that guy?"

I raise my eyebrows at him. Who does he think he is to be questioning me?

"Excuse me? Why is that any of your business?"

"I guess it's not. But you told me you weren't ready to date when I asked."

"It's not a date. He's a co-worker."

"It looks like a date." He looks back at Tim sitting at the table and then at me. "You could've just told me you were dating someone, Ivy."

"I am *not* dating him. And what about you? You're not here alone, either."

"She's just a friend. She's actually dating one of my good friends. I stopped by here on my way home to grab a quick drink and say hello."

Relief that I have no right to have washes over me.

Suddenly, he moves and traps me against the wall with his body and lowers his face close to mine.

"Look, Ivy. We can stay here and eye-fuck each other across the room all night, or you can ditch this boring date you're with and meet me back at my place in half an hour."

I lick my lips and look nervously back at the table where Tim is waiting. I have zero interest in him. I never should have agreed to have dinner with him.

"And then what, Lukas?" I ask, turning back to him, our noses touching. "We shared one kiss, and it was probably a mistake."

A sexy defiant grin spreads across his face.

"I told you already, Sunshine. I don't make mistakes." He bows his head down lower until his lips brush across my cheek. "I make memories," he whispers. "Memories you'll never forget."

My heart pounds harder and faster in my chest.

"Lukas . . . please . . . you're twenty-four. I'm thirty-six-"

His lips on mine quickly shut me up.

"Shh . . . be a kitten tomorrow," he whispers, his hand sliding slowly up my arm. "Be a cougar tonight."

I giggle in his face. "Oh my God, Lukas, seriously? Did you just say that?"

He laughs with me and leans his head against mine. "I did. I'm losing my mind over you. You have to agree to have dinner with me before more cheesy shit starts coming out of my mouth."

I try to suppress more giggles. "You're crazy, you know that?"

"I know."

"You have to stop this," I say, although I can't stop smiling at him.

"I don't think I can."

I pull away from him and straighten my sweater.

"You look pretty," he says. "That sweater brings out the teal in your eyes."

"Thank you." I love that he used the word teal. How many men know what color that really is? Of course, he does because he's an artist, and I absolutely love that about him.

"Lukas, I can't just leave Tim. I work with him. I have to see him every day. I'm not a rude person, and I'm not going to start being one."

He looks defeated.

"Don't make that face, please," I retort. "You look just like my son."

He pouts some more, making me laugh. "You better stop," I say.

"Ivy, this sucks. We could be having a really nice dinner right now, at a nice quiet place, I might add, and instead, you're with that poser and I'm bored out of my mind. Now, I'm going to go home alone and think about you all night. There's no telling what I might do to myself thinking about you." He grins deviously and raises his eyebrows.

Lordy. I can feel my cheeks getting redder by the minute.

"You are naughty," I tell him, shaking my head at him. He's so damn playful, but I'm starting to love it.

"Come to my place after your non-date then," he offers. "I'll be there, just drawing probably. I'll show you all my artwork. I have books of it. And we can eat the cookies and brownies my Gram sent me home with."

I really need to get back to my dinner, or Tim is going to think I left him here.

"Lukas, no. I'm going directly home after this dinner, and I'll see you at our appointment. I told you I would consider having dinner with you, since you're being so crazy persistent, although I cannot for the life of me figure out why."

"Because I feel like we're meant to be together. That's why." He shrugs. "Laugh all you want. I don't care. I felt it the first day I saw you, and I don't fucking get it either, but you're like a magnet. I just keep getting pulled back to you. Even when I'm not around you, I can't get my mind off you. And when I *am* with you? All I want to do is get closer to you."

I want to tell him he's crazy, but I can't, because I feel the same way. So maybe we're both crazy. Whatever it is, it's scaring the hell out of me.

"I really have to go," I whisper, looking up into his eyes. "And I'm not laughing at all."

Once again, as I walk away from him, that familiar ache from leaving him comes back.

"I was just about to come look for you," Tim says when I return. "Is everything okay?"

I sit down and drink some of my wine. "I'm so sorry. My daughter was having some drama that I had to straighten out."

"I think your food is cold. Do you want me to flag the waitress and get it warmed up?"

I shake my head and pick up my fork. "No, it's totally fine. I'm so sorry I was gone for so long."

He smiles across the table. "You can make it up to me."

My insides cringe. There is no way that will be happening.

I force myself to eat. Time drags as we order coffee and

dessert, while Tim tells me about his new flat screen television, which he seems way too excited about.

Just as our dessert comes, I look across the room toward the bar to see Lukas saying good-bye to his friends. He looks back at me, does his little wave, and then leaves. Alone.

"You seem distracted," Tim says.

"No, it's just a little noisy here. It's hard to focus," I reply, but I'm pretty sure he's noticed me looking over at Lukas several times. Did he really tell me that he thinks about me all the time, or did I dream that up?

When we leave the restaurant, Tim asks me if I want to go back to his place, which I wasn't expecting at all and definitely have no interest in doing.

"No, thank you. I really should get home."

He looks at me across the dimly lit car as if I'm nuts. "It's not even ten yet. Why do you have to go home?"

"My daughter is home alone. I don't like to leave her alone at night."

"She's seventeen. I think she can manage for a few more hours. Or until the morning."

"Tim . . . I don't think I can do that. I'm sorry."

"I didn't think I'd be taking you out to dinner and then taking you home right after."

"Really?" I say, annoyed. "How many times have I said over the past few weeks that I wasn't interested in dating yet? I'm sorry, but I'm just not ready for anything more. I didn't mean to lead you on."

He takes his eyes off the road long enough to frown at me. "I figured when you finally said yes that it meant you changed your mind." He reaches across the car and puts his hand on my leg. On my thigh!

I want to jump out of the car to get away from him. "No, Tim, I'm sorry. I was just trying to be nice. I thought we could have dinner as friends."

"Well, yeah . . . but usually there's a little bit more than that. You know, friends with benefits? You really have no idea what goes on in the real dating world, do you?"

I refrain from telling him to go fuck himself in the real dating world, because no matter what, we still work together and I'm still the HR Manager, regardless of my bad decision to have dinner with him, and I'm not going to sink to his level. If the dating world consists of sleeping with people on the first date just for the hell of it, then I want nothing to do with it.

We don't speak at all until he parks in my driveway, where I thank him for dinner and get out of his car, slamming the door behind me.

"Mom, what are you doing home so early?" Macy asks when I walk through the front door. She and Shelly are lounged on the couch eating popcorn, engrossed in the television.

"It was just a quick dinner with someone I work with. Can I get you two anything?"

They both shake their heads simultaneously.

"Okay." I take off my coat and hang it in the hall closet. "I'll be upstairs. Enjoy your vampire marathon."

After a hot shower, I curl up in bed and put a romantic comedy on, realizing Tommy didn't call me to say goodnight. I hope that means he's having a good time with his father, but I also feel a little bit forgotten about. I hate this separation of my family, but it looks like I'm going to have to get used to it.

At midnight, my phone beeps on the bed next to me. Picking it up, I swipe my finger across the screen, squinting at the glare in the darkness of the room. It's a text from Lukas. I recognize his number now and quickly save it in my contacts.

Lukas: Hey

Me: It's midnight

Lukas: And? You gonna turn into a pumpkin? ;-)

A smile spreads across my face as I type back.

Me: Very funny :)

Lukas: I wanted to make sure you got home okay. Your date looked like he was either going to bore you to death or grope you on the way home.

Me: Yes to both, but I survived. I came home and went right to bed. Exciting, huh?

Lukas: Same here. Came home, been sitting in bed drawing.

Me: What did you draw?

A few minutes go by, and just as I think he's fallen asleep, I receive a picture message of a colored pencil drawing of a beautiful girl with long brown hair, her hair blowing to the side and fading into a butterfly wing. It's breathtaking. The colors are gorgeous, and even viewing it on my tiny phone screen, I can see the details are incredible.

Me: Wow. It's beautiful. Your talent is beyond words.

Lukas: It's for you

Me: Really?

Lukas: Yes. I'll give it to you when I see you at your appointment.

Me: Thank you. I love it.

Lukas: So he groped you?

Awww. Is he actually jealous?

Me: He put his hand on my leg and kinda hinted that he was hoping for more since he bought me dinner.

Lukas: WTF! This is why chicks don't trust guys. Dinner isn't exactly a trade off for a blowjob. Not in my book, anyway.

Me: I agree, and this is why I don't feel comfortable dating. I haven't dated since high school. That was a long time ago, and things are definitely different now.

Lukas: You can trust me, Ivy. You know that, right?

I stare at the phone and his tiny words in the green bubble. Yes, I do believe that he wouldn't rush or hurt me. Even though he's persistent, he knows when to stop, and he doesn't get mad or make me feel like there's something wrong with me. That's what I need right now.

Me: I trust you as much as I can right now.

Lukas: Well, that's a start. ;-)

Me: I wasn't exactly expecting all this with you. I just wanted a tattoo. :/

Lukas: You got the bonus plan. And I wasn't expecting this, either.

That shaky feeling comes over me again as I read his words.

Lukas: I felt like someone punched me when I saw you with that guy. Truth.

Funny. That's exactly how I felt when I saw that beautiful girl with him.

> Me: I don't know what to say. I'm confused by all of this.
> Lukas: I am, too.

The keyboard beckons me to type something, but I'm at a loss. I feel so much but have no idea how to say it, or if I even should. I feel like I'm playing with fire here, letting him in. The last thing I want to do is lead him on or get myself into something else I can't deal with, like the mess I created with Tim and dinner.

> Lukas: I know the age thing bugs you. I know you're used to being with guys with short hair and no piercings who have swanky office jobs. I know I'm not what you would ever look for or want. I get it.

My throat tightens. It's true . . . but he's so much more than that. Slowly, I'm seeing that. He's special. Unique.

My phone buzzes again.

> Lukas: Just give me a chance. I'm not a fuckup. I know what I want. Stop thinking about ages and looks. None of that matters.
> Me: I have never thought you were a fuckup. Quite the opposite, actually.
> Lukas: Good
> Me: I should go to sleep. Thank you for the drawing. I can't wait to see it.
> Lukas: Sweet dreams

I toss my cell phone to the side of the bed and roll over, hugging my pillow. It's still hard to sleep in this room without Paul. We lived and slept here together for so many years that now it feels haunted with memories of him, like he's going to

LUKAS

walk through the door at any moment. I'm starting to believe I really do need to sell this house and start over with new surroundings that aren't tainted with memories.

My phone beeps again. Shaking my head and smiling, I reach for it, and what I see makes my heart literally jump. It's a black and white photo of Lukas, lying against a black pillow, his hair falling over half his face. He's naked from the waist up, covered in tattoos. A large cross hangs around his neck, resting against his muscled chest. He's got a finger held to his lips. The room is dim and shadowy, and he looks hot as hell. I tear my eyes from the photo and read the words he's typed in the next text message.

Shh...
Rest your mind, my love
I shall see you in our dreams
Open your heart, my love
I shall cherish you always
Shh...
There is only you and I
No need to be afraid, my love
Shh...
If you stumble or fall, my love
I shall catch you every time

No one has ever sent me a poem before. I read it ten times . . . no, twenty . . . okay, maybe thirty. I love it, even though I'm not sure what it means. I open up the photo again, drawn to the sensuality of it, wanting to be in that bed with him. Of course he has black pillows and sheets; somehow, I knew he would.

I should reply, but what do I say to this?

I poise my fingers over my phone. Do I say something silly to diffuse this, or say something more in line with his romantic flirting?

Lord help me. Tim was right. I have no idea how to do any of this. We didn't have cell phone flirting when I was dating years ago. Is this why Macy is attached to her phone 24/7? This is so crazy.

> **Me:** Between the photo and the poem, you've rendered me speechless. I can't even think straight to reply.
>
> **Lukas:** Mission accomplished then. ;-)

Ack! He makes me crazy, and I can't deny the fact that I'm enjoying every minute of it.

CHAPTER 10

IVY

Today I took a personal day, something I haven't done in years. I thought I could see my hairdresser and get my hair cut and colored, but she's booked for two weeks. So now, I'm standing in the hair color aisle of the local beauty supply store, confused and overwhelmed.

"You just mix two of these with this and put it on." The salesgirl tells me, handing me three little boxes. "Mix it in this," she says, handing me a little plastic dish. "And put it on with this." She throws in a little brush thing. "And wear these." She adds some black gloves. "Then use this conditioner."

"That's it?" I ask, skeptical. "Is it hard?"

She shakes her head of pink hair. "Yup, that's it. It's not hard at all. I do mine all the time."

I'm not sure if that's a good or bad sign. She kinda looks like twenty things *not* to do to your hair.

"I've never had my hair colored before, not even at a salon," I say as I follow her to the register, clutching all the products she piled in my arms, and she glances back at me like I'm an alien.

"Leave it on for half an hour then rinse it. Don't use shampoo. Leave the conditioner on for five minutes. Then just dry it and style like you normally do. Piece of cake."

Okay. That sounds easy enough.

Next, I stop at the mall and buy a few new outfits and shoes, as well as a cute pair of black boy shorts with red hearts on them. I'm seeing Lukas tonight for my tattoo appointment, and I'm going to agree to have dinner with him tomorrow night if he still wants to. I haven't been able to stop thinking about him, and he continues to send me flirty text messages at all hours of the day and night. Screw the age difference; I'm determined to have some fun for once.

※

The house phone is ringing as soon as I walk through the front door after my shopping spree. "Hello?" I say breathlessly, wondering who would be calling me at home now, when normally I would be at the office this time of day.

"Hey, it's me," he says. "What are you doing home?"

I throw my shopping bags on the couch, annoyed that he had to call today of all days. "How did you know I was home, Paul?"

"I called your office, and your assistant told me you didn't come in today. What's wrong?"

"Nothing is wrong. I just felt like taking a personal day off."

"Hmm. That's not like you."

"What do you want?"

"I wanted to talk about Christmas. It's next week."

"I know when Christmas is," I reply, kicking off my shoes and sitting down on the couch next to all my new clothes.

"We haven't talked about what we're going to do with the kids."

"What do you mean?" I ask, my stomach already burning just from hearing his voice.

"Do you want them on Christmas Eve or Christmas Day? I'll let you pick."

Let me pick?

"Paul, what are you talking about? The kids are staying with me both days. We're going to my mother's house on Christmas Eve, just like we've been doing for the past eighteen years, and Christmas Day, I'm making breakfast and dinner, like we've always done."

Does he think I'm going to let him take the kids away on the first holiday since this mess started?

"So when the hell do I get to see them?"

"You can see them the day after Christmas."

His voice rises. "What the fuck? That's not the same."

"Well, you should have thought of that before you left us for your girlfriend. Think of the kids for once, Paul. I'm sure they'll be much happier doing what they've always done on Christmas. They love seeing my parents and getting all their presents." I press my fingers against my forehead, my head starting to pound. "And where are they going to sleep? Macy said you have one extra bedroom, and it's filled with Charlene's clothes."

"There's a bed in that room. We just have to straighten it out and put some things away."

"Okay, you have *two* kids."

"Then one will have to sleep on the couch."

"Neither one of them is going to like that. Why disrupt them on Christmas? Just let them be to get used to all this before you go disrupting even more of their lives."

He sighs on the other end of the phone. "Fine. This time, we'll do it your way, but I'm going to talk to my lawyer about a set visitation, holiday, and summer schedule for Tommy. And the divorce. Have you gotten a lawyer yet? We're going to need to sell the house and divide our assets and money. You can't just keep everything."

"I'm not trying to just keep everything. You left. I didn't have a choice, remember?"

He sighs. "You're right. I'm sorry. I'm just stressed out."

I laugh sarcastically. "Stressed out from what? All the fun you're having with your new girlfriend?"

"Look, this has been hard on me too, Ivy."

"I'd like to feel bad, Paul, but I can't because all of this was your choice. The kids and I are the ones who have had to deal with the side effects of your affair."

"I'm not going to argue with you, Ivy. We never used to fight."

I can't believe he just said that to me. It's true, though. Paul and I rarely ever fought the entire length of our relationship. We always talked things over calmly and reached decisions together. Neither one of us were ever the type to get mad and yell at each other. It wasn't until he started to 'work late' that the arguing began.

"Isn't that strange?" I ask him. "We never fought and were always happy together, yet you still had an affair and left." I know I should stop making comments, but I can't seem to control myself.

"Ivy, please."

"Fine. You can pick the kids up the day after Christmas. You're supposed to have Tommy this weekend. Are you picking him up today from school? He has a bag of clothes with him."

Macy has decided she doesn't want to spend alternate weekends at her dad's house, and I'm not making her. She'll be going to college soon; I can't force her to spend weekends with Paul and his girlfriend.

"Yes, I'll be there to pick him up."

Biting my lip, I'm not sure if I want to ask him what I'm thinking about. "Paul... How is Tommy when he's with you?"

He takes a few long moments to answer me, which fuels my suspicions that I'm not going to like his answer.

"Well... he seems confused. He asks me to bring him home a lot. He asks me why I won't come back home. He's only seven, Ivy, so he really doesn't understand what's going on, but I think in time he'll be okay. Charlene is trying really hard to be nice to him."

I empty the bag from the beauty store onto the coffee table. "Trying to be nice?" I repeat. "Is it hard for her?"

"She's not really used to kids. She wasn't expecting to have a seven year old every other weekend. We're working it out."

I want to smack both of them for being so selfish and thoughtless.

"She was having an affair with a married man who has two kids," I say, trying to keep my tone calm. "Obviously, she thought, someday, she was going to get you to leave me. What did she think was going to happen to your children?"

"I don't know."

"I suppose this is what happens when you date someone so much younger without any children," I reply, and immediately turn those words around on myself. Would I be getting into the same mess by dating Lukas?

"Charlene likes kids. It's just a lot all at once."

Poor Charlene.

"I have to run. I have plans tonight, and I have some things to do. Try to remind Tommy to call me before he goes to bed. I like to say good night to him."

"Where are you going tonight?" he questions, suddenly sounding interested in the conversation, but I'm not going to give him any information about my personal life. It's none of his business anymore, and I don't need to hear his negativity. It will just ruin the confidence I've worked so hard to build in myself.

"None of your business. Goodbye." I end the call and immediately notice that I have a text from Lukas on my screen.

Lukas: Knock knock
Me: Who's there?
Lukas: Orange
Me: Orange who?
Lukas: Orange you glad you're gonna see me tonight? ;-)

Laughing, I type back.

Me: Yes, I am. You're a goofball. ;)

His cute text has instantly lifted my mood, something he definitely has a gift for. It's impossible to be in a bad mood with Lukas around.

I grab all my hair stuff and take it into the bathroom, placing it all on the vanity. I mix up all the bottles, take my blouse off and put an old tee shirt on, comb my hair straight, and then put on the black latex gloves, which remind me of the ones that Lukas uses.

The mixture is thick and a weird reddish-pink color, but the girl assured me this would come out the cool auburn color that I want. Using the little black brush, I start to paint it onto my hair. The front around my face is easy, but when I start to get it on the sides and back, it becomes increasingly difficult to figure out if I'm actually getting all of my hair because my hair is so long and thick. The brush seems useless, so I put it aside and use my fingers instead to spread gobs of the colored goop through my hair. But it quickly becomes sticky, stiff, and weird, making it hard to spread apart. How the hell is my hair ever going to be soft and silky after this? There's just no way!

I have no idea if I've gotten the color onto the back part of my head, so I flip my head upside down and spread more of the mixture with my fingers, panicking at how long this is taking. What if I've gone past the half hour? And do I start counting the half hour when I'm actually all done or when I started? I start to cry, thinking I'm going to be bald when this is over. Why did I do this? Gray hair has got to be better than this mess.

"Mom, what are you doing?"

I flip my head back up to see Macy standing in the doorway, her eyes wide.

"I wanted to dye my hair, but I don't think it's working. I think I've missed a bunch of spots, and I can't tell where, and now it feels all sticky and . . . hard." I hold out my gloved hands, covered in stray hairs and pink goop. "And I think my hair is all coming out!"

She rushes forward. "Geez, Mom, you totally need supervision!"

I nod, feeling ridiculous. "I'm scared I ruined it. And look at all the strands that are coming out!"

My daughter's sweet side makes an appearance. "Mom, it's okay. I dye Shelly's hair all the time. This is normal. Let me just finish it for you."

I sit down on the toilet lid while she takes over my messy

situation. "I don't think I've ever seen you cry before," she says softly.

I reach for a tissue and wipe my eyes with it. "I know. I just didn't think it would be so hard. The girl at the store made it sound easy. She just said mix this stuff, put it on, and rinse. She never said it was going to get all sticky. I thought it would just go on like conditioner."

"Don't worry. I'm gonna make sure it looks gorgeous."

"Are you home early?" I ask, not sure what time it is. How long have I been in here messing with my hair?

"No, I get home at two every day. I was worried when I saw your car in the driveway."

For the first time, I see my daughter as a grown up, easing my fears as she works on my hair, telling me about her day as we wait for the color to process, then walking me to the kitchen sink to rinse the color off.

"Do you think it's going to look okay?" I ask her, still worried about what color it's going to be.

"I think it's going to be awesome, Mom. I'm going to get some cold cream. You have the color all over your neck." She runs to the bathroom while I wonder what that means. "You're supposed to put cream around your face and neck because the color dyes your skin, too," she says when she comes back.

I'm pretty sure I turn white. "What? Are you serious? The girl didn't mention that."

"Yes, it's all over your face and the side of your neck."

"Oh, shit. Can you get it off?"

She laughs. "Mom, you never swear. What's going on with you? Crying and swearing? Dying your hair?" She uses a cotton pad to wipe cream along my forehead. "Is this about Dad? Did something happen?"

I shake my head. "No, nothing happened."

She continues to scrub at my face and neck. "You have your tattoo appointment tonight, don't you?" she asks, quirking a perfect eyebrow up at me.

"Yes, so?"

She stands back and looks at me. "I think you're going to have to take a shower to get the rest of that off, and maybe use some witch hazel. I've used that before to get it off."

"All right." I look up at the clock to see that its three pm. My appointment is at six, so I still have enough time to shower and eat without being late.

She throws away the cotton and rinses out the sink. "Mom. It's okay for you to have fun, ya know."

"Macy-"

She interrupts me. "I've seen you smiling at your cell phone. I saw the new clothes in the living room. You don't have to hide from us. Tommy and I want you to be happy."

I give her a quick hug. "Thank you, sweetheart. That means a lot to me. Life is just a little hard right now."

When I go back to the bathroom to shower, I'm horrified to see that I dripped the hair dye onto the floor, and some is on the wall and in the porcelain sink. *How the hell did I do that?* I grab a bottle of spray cleaner from the kitchen and scrub at the splatters, but most of it is not coming off, leaving a faint red stain in several places on the floor and wall. *Shit.* Paul will freak when he sees this if he wants to sell the house.

I vow never to try to do things with my own hair again. Grey hair seems much safer than this art project I turned my head into. The new color probably won't even be noticeable.

CHAPTER 11

LUKAS

My cousin Storm is the lead guitarist of Ashes & Embers, a rock band his brothers and my brother, Vandal, are members of. When Storm found out that I play the violin and the piano, he had this cool idea to add some classical elements with a metal edge to a few songs the band was working on. I laid some tracks with them at the studio for those songs, and agreed to play live with them at the local clubs where they play occasionally.

I love music, but I love the tattoo parlor more. Owning my own business and having steady income is something I've always dreamed of and never thought I would have. Call me boring, but I like stability. While some people may think living the rock star life, and touring around the country—or the world—would be amazing, it's not a lifestyle I want. It would only feed my demons and dredge up my past issues with feeling unsettled and unwanted. I've seen how Vandal has to juggle the band, working at the shop, and his daughter. I just don't want to split myself that way.

So now, Storm is here to make sure I'm going to play live with them in a couple weeks at a club across town.

"I said I'll do it, man," I assure him for what must be the tenth time.

He's excited and jumpy, as usual. "This is special. I'm singing a song to Evie," he says, following me around like a little kid.

I look up at him as I clean my work area, trying to remember why that name sounds familiar. "The girl from the blizzard incident?" I ask him.

He nods, clapping me on the shoulder. "That's the one. I gotta get this girl, Lukas. I'm fucking mad crazy over her. And your intro to the song is gonna kick fucking ass."

"It's gonna be sweet. No worries. So what's the deal with the chick?"

He leans against the wall, right on top of one of my paintings. "She's got a fucking douche-bag boyfriend she's been with for like half a fucking century," he says, rolling his eyes. "But she's not happy."

"Are you sure about that? Is that your assessment or her own?"

He glares at me. "Don't use big fucking words with me, Lukas. She's not happy. Period. I know it, and she knows it. I just have to get her to admit it."

"I think I know the feeling."

The front bell rings, meaning Ivy is here. Finally. "Look, that's my next appointment, so you gotta go, Storm."

He turns toward the waiting area, grins at me, and leans toward me, lowering his voice. "The one you were telling me about? The older chick?"

I push him out of my work area. "Yes. Be gone."

I follow him to the waiting area, where Ivy's sitting in one of the red velvet chairs, looking fucking amazing. Her hair is now deep burgundy, and her face is glowing as she smiles up at us.

"Hi," she chirps happily when she sees us.

"Hey, Ivy, I want you to meet my cousin, Storm. And Storm, this is Ivy."

Storm shakes her hand and looks back at me. "Dude, you were right. She's beautiful." I'm going to kick his ass if he embarrasses me. Or her.

Ivy laughs. "It's nice to meet you, Storm. I love your name."

"Yeah, it's very fitting," I interrupt, grinning. "He was just leaving."

Storm puts his arms up and waves his hands. "I get it. I'm going. I'm going." He turns to me. "I'll see you soon, man." He looks down at Ivy. "And hopefully you, too. Have a great holiday."

"You too."

I lock the door behind Storm, so no one else wanders in, and finally turn my full attention to Ivy.

"You look gorgeous," I say. "You are rocking that fuckin' hair color."

She smiles and looks down a little, her cheeks blushing. "Thank you. My daughter helped me color it."

"I love it. Come on. Let's go back."

Damn, I want to pull her into my arms and kiss her, and just forget about her tattoo for now. This time, when she changes her clothes, she comes back wearing these cute little black shorts with red hearts. I'm loving the changes I see in her today. She's growing confident, and I'm hoping I've helped bring that out of her.

After she settles down in the leather chair, I wheel my stool closer to her and run my hand gently over her tattoo, which looks awesome spanning her leg.

"Did you wear these for me?" I ask her, my voice low, my fingers skimming the edge of the shorts. She nods and smiles shyly, and that just ignites my desire for her even more. Her shyness turns me on wicked bad.

"I like." She watches my hand move to rest on her outer thigh. "I'm gonna finish this tonight, and I don't want this to be the last time I see you." I look up at her face, finding her eyes wide, and she's chewing her bottom lip. "So what's it gonna be, doll? Will you have dinner with me tomorrow night? I'd like to get you out of client mode."

She nods, still not saying a word. "You sure?" I ask her, and she nods yet again, her eyes glazed as I let my fingertips brush just beneath the edge of her shorts, touching her silky thigh.

I bend down and kiss her leg, right above her knee, and a small gasp escapes her. Fuck, she's so easy to turn on. Bending her leg up, I kiss the sensitive spot behind her knee then slowly drag my lips up the inside of her thigh, tasting her sweet flesh. I stop just a few inches from the apex of her thighs and gently graze her with my teeth.

"Lukas . . ." she whispers. Her hand goes to my head, her fingers in my hair, and all I want is to feel her yanking my hair and hear her moan my name while I give her all the attention she's starving for and deserves to have. I want nothing more than to give this woman my heart, body, and soul, and hope that she'll give me the same in return.

Lifting my head up, I catch her eyes with mine. "I'm not going to do this here." I sit up and reluctantly pull away from her, which is sheer torture for me. As much as I want her, I'm not going to fool around with her on my tattoo chair. This is where I work, and I've already crossed way too many inappropriate lines. More importantly, she deserves so much better than this. When I touch her and kiss her, I want it to be in the right place at the right time.

"What's wrong?" she asks me, nervousness lacing her voice.

"Nothing at all. I'm just not going to start something I can't finish the right way. I want to have a real date with you, and if we go further, I sure as hell don't want to do it here in my work area. I want you in my bed, and I want a lot of time."

Her lips part, but no words come out. She nods silently instead. I wish she would talk to me instead of nodding all the time, but the idea that I have such an effect on her that she can't speak intrigues me. It means she *feels* something, and that's what I really want.

Reaching across my worktable, I hold up the framed drawing that I made for her of the girl with the butterfly hair.

"This is for you. Don't forget to take it home."

"You framed it for me? You didn't have to do that." She takes it from me and holds it in her lap, studying it. "I love this so much, Lukas. It's gorgeous."

"It's how I see you."

Her mouth drops, and she's speechless again. I've never met a woman so easy to make happy.

"My cousin Storm that you just met?" I grab my gun and prepare to get to work. "He was stuck in a truck during that bad snow storm we had a few weeks ago, with a girl he picked up on the side of the road whose car got stuck in a ditch."

"What? Are you serious?"

"Yup. They were trapped in his truck for an entire weekend." I would love to be trapped in a truck with Ivy for two days. The things I could do with her to keep her warm.... Fuckin' Storm has all the luck.

"Did he know her?"

I shake my head. "No, not at all, and I guess things got a little heated, if you know what I mean. Now, he's got a thing for her, but it turns out she's got a long-term boyfriend."

"Oh, wow. That's crazy. What's he going to do?"

"The same thing I'm trying to do with you. Make her fall in love with him."

I swear I can see her stop breathing as she absorbs my words. Then finally, she reacts with a hesitant smile.

"I don't think either of you are going to have to 'make us', Lukas."

My hands shake and my brain derails at what she's hinting at, making me stop working before I screw up her tattoo.

"The weekend after Christmas, his band is playing at a club not far from here. I'd love it if you came with me?" If she says yes, it will be the perfect opportunity for me to show her that I'm also a musician, rather than telling her. I kinda want to surprise her and just let her hear me play.

"Like a concert?"

"Yeah, but small scale. It's in a club. I think you'll like it. My brother's in the band, and all my cousins. And the girl from the blizzard is gonna be there."

"All right," she says hesitantly. "I'll go with you. I'd love to meet some of your family and hear them play."

I look up at her from under the shroud of hair hanging over my face, my gun poised just over her calf. "You don't know how fucking happy I am that you're saying yes to me now, Ivy. I was starting to feel like a creepy stalker, asking you a hundred times."

She fidgets a little, moving her legs. "I'm still a little freaked about the age difference, but you asked me to give you a chance, so that's what I'm doing." She grips the edge of the chair as I tattoo the spot right above her ankle. "You kinda made yourself irresistible," she adds.

"I know it hurts here, but it will be over in a sec," I say, trying to hold her leg still. "So you think I'm irresistible?"

She flashes me a beautiful smile. "Are you fishing for compliments, Lukas?"

"Shamelessly."

"Yes, you're irresistible. Happy now?"

"Incredibly. And guess what? We're done." I wheel away from her and lay my gun on my workbench.

Surprise and excitement light up her face. "Really? It's really done?"

"Yup. Go over to the full-length mirror and check it out. Let me know if you want me to add anything."

She runs to the mirror and examines the tattoo that starts just below her hip and travels down to her ankle. It's gorgeous, and I'm so proud of her for getting through such a big piece as her first.

"I love it!" she squeals.

I come up behind her and put my arms around her, looking over her shoulder at us in the mirror. She stills then leans back against my body, fitting perfectly against me.

"You're beautiful," I whisper against her ear. "Look at us together, Ivy." I slide my hand slowly down to rest on her hip. "We look perfect together." She nods, mesmerized, watching my hand move across her stomach in the mirror. My inked arms look wild against the white of her blouse, and I wish I could take a picture of us like this. I slide my hand up between her breasts, over her throat, and to her cheek, turning her face to mine. Her aqua eyes darken, and her lids fall closed as I kiss her softly on the lips, stealing a sigh from her.

When I pull away, her eyes open slowly and she blinks at me. "How do you do that?" she whispers breathlessly.

"Do what?" I turn her in my arms so she's facing me.

"I don't know . . . you make me feel like I'm in a dream. I don't know how else to explain it."

I push her hair away from her face and tuck it behind her ear. "Think about how it will feel when I make love to you."

She puts her hands on my chest and stares at the black crucifix hanging around my neck.

"I'm afraid to think about that." Her voice is uncertain, her fingers shaking as she touches my necklace.

"Why?" I stroke her hair, not forcing her to look at me but wanting to comfort her because I can see she's fighting an inner battle again.

"I just . . . This is so hard."

I kiss the top of her head. "Ivy, you can tell me anything. I hope you've figured out that I'm a communicator. Don't shut me out—that drives me crazy. Whatever's on your mind, just spit it out and we'll deal with it."

She takes a deep breath. "I'm just . . . worried. I've only been with one man, and you're a lot more . . . experienced than he was. Or is. I can tell you are, just by the way you touch and kiss. And my body . . . I've had two kids . . ."

I don't tell her that my first lover was a twenty-two-year-old fitness model, and I was just sixteen when we hooked up. Erika was my best friend Finn's older sister, and I spent a lot of time at their house. Yeah, it was wrong on more levels than I can count, but I learned a lot about what women want, how to make them crazy, how to go slow when the time is right, and how to pound the shit out of them when they want it hard. Erika brought me out of my shell, and helped me find some much-needed self-confidence. There was no love there, but we liked each other and had a lot of fun. She moved to England years ago, and is now happily married.

I gently lift her face with my hands so I can look into her eyes. "You have nothing to worry about. I'm already attracted to you like fucking crazy, and I'm not a shallow person. I'm interested in a lot more than looks, but just for the record, I think you're beautiful and sexy and adorable. I've jerked off about a hundred times thinking about you."

"Lukas!" The look of utter shock on her face is priceless.

"Hey, you need to know these things so you believe what I'm telling you." I take her hand in mine and bring it between our bodies, pressing her palm against my rock hard cock. "Feel that? The cock doesn't lie, baby. That's all from you."

Her eyes go wide like silver dollars. "Holy shit . . ." she says under her breath, pulling her hand away, all flustered.

"I want you to touch me, but only when you're ready. I might push you a little, but that's only because I want you. Anything that happens between us will be at your pace, okay?" She nods and swallows. "You say stop, I'll stop. Always. And you should know, I actually have always wanted to be with someone who hasn't had a ton of experience, but I also don't want to date a kid or someone immature. So . . . You. Are. Perfect."

She shakes her head at me and grins. "You're too good to be real. There's gotta be something wrong with you . . ." Her hands slowly slide up my arms and rest on my biceps.

"Trust me. There's a lot wrong with me, Ivy. I have a hardcore jealous streak. I've battled depression for most of my life. I lived in a dumpster for three months. I believe in things most people don't. I'm an outcast. I don't love much, but when I do, I love hard and fierce."

She hangs on every word, her grip tightening around my arms.

"I want to know what fierce feels like," she whispers, her eyes looking up at me innocently through her long dark lashes.

I pull her body closer to mine, holding her tight against me so she can feel me again. "I have a feeling you will, doll."

She goes up on her tiptoes and kisses my cheek. "I want one more thing on my tattoo," she says, moving out from under my arm and heading back for the chair.

Frowning, I follow her. "Okay, tell me."

"I want a little x and an o, to remind me of you, because you give the best hugs and kisses."

I wasn't expecting that at all. I was thinking she was going to want another butterfly, or maybe another little flower, but I never imagined she'd want something that was special for us. "Are you sure?" I ask her.

She nods enthusiastically. "Definitely. I'll let you pick where."

"I'm really honored by this, ya know," I grab my gun and find a nice place on her leg where I can add the two letters without detracting from the design. "There," I announce when I'm finished. "Now, my hugs and kisses are on your body for the rest of your life," I tease.

"Just what I wanted."

I get up and put my tools away, afraid if I don't put some distance between us that I'm going to ravish her right here. "You better be careful what you wish for," I say, glancing over my shoulder at her. "You just might get it."

LUKAS

After sharing a sizzling kiss good-bye with Ivy in the parking lot again, my blood is racing through my veins. I know I won't be able to sleep, so I take out my violin and play a few of the new songs I've been working on. The resonation of the strings calms me, always has. Even though I bought a brand new violin a few years ago with a little bit of my inheritance, I still play my first violin—the one I found in my great-grandparents' attic when I was seven years old and taught myself to play. It's ancient, and I have no idea who it originally belonged to, but it's one of the best—a Strad. Two years ago, I shipped it to London to have a renowned violin maker repair it for me, who begged me to sell it to him and offered me an insane amount of money. I refused. This violin is too much a part of me to let go, no matter how much it's worth. I don't need money, but I do need the things that calm me and bring me peace.

And now, Ivy excites me but also brings me a new sense of peace I've never felt before, not even from my music or art. Fighting the urge all night to carry her up here to my apartment was exhausting but worth it. Tomorrow night, she'll be here, and I can't wait to see her in my personal space, surrounded by the things I love.

Later, after I put my violin back in its case, I send Ivy a text.

Me: Is it tomorrow yet?

By the time she replies eight minutes later, I'm already in my bed.

Ivy: Technically, yes, it's after midnight yesterday, so it's today, which is tomorrow.
Me: Holy fuck, that hurt my brain.
Ivy: LOL
Me: What are you doing?
Ivy: I'm in bed.
Me: Me, too. Were you thinking about me?
Ivy: What do you think?
Me: I think yes. ;)
Ivy: Then I guess I was :)
Me: Don't stop.
Ivy: How could I? You're irresistible, remember?
Me: Did I tell you how beautiful you looked today?
Ivy: Yes, thank you. You make me feel all shivery.
Me: Good shivery or bad shivery?
Ivy: Definitely good :)
Me: Then get ready for more. I have a lot more shivers to give you. ;)~

CHAPTER 12

IVY

Lukas wanted to pick me up and bring me to his place for dinner, but that felt silly to me, so I insisted on driving to his place. I think his chivalry is sweet, but I feel better having my own car in case I want to leave for whatever reason. Lindsay yelled at me when I told her earlier, telling me I was being difficult and that I should be grateful he has manners. She then ended the call reminding me to get on top of him.

I fall a little bit in love with him when I see what he's wearing as he lets me in his door. He's got on a black button-down shirt that's unbuttoned to the middle of his chest, faded jeans, and black and white Converse. He pulls off casual and sexy so effortlessly, and the Converse tug at a little piece of the high school girl that still lives inside me.

"You look pretty," he says, pulling me inside and shutting the door behind me. Taking my hand, he leads me to the living room. "Make yourself comfy. I'm just gonna go check dinner."

"Okay." Taking off my coat and laying it over the arm of the couch, I look around his house, which is beautiful and exotic, just as I imagined it would be. Just like him.

The old stone church he lives in has been turned into a two story house, with the tattoo parlor taking up about half of the first floor, and the other half being this huge living room, kitchen, dining area, and bathroom. The tattoo parlor is completely separate, with its own entrance at the front of the house. A beautiful stairway leads upstairs to where I assume the bedrooms are. Part of the second floor is open with a wooden railing to a loft area, giving the house a very open feel.

"Do you need any help?" I call out toward the kitchen.

"No," he hollers back

I continue to gaze around his house. Stained wood beams run across the ceiling and walls. The floors are dark hardwood with colored rugs beneath a large, black leather sectional couch and mahogany coffee table. Two purple velvet accent chairs sit off to the side, turned toward a huge flat screen television mounted on the wall. The tall stained glass windows are beautiful and timeless, and give off a warm, colorful glow to the room. Wide archways with stone accents divide the rooms. It's just breathtaking and so rich looking, the kind of house you would see in a fantasy movie.

I slowly walk around the living room, admiring the artwork on the walls and the statues and trinkets perfectly displayed, lightly running my fingertips over the beautiful antique accent furniture, remembering how he told me he also liked to feel the depth of these treasures, and I want to feel what he feels.

"Hello."

I jump about a mile, and then lean forward, not quite believing what I'm seeing . . . *and hearing*. In front of me is a huge black metal birdcage sitting atop a marble stand, and inside is a raven. A *real* raven. I step closer to the magnificent bird, who's also eyeing me with his amber eyes.

"Well, hello there," I say, captivated. The bird is beautiful, as black as night, tilting his head at me.

"Don't talk to him!" Lukas shouts from the kitchen.

"I'm a pretty bird," the bird says.

Oh, wow! He's incredible. "Hi, pretty bird," I say softly.

The bird cocks his head at me. "Don't talk to him," he says, mimicking Lukas. *Exactly.* Somehow, the bird has impersonated Lukas' raspy voice perfectly, which is creepy and cool and pretty wild.

"I see you met Ray." Lukas crosses the room and stands next to me. "You have to be careful around him. He repeats everything."

I turn to him in awe. "Lukas, he's amazing! Why didn't you tell me about him?"

"He's amazing," the bird says, impersonating my own voice almost exactly now.

"Oh my God!" I exclaim. "I've never seen anything like this."

Lukas runs his hand through his hair. "Yeah, he's cool, but he's a fucking pain in the ass. When he gets in a mood, he talks non-stop and repeats everything I say. It's only cool sometimes. Trust me."

I stare at the bird, waiting for him to say something, and I think he's doing the same to me. He raises his little wings a bit and skitters across his perch to come closer to me.

"I love him! I had no idea they could talk. Is he a raven?" I poke my finger through the cage bars and gently stroke his wing.

"He is. I found him when he was a baby, years ago. He had a broken wing, so I brought him home to take care of him, and when he started repeating everything I said, I couldn't let him go. I got attached to him. He's kind of a runt, I think. He hasn't grown much at all. And, yeah, some can learn to talk, and as you can see, they have an uncanny ability to mimic voices and sounds. For a while there, he could mimic my ring tone."

"Amazing," Ray squawks, clearly excited.

Lukas grabs my hand and pulls me away from the bird. "Okay, that's enough of him. If we give him too much attention, he won't shut up. I'd like to be able to talk to you without him babbling in the background."

I can't help but laugh. "He's hard to ignore. Your house is gorgeous. I can't stop looking at everything. It's such a unique place." I smile at him. "Just like you."

He grins. "I hope that's a compliment?"

"It is, and something smells great. What are you making?"

He leans down and whispers into my ear. "Chicken à la king."

"Why are you whispering," I whisper back.

"We don't want the bird to know we're eating one of his kind."

"Lukas!" I cover my mouth and try to suppress my laugh. "That's not funny."

"I know. That's why I whispered. Let's go eat. It's ready."

I follow him to the kitchen, which is a classy mix of modern appliances with an antique table and chairs, granite counter tops, stone backsplash, and more gothic wall decor.

He pulls out a chair and motions for me to sit. "Can I help with anything?" I ask him, feeling spoiled. I've never had a man cook for me before, and I have to admit, it's definitely a nice feeling.

"Nope, I've got it all under control."

I watch him move around the kitchen, setting bowls and plates of food on the table in front of me.

"White wine?" he asks, holding a bottle up.

"Ooh, sounds great."

He takes his seat and pours two glasses of wine. Everything he's prepared looks and smells delicious. All his serving dishes are black with a marble pattern—very different from the cream-colored set I have at home. He's made a spring mix salad, and the chicken à la king is arranged on my plate with a side garnish of orange peel slices in the shape of a flower. I feel like I'm sitting in a five-star restaurant and not some young goth guy's kitchen.

"I'm very impressed," I say, smiling across the table at him. "You did all of this?"

"I sure did. I love to cook."

"It shows. It looks too pretty to eat."

"Don't be shy. Dig in. I have extra forks, and I can make you lots more pretty food."

I shake my head and smile as I cut up my food, loving how he teases me. "This house is so big. Do you get lonely here?" I ask him before taking a bite of the chicken. "Mm . . . this is delicious!" I exclaim, and it really is yummy perfection. Is there anything he can't do?

"I have the bird to keep me company," he says simply, and I can tell that he means it sincerely, like having just the bird is totally okay, nothing and no one else needed. I'm not sure if it's sad or admirable.

"Can I ask you something personal?" I have so many things I want to ask him, but I hate feeling like I'm prying into his life and possibly digging up bad memories for him.

He tips his glass at me before raising it to his lips. "That's why we're here, baby doll, to get to know each other better. Ask away."

"Have you ever been in a long term relationship?"

He nods and swallows. "Yup. I was with a girl for almost

three years, seventeen to twenty. We had a pretty great thing going, but unfortunately, money changes people."

"Your inheritance? Did getting all that money so young change you?"

He shakes his hair out of his eyes and smirks a little. "No, me getting all that money changed *her*."

"Oh," I say. "I'm sorry to hear that."

"Hey, better I found out before it went any further and she spent every dime, right?"

"True, but it's still a shame."

"It is, because I really loved her, and I thought she loved me. I guess she did, at least for a while." He props his elbow on the table and rubs the side of his face. "As soon as I got the money, she changed. She went from being a fun, sweet girl to a demanding bitch. And ya know what? I would have given her anything, but the way she treated me? No fucking way. She just assumed, and expected, that she had free reign to my money and could spend it on whatever she wanted, and demand all sorts of crazy shit from me, like she was entitled to it."

"That's terrible. My faith in people just dwindles the more I hear stories like that. Doesn't anyone value love and commitment anymore? Or is everyone just about getting something better for themselves?"

"That's basically how it seems to be."

"Are you still in love with her?" I blurt the last part out before I can change my mind about asking. As much as I'm afraid to hear the answer, I need to hear it, because I'm slowly falling for him and I don't think I can compete with the memory of a girl he might still be in love with. I can't take another hit to my heart just when I'm finally starting to feel a little bit of happiness again.

He leans back in his chair and looks up at the ceiling. "I'll always care about her, but no, I'm not in love with her anymore." Sitting forward again, he studies me silently. "And how about you? Are you still in love with him?"

I've reached a point where I can answer that question with certainty. "No, not anymore. Like you, of course, I'll always care about him, but he's just hurt me too much and destroyed too much. He's not the man I fell in love with." Lukas listens intently, relief evident in his eyes at my admission. "I guess my parents were right," I continue. "They told me years ago, when I got pregnant and married, that we were way too young to make such a big commitment, that people change too much, especially in their twenties, and don't really know what they want in life yet. And looking back on that, I think that's true in a lot of ways, although I hate to admit it to my parents."

He runs his finger over the rim of his wine glass, his eyes following the circle he's making on the crystal edge. "Do you feel that way about me?" he finally asks, shifting his eyes up to meet mine. "Do you think, because I'm in my twenties, that I don't know what I want? That in a few years I'll be different?" He tilts his head to the side. "That I might grow away from you?"

I look down at my plate, needing a break from his intense gaze for a few seconds, having to remind myself to breathe. Sometimes, like just now, when our eyes meet, that intense, warm vibrating feeling rushes into me again, making me feel like I've forgotten *something* and then all of a sudden remembered it again in one turbulent shudder of my heart.

"You felt that just now, didn't you? It scares you," he states.

I shake my head, ignoring what he just said for now because that feeling *does* scare me, but not exactly in a bad way. "Yes, I admit I'm worried because you're still in your early twenties, and what you want, *who* you want, is most likely going to change."

He shakes his head. "Not gonna happen. I know myself."

"People change sometimes as they get older. It doesn't mean it has to be negative, just different. People grow and evolve and sometimes want different things than what they thought they wanted."

"I could say the same about you. In five years, you might change what you want in life, too."

I smile across the table at him. "That's true."

"Is what you want now the same as what you wanted when you were in your twenties?" he asks.

I take one last bite of my dinner and weigh my answer carefully. "*What* I want is the same. *Who* I want to share it with has now changed. Love, family and commitment has always been the most important things for me. Unfortunately, the person I thought I was going to have it with didn't feel the same."

He winks at me, picks up our plates, and carries them across the room to the sink. "Don't even try to help," he quips, not looking back at me. I watch him rinse the dishes and place them in the dishwasher, checking out his ass as he bends down. I tried not to, but his body just commands attention.

"I value those things, ya know," he calls back over his shoulder.

"What things?" I ask, quickly looking away from his sexy rear.

He turns and leans back against the kitchen counter, crossing his muscled arms in front of him.

"Love, family and commitment," he answers. "Bring your cute self over here." His sultry voice drifts across the room and intoxicates me, and I bask in it for a few moments before I get up and walk across the room to him.

"Getting demanding, are you?" I say playfully, peeking up at him. He grabs me around the waist and pulls me against him.

"Would you like it if I was?" His voice takes on a whole new level of raw sexiness, making my legs go wobbly. I rest my hands on his arms and try to answer him in my own hopefully sexy voice.

"I think I would, Mr. Valentine."

Leaning down, he kisses me softly.

"Dinner was perfect," I say when we part. "And I do still value those things. A lot."

"I know you do, Ivy." He kisses me once more. "Come upstairs with me? I want to show you the rest of the house."

"I'd love to," I answer, wondering if that's secret code for let's go upstairs and have sex and I just unknowingly agreed to it. Taking my hand in his, he leads me up the wide wooden stairway.

"My bedroom is down the end of the hall," he says, gesturing in that direction. "But I'm not going to take you there, so stop looking like you want to run away. I have these two other bedrooms, which are never used unless my niece sleeps over, or sometimes my buddy Finn stays over."

"Finn?" I repeat.

"Yeah, he's my best friend. Hopefully, you'll get to meet him sometime, and my niece, too. She's the cutest thing ever."

We walk toward the loft area, which is set up like a sort of office and art room, with a large desk, easel, and ceramic cups filled with all sorts of different charcoal pencils. More of his framed drawings and paintings decorate the walls.

"Is this where you draw?" I ask, perusing everything. I've

always been awed by artistic people, and he is one of the most talented I've ever had the pleasure of meeting in person.

"This is where I'm *supposed* to draw, but I usually end up drawing in bed or on the couch. Now, I'm going to show you my favorite part of the house." He draws the blinds back to reveal sliding glass doors.

"Oh! Is this the balcony I saw from the parking lot?"

"It is."

The balcony is set up like a scene straight from a romance novel. A small electric fireplace is in the corner, which at first seems odd to me since we're technically outside, but I quickly see the point of it when I notice the loveseat over to the right, and the small table in front of it that's set with lit candles and a vase of purple flowers. A string of tiny white lights runs along the balcony edge and outlines the glass doors. It's dark outside, but the candles, lights, and fireplace give off just enough light for us to see each other.

"Wow," I exclaim, eyeing all the little details that he's obviously put time and thought in to. "This is beautiful . . . I can't believe you did all this."

"I was hoping you would like it out here." He picks up a big thick black throw blanket that's draped over the couch. "Sit," he says, nodding to the couch. "We're gonna snuggle."

"Oh . . . okay then," I say, startled by his plan.

"Why do you look so surprised?" He looks at me with that smile on his face that makes my insides go to jelly.

I shake my head as we sit on the loveseat and he drapes the blanket over us. It's cold out, but I don't feel it at all with the heat from the fireplace and the blanket covering us, not to mention the warmth coming off his body being so close to mine.

"This . . ." I say, looking around. "It's just so . . . romantic and thoughtful. You do things that most men don't." He wants to snuggle. Without being asked or forced. He's the equivalent of a unicorn.

"I wanted to be under the stars with you."

He makes my heart clench. Is this real? Is *he* real? I want to believe he is. I *need* to believe he is.

"I have something for you," he says, reaching behind the loveseat and coming back with a tiny box.

"What? For me?" I stammer, surprised. Is he really giving me a gift?

"Open it."

I hold the small box in my hands, afraid to open it. I can't remember the last time someone gave me a surprise gift.

"Why did you get me a present? You shouldn't be buying me things."

"Why not? I wanted to give you something, so I made something for you."

"You gave me a drawing." There's no way there's another drawing in this tiny box. This is like a jewelry box.

"And now, I'm giving you something else. Just open it."

I open the little red box and push the tissue paper away. Inside, I find a silver necklace with a little tiny fork charm hanging off it.

"Lukas! Oh my God, I love it!" I lift it out of the box, smiling. "You made this?"

He takes it from me and gently puts it around my neck, lifting my hair and clasping the chain.

"I made the little metal fork," he answers.

I hug him. "Thank you. I love it." I want to never take this little tiny fork off. His sweetness just gets better and better.

He turns his body toward me, resting his back against a big pillow that's leaning against the arm of the love seat, and finds my hand under the blanket, lacing his fingers between mine.

"Do you believe in soul mates?" His voice is low and soft, with a hint of hesitancy, like he's afraid of what I might say.

Lukas doesn't belong here, I realize right then. He's a Knight. A prince. A warrior. A Viking. He's one of those men that fight for love 'til the end of time. One who would carry a woman away on his horse and make mad passionate love to her on the grass. A man who takes what he wants and makes it his forever. A man not afraid to dream or believe in what can't be seen, but can only be felt. His heart is lost in this time, where people no longer live to love or believe that love can transcend time.

And me? *"Who am I,"* I wonder.

As a little girl I dreamed of the fairytale love, like we all did. I dreamed of a love that would last forever. I hoped for bouquets of roses for no reason other than to say I love you. I fantasized about a magical marriage proposal and a beautiful wedding gown. None of that happens in real life, though. At least not in mine. I had happy moments, but no magical moments.

Until now.

I sigh dreamily and look up at the stars in the dark winter sky. "I love the idea of soul mates," I finally say, squeezing his hand. "To think that there's someone out there that has loved you before, loves you now, and will love you again? It's a pretty intense idea, but I think it's only something that happens in movies and books, unfortunately."

He pulls me against his chest and wraps one arm around my waist, his other hand letting go of mine, sliding up my arm, over my shoulder, and stopping to rest at my neck, holding me so he can look into my eyes.

"Maybe." He kisses my lips softly. "Or . . . maybe not." His lips come down on mine again, lingering longer this time.

"If soul mates are real, I want you to be mine," I whisper against his lips. And I do; I really, truly do. Maybe that's what we keep feeling . . . that spark, that heart-jump, that odd recognition. A low groan comes from his throat, and he pulls me even further on top of him, sliding his body down on the couch until he is completely under me. He pulls the blanket over us and finds my lips, kissing me hungrily. His hands slowly roam my body, giving me time to get used to his touch. Turning us both on our sides, he lifts my leg over his waist, his hand sliding up my outer thigh to my ass, pressing my body against his so I can feel his hard cock through his jeans. My heart rate quickens as I touch the exposed part of his chest, and I lower my head to kiss him there.

"Unbutton my shirt," he whispers, his breathing heavy. With a shaky hand, I undo the remaining buttons of his shirt and push the dark fabric aside, letting my hand roam across his chest and down over his hard toned stomach. My brain and body are fighting a battle . . . my brain saying I'm not ready to go further than this right now and my body saying go, Go, GO.

He reaches for me and pulls the hem of my sweater up, and I freeze.

"I just want to feel you against me. That's all," he says reassuringly, sensing my panic. Leaning up, I let him pull my sweater over my head, and he wraps his arms around me, holding me tight against him. His skin is so warm, even in the cold night air.

Our lips meet again, our hands slowly exploring each other with gentle caresses, our bodies moving in a drowsy rhythm. Winding my hair in his hand, he gently pulls my head back and kisses my neck, moving his lips down to kiss the sensitive flesh between my breasts, his fingers grazing over the edge of my new black lace bra. His soft, slow touches and kisses are exactly what I need and want, and somehow he knows this. My eyes flutter closed, and I let myself relax into his touch, bowing my head down to kiss the top of his head as his lips and tongue roam my chest. His hair is soft and silky against my lips, and smells of sage. He is so easy to get lost in. He ignites all of my senses, awakens all my desires, and calms my fears and insecurities. He is quickly finding his way into my heart.

He drags his tongue up over my throat and back to my lips, making me shiver.

"Are you cold?" he asks, pulling the blanket up.

I shake my head. "No . . . not at all. You're just making me all shivery again. The way you kiss . . . Lukas, I have no words."

He sucks in a breath and touches my cheek. "Can you stay with me tonight? Do you have to go home?"

Oh, God. I don't want to leave the cozy warmth of his arms, or break the closeness that's growing between us. I'm afraid it will stop and never come back again, and I don't want this moment to end. *Ever.* Tommy is with Paul, but Macy is home alone, and I told her I would be home. Yes, I could call her and tell her I won't be coming home tonight, but what will she think? She knows I had a date with someone new tonight. How will that make me look as a mother if I don't come home? I don't want my kids thinking both their parents have just started hooking up with random people. And if I did stay . . . am I ready for this to go further?

No. I'm not. Not yet.

"I can't," I finally say. "I'm sorry. Macy is alone, and I told her I'd be home. I know she's almost eighteen, but I've never stayed away from home over night before, and she knows I had a date tonight and I don't-"

"Shhh . . ." He touches my lips with his finger and smiles at me. "I understand, Ivy. I know there's a lot of new going on here for you. And your kids."

"I'm sorry . . ." I feel like the immature one here, having to run home all the time, shying away from sex.

"Don't be sorry. I can be patient." He takes a deep breath and exhales. "Will you keep seeing me?"

"Yes, I want to see you again."

A big smile lights up his face, and it's contagious. "You're really cute when you smile," I admit, tracing my finger over the tattoo on his chest.

"You're pretty cute yourself. So . . . can we go steady? Is that the term you use?"

I smack his arm and gape at him. "Lukas! I'm not from the fifties! Jesus!"

Laughing, he hugs me closer to him, his big arms circling me. "Well, how the fuck do I know how to say this right?"

"What are you trying to say exactly?"

"I'm trying to say I want you to be my girlfriend, and I think I'm failing miserably."

My heart soars from cuteness overload. How could I say no to such sexy adorableness? It would be seriously impossible.

I reach up and push his hair out of his eyes. "You're not failing at all, Lukas. I don't think you could fail at anything."

"So, is that a yes?"

With a big smile and my heart beating faster, I lean forward and kiss his lips. "It's a yes."

CHAPTER 13

LUKAS

My first date with Ivy could not have been more perfect. Dinner came out great, she looked beautiful, Ray kept his beak shut, and kissing her under the blanket—with the stars above us—was simply exquisite. I didn't want the night to ever end. If I close my eyes, I can still taste her on my lips and feel her soft skin pressed against mine.

That was over a week ago, and I haven't seen her since.

I practically begged to see her for Christmas, but family obligations kept her from me, which I totally respect and understand. But I wish I was part of her family and not an outsider. Maybe someday that'll happen.

A couple hundred text messages and a few phone calls later, I'm on my way to pick her up to take her to see the band play tonight. I feel weird when I pull into her driveway, sorta wishing I let her come to my place like she wanted to, but I insisted on picking her up here. It feels fucked up, though, ringing the doorbell of the house she lived in with her husband. After a few seconds, she opens the door and comes out on the front steps but doesn't invite me inside, which probably would have been really uncomfortable. Instead, she throws her arms around my neck, clinging to me.

"I really missed you," she murmurs.

Fuck, less than five seconds, and she's already got my brain going gushy.

I hug her close to me and lift her off her feet, making her laugh and hang on to me tighter. "I missed you, too. I was starting to think you were gonna friend-zone me." I set her down on her feet and study her face, afraid to see some kind of change in her, but I don't. Her eyes are still sparkling at me, just like they were when we said good-bye over a week ago.

"No, Lukas, I'm not friend-zoning you, silly. I'm sorry I couldn't see you for Christmas. I wanted to, really, but I just needed to focus on the kids and keep their routine normal."

I take her hands in mine. "I understand. You're a great mom, and I love that about you."

We walk to my car, and I open the passenger door for her, then go around and get in behind the wheel. Leaning across the console, I turn her face to mine and kiss her lips, and she makes a little startled sound, fueling me to want more of her. I pull her over to me until she's half lying on my chest, her body stretched across the console, and kiss her deeper, my tongue searching out hers.

She pulls away. "This car is really small," she jokes. "Not really conducive to making out in the front seat."

"I don't care. I'm dying to kiss you." I cup the back of her neck and pull her back to my lips, wishing we didn't have to go to the club so I could just take her home with me. Right now, I'd love nothing more than to stretch her out on my bed and explore every inch of her until she's crazy stupid for me.

"I've been thinking about your kisses a lot," she says, her voice small and sweet. She may be older than me, but truthfully, she's so cute and shy that she seems younger than she is. I don't think she sees that in herself, but I do.

"Oh yeah? What have you been thinking?" I nip her bottom lip and let my hand slide over her jeans to rest on her ass.

"How good you make me feel."

Even in the dimness of the car, I can still see her aqua eyes shining at me, and the glint of her lips, moist from my kiss.

"I want to make you feel things you've never felt before, Ivy."

She closes her eyes, as if she's taking my words into her to keep, then slowly opens her eyes again. "You already have," she whispers, then presses her lips to my cheek.

Sighing, I help her back over to the passenger seat. "We should go, or we'll be late," I say. "Although, I kinda just want to stay here and be alone with you."

"I do, too, but I really want to see the band. I've been looking forward to this since you told me about them. We can be alone after. Macy is staying at a friend's house tonight." She smiles shyly over at me, and I think I know what she's hinting at. What she doesn't know is that, in a little while, she's gonna see me on stage with the band, and I hope to hell it doesn't change her mind about me.

The club is crowded, and there's a line at the door, so I text Vandal to meet us at the back door to let us in.

"Well, well, well . . . you finally found someone I haven't had the pleasure of," he says, checking out Ivy, his eyes roaming all over her. I know he's doing it just to get me riled up, but I ignore his stupid shit because I'm in too good of a mood tonight to let him ruin it.

"Ivy, this is my brother, Vandal. Van, this is Ivy."

Ivy looks petrified of him, which is a typical reaction for most women. First, they look scared, but then they become oddly attracted to him. I've watched it happen more times than I can count. Vandal is a big guy at six-foot four, with a muscular build like a wrestler. He has long black hair almost down to his friggen' ass, dark skin, and lots of tats. We do look alike in some ways, but he's bigger than I am and almost always has a menacing look on his face.

"It's nice to meet you," she says politely. I put my arm around her, and she presses her body into mine, fitting against me like she was made from a part of me.

Vandal actually smiles at her, something he doesn't do often. "The pleasure's mine, sweetheart. Hope you enjoy the show."

I pull her away from him before he blurts out anything annoying or inappropriate, and lead her down the hall to the door that will take us into the club.

"Wow, he's a big guy," Ivy says when we're away from him. "He looks Native American."

"Yeah . . . we have different mothers."

"You mentioned a niece . . . Is she his?"

Nodding, I find our reserved table by the stage. "Yeah, Katie is his. He's a good dad. I'll give him that. Her mother's a crazy bitch, though." I help her get her coat off, and hang it over the back of her chair before we sit together. "Katie's just a little younger than your son. Maybe next time I babysit her, we could let them meet?"

I know she's nervous about me meeting her kids, but if

we're going to continue dating, she's going to have to let them meet me and get to know me at some point. I don't want to be treated like a dirty secret. She doesn't know me well enough yet to understand how important it is for me to be part of a family . . . and to have my own family. If her kids end up hating me, I'm not sure how I'm gonna deal with that.

"Okay," she promises. "That would be fun. Macy is really good with kids. She'll probably love your niece."

I lean into her neck and kiss her ear. "You look gorgeous tonight." She's got on a black lacy jacket over a red silk top, skinny jeans, and black leather boots. Her hair is straightened tonight, different from her usual loose waves, and it looks even longer, almost reaching her waist. I'd love to draw her naked, with just her hair flowing over her body, and frame it for my bedroom. I file that wish away with the rest of the things I want to do with her.

She beams at my compliment. "You're lookin' good, too . . . I have to tell you, the shoes kinda really get to me," she admits, her lips curving into a sensual smile.

"I'll never take them off, then." We're interrupted by a crowd of three people just as I'm about to kiss her. I look up to see two chicks and a guy standing by our table.

"Hey, I'm Lukas. You guys must be Evelyn, Mike, and Amy?" I stand up, and the shorter girl nods, her eyes darting around nervously, like she's looking for someone or hoping not to be seen. I can see why Storm likes her, though; she's cute and has huge round, expressive eyes like a baby owl.

"That's us. You're Storm's cousin?"

"Yup. This is Ivy."

After introductions, we sit and I watch Evie's boyfriend scout out every hot chick in the place, while Evie talks to her friend and Ivy. Storm's right; the boyfriend's a douche and obviously a whore-hound. He could at least attempt to hide it. Dumbass.

Storm shows up at our table to say hello, and I can't tell who's more in love with him—Evie or her boyfriend. He's fanboying over Storm so bad that he's oblivious to the fact that Storm's got his hand on his chick's neck and is whispering in her ear, making her blush. Ivy raises her eyes at me as we witness the train wreck going on in front of us, and I just shake my head. How Storm is gonna unravel this mess is beyond me, but I hope he does, for his sake. I'm one of the few people who know he still has nightmares from losing his first wife years ago to suicide, an evil our family seems to be plagued with. I glance at my own inked wrists, and I can still see the raised scar tissue there. I wonder how long it will be before Ivy notices them and questions me.

For some, body art is to display things we're passionate about. For others, it's a camouflage to hide who we really are inside.

CHAPTER 14

IVY

It's been years since I've been to a concert or seen any kind of live band play, and I didn't recognize the band name when Lukas asked me to come. Now that I'm looking around, and seeing people milling about wearing the hoodies and t-shirts with the Ashes & Embers logo, I realize that Macy has one of their posters hanging on her wall. She also has several of their t-shirts. *Great.* Of course, my daughter would be a fan of the band that Lukas is so close to, because her being attracted to the man I'm dating isn't awkward enough. Now, I'm going to have to deal with her obsessing over the entire band.

The lights go down, the curtain goes up, and the band starts to play; they're a plethora of muscle, long hair, tattoos, and sexy voices. Their sound is great, and the crowd is going wild over them. Vandal stands off to the side of the stage, playing bass, and he's a whole lot of scary with a side of wow. It's easy to see why Evie is so taken with Storm; he's hot and playful and absolutely full of personality on stage. The singer looks like Storm but is much more serious, swaying with the mic, his voice deep and emotional, pulling us all in. He could sing the alphabet, and it would be amazing. He's that good. There's another guitarist strutting around the stage, banging his head of long dirty blonde hair. He's shirtless and his ripped, faded jeans are hanging low on his hips, revealing toned abs and that V—*the same Lukas has too*—that women go crazy for. I can barely see the drummer, but from what I can see, he's a wild man back there, his hair even longer than the rest of them, tossing his sticks in the air and catching them every time.

A crowd of women have made their way to the front of the stage and are screaming, grabbing at the guys' legs, especially Storm's. I glance over at Evie, wondering if she knows what she's getting into, getting involved with a rock star. I don't know if I could deal with women constantly coming on to my man, groping him, offering to do God knows what just to be with him. If Paul was so easily swayed by a younger, sexy girl, how do men react when it's happening to them on a daily basis? I don't even want to know.

Right after the second song, Lukas leans close to me and plants a kiss on my cheek. "I'll be right back, doll." I nod and watch him walk over to the side of the stage, talk to a blonde girl, and then disappear down a hallway.

"How long have you been dating?" Evie asks me.

"Oh . . . well, we're not really dating. It's kinda new. I'm a thirty-six-year-old new divorcee. I met him to get a tattoo done, and we sorta hit it off."

"That's great! He's really cute."

She's so right, and he seems to get cuter every time I see him. "I guess." I smile at her. "I don't know . . . he's much younger than me. He's only twenty-four. I have a teen daughter who has a crush on him, and she loves this band. This is all really new for me. I think I'm kinda too old for this."

She waves her hand at me, dismissing my comment with a smile. "Get out of here! You don't look thirty-six! And who cares about age anyway? Storm speaks really highly of him. He's a good guy. If you're happy, just go for it! "

"Look who's talking!" Evie's friend interjects, nudging Evie's arm.

I lower my voice, so her boyfriend can't hear me. "I heard about you and Storm. Lukas told me what happened."

"What did you hear?" she asks, her big eyes growing wider with fear.

"About the blizzard and how he fell for you. Don't worry. I won't say anything. Lukas really wants to see Storm happy."

Her eyes soften. "I do, too."

I look up at the stage as the song ends. The singer grabs the mic off the stand and walks a little closer to the edge of the stage.

"So, as you guys know, my brother got stuck in a blizzard a few weeks ago, right?" He turns to Storm, laughing in his direction. "Like trapped in his truck out in the woods."

The crowd screams, and Evie looks like she is going to pass out.

The singer continues. "So, this chick he was stuck with had no fucking idea who he was. Can you believe that shit?"

"No!" the audience yells.

"Fuckin' A, right! So Storm gave her one of our sweatshirts to wear, because he steals them all and he had one in his truck." He looks over at Storm, who's shaking his head and laughing over on his side of the stage. "And she says, 'oh is this one of those bands that just yell, and you can't hear the fucking lyrics?'"

The crowd roars and laughs. Evie's friend, Amy, laughs

hysterically, while Evie sips her drink. I feel bad for her. She looks like she's going to be sick.

"So we decided to do a song with no fuckin' yelling, just for Blizzard Chick! And as a special treat, Storm's gonna sing this one. It's one of his favorite songs."

"Oh, God," Evie says as the audience jumps up and down.

Storm's brother continues. "Now, you all know he can't sing as good as me, so let's go easy on him, okay?" He puts the mic back in its stand and walks away as the lights go down.

Evie's boyfriend turns to her. "This ought to be good," he says, with a slight smirk on his face. Honestly, I think he knows that Evie and Storm have something going on, and he just doesn't care. He has that jerk look to him. *Resting jerk face.*

The stage is dark and quiet for a few moments, and then a violin starts to play a few soft notes in the dark. Suddenly, a blue spotlight shines down on one member on the right side of the dark stage, holding the violin, moving the bow softly over the strings, the sound haunting and beautiful.

It takes me a few stunned moments to realize it's Lukas glowing under the blue light like an ethereal angel, his eyes closed as he plays the slow intro of the song. He looks incredible up there on stage, and the way his arm muscles flex as he plays is making all the women drool. Including me.

A purple spotlight shines down and lights up Storm, who's sitting on a stool center stage, holding his guitar, and he starts to sing a beautiful love song. Storm's voice coupled with the lonely, romantic sound of the violin is mind blowing. I can't take my eyes off of Lukas. He's so beautiful, oozing sensuality and confidence, the music flowing from him like he was born with that violin in his hand.

I grab Evie's hand under the table, and we hold on to each other, bonding as we watch the men we're falling in love with on stage, knowing we're never gonna be the same after this. I recall Lukas' words about trying to make us fall in love with them. How could we not?

I can't believe Lukas never told me he plays, or that he would be playing tonight. I wonder if he's actually a full time member of the band. I have to admit, I'm getting turned on watching him up there, the way his head is bent down, his hair falling over his face and shoulders, his arms and chest flexing as he plays that beautiful instrument. He's a dazzling mix of dark goth, adorable, and classical, all rolled up in a damn fine sexy ball.

Oh, shit. Am I really dating a twenty-four-year-old tattoo artist who's also a rock star? How did this happen? I'm just a boring, plain, human resources manager. Lukas is way out of my league.

The next song they play is heavier, and the rest of the band joins in as the lights brighten and fog wafts across the stage. I watch as Lukas saunters around the stage, adding some fast metal solos, shaking his head with sexy attitude as the bow flies over the strings of the violin. Hot does not even begin to describe him. I've never seen anyone play a violin so fast and hard before. The audience is going wild over him, forcing me to tear my eyes off him and shift my eyes over to see the crowd of gorgeous women trying to get closer to the stage, gawking at both Storm and Lukas, reaching for their legs and taking pictures.

So not only does he have half-naked, beautiful women sprawled out in front of him at the tattoo shop all day, but he's most likely got fans of the band after him, too. I swallow hard, a myriad of fears and insecurities swirling inside me.

If a pretty girl was able to swoop in and take my average-looking, office-working husband from me, how in the hell could I hold on to someone like Lukas?

The band takes a break, and Lukas jumps down off the stage and pushes his way through the pile of women pawing at him to get back to our table. I try to swallow my jealousy down. *He only smiled at them. He didn't stop to talk to anyone or let anyone flirt with him. He's not a man-slut.* He's all smiles when he approaches the table, his hair sticking to his damp forehead.

"Well?" he asks, out of breath, the adrenaline obviously still thrumming through his veins. I hand him my glass of water, and he gulps some down.

"Lukas, that was amazing!" Amy screeches before I can even open my mouth. "Holy shit, you rocked it!"

"Thanks, it was fun." He smiles at her and then turns his attention back to me. "You're not saying anything," he says, sitting and pulling my chair closer to his, trying to catch his breath at the same time. "Those lights are fuckin' hot."

I force a smile onto my face, still not sure how I feel about all of this. "I'm just surprised . . . I had no idea you played the violin . . ."

"And the piano," he adds, grinning.

"And the piano," I repeat, " . . . in a rock band. Why didn't you tell me?"

He looks around at the crowd and then back at me. "I was afraid it might scare you away. And I kinda wanted to surprise you."

LUKAS

"You definitely surprised me. It was awesome, though. Going from that slow beautiful classical tune, then to metal was just incredible. I loved it." I lean a little closer to him and lower my voice. "You looked really sexy up there strutting around."

"Oh yeah?" He quirks his eyebrow up. "Did it turn you on?"

"Lukas . . ." I look around the table to see if anyone is listening to us.

He touches my cheek and turns me back to him. "Hey, don't try to back pedal into shyness."

"You're so bad." His teasing has become a sweet addiction for me. "You love to make me crazy."

"You have no idea how bad I want to make you crazy, Ivy." His gravelly voice caresses my senses, and I squeeze my thighs together. Verbal foreplay is something I've never experienced before, but wow, does he make it work.

He clears his throat. "I want you to know, I only play the intros and solos on a few songs. I don't go on tour with the band or go to all the practices. I only play some of the local clubs with them." He looks me dead in the eye. "My commitment is to the shop. And you."

"Oh," I say, shocked by his words. "Me?"

"Yes, you . . . I don't want a fling, Ivy." I love his serious voice. It's deep, calming, and permanent. He doesn't ever lie or say something he doesn't mean, and I admire that about him more than anything else.

"I don't, either," I answer, hoping he can feel that I mean my words just as much as he does.

We stay for the rest of the set, and when the last song is played, he nuzzles into my neck and whispers in my ear, "Let's go. I need to be alone with you."

He's like wildfire on the drive back to his place, playing metal music on the radio and tapping his hands on the wheel. It's obvious the music really gets him going and makes him feel alive. I don't mind because I'm still replaying the night in my mind, trying to sort out my feelings; who he is, and what he does, makes me nervous. His work, his hobbies, and his passions all put him directly in front of women who want the novelty of a man like him. Sexy. Unique. Talented. Popular. Creative. *Romantic.*

After losing my husband to another woman's shameless sluttery, giving my heart to a man who has a target on his body and heart by probably several hundred women scares the ever loving shit out of me. Could I deal with it without feeling paranoid all the time?

On the other hand, I'm extremely drawn to those unique aspects that make him so special. Watching him on stage and hearing his music was a total turn on, and that surprised me. It was a little bit exhilarating to know that so many of those women wanted him, but he was coming home with me. It made me feel special and wanted. It made me feel young again.

Reaching across the car, he takes my hand and raises it to his lips, then rests our clasped hands together on my leg. "You're quiet," he says, over the music. "Are you all right?"

"I'm great. I was just thinking about how amazing you were tonight. And Evie loved the song Storm sang to her. She was really touched by it."

"I was hoping you would like it. Maybe Storm's plan of wooing Evie worked."

I smile over at him and tighten my fingers around his. "I'm pretty sure it did. It was a really sweet song, just like you."

He chews his lip ring for a few seconds, then glances at me briefly before turning his attention back to the road. "I'm not always sweet and quiet, Ivy."

The tone in his voice is now deeper, mysterious, and dark, making my stomach do a slow flip.

I lick my lips nervously, because I love my sweet Lukas and can't imagine him any other way. "Okay," I murmur, but I'm not sure he hears me because he doesn't say another word for the rest of the drive. He just holds my hand and nods his head to the rock music thumping from his stereo.

Earlier, I told him Macy was staying over at a friend's house, and he knows that Tommy is with Paul this weekend, thus leaving me free for the entire night.

Free to not go home.

Free to stay at his place.

Free to sleep with him.

Free to be . . . free.

CHAPTER 15

IVY

He opens my car door and then puts his arm around me, protecting me from the cold air as we walk across the dark parking lot to his house. Snow flurries are falling softly as he unlocks the door and lets us in.

Helping me off with my coat, he also removes my lace jacket and lays them on the wooden bench in the foyer by the door.

I shake the snow off my head, laughing. "I didn't know we were supposed to get sn—"

I'm cut off by him grabbing me around the waist, spinning me around, and pushing me up against the wall. His hand fists my hair, pulling my head to the side, my cheek pressed against the stone wall. His body engulfs mine, his muscular chest pressed against my back, his hard cock against my ass, his thighs flush to the back of mine. I feel trapped between his body and the stone wall of his foyer, and I relish in it, my heart pounding hard against my ribs. I want to be in his prison.

"Put your hands on the wall." His voice is breathless and raspy, just above a whisper in my ear. A shiver trots down my spine, but I do as he says, simply because he told me to. And right here, in this moment, with his beautiful hard body against mine, his hand tangled in my hair, I would do anything he asked of me. I press my palms against the wall—*the wall that was once a church.*

"Ask me why I live in a church," he says, as if reading my mind, gathering more of my hair in his hand and gently pulling it all away from my face and neck.

"Why do you live here?" I ask breathlessly.

"So you can worship *every . . . fucking . . . inch . . .* of me." He grinds his hips against my ass with each word, making every hard inch of him very known.

Oh, shit. Sweet Lukas has left the building.

"And I plan to do the same to you, doll."

He touches his lips against the side of my neck, while his free hand goes to my waist, holding me as he begins an oral assault like I have never imagined. He moves his mouth down to the side of my throat, kissing, sucking, and nipping at my flesh, slowly dragging his tongue down to my collarbone. He continues raining more kisses upon me, tugging my hair, forcing my head to arch back more so he can lick and suck my exposed neck like a hungry vampire, the piercings on his lip and tongue flicking over my flesh. I practically go limp against his body, the feel of his warm, wet lips intoxicating me, rendering me drunk and woozy.

Pushing my silk top up until it's bunched up at my shoulders, his lips come down on my bared back, kissing and licking between my shoulder blades, igniting warm tingles throughout my entire body. I feel him unhooking my bra, the fabric falling to my sides, and his tongue slithers down my spine, slowly tasting me, until he's kneeling behind me, kissing the small of my back. Letting go of my hair, he grabs the waist of my jeans in his hands and pulls them down, along with my panties, in one swift yank, making me gasp. They pool around my ankles, leaving me naked against the wall. I've never been so incredibly exposed, and I'm caught some place between incredibly flustered and wildly excited.

"Lukas..."

"Shhh . . . trust me, and you won't walk out of here the same, baby."

His hands slowly caress my thighs, while his lips travel over my hip, then down further, kissing my buttocks, lightly nipping me, making me jump.

"Turn around," he whispers, his hands on my hips, guiding me around, leaving me no choice but to turn to him. I lean my back and head against the wall, lightheaded, and look down at him, kneeling in front of me like a sexual God, his eyes glazed and full of smoky desire and passion. *My God, he actually wants me. Me.*

"You're beautiful," he says, skimming his hands up my calves, then up my thighs, and finally resting on my hips. Leaning forward, he kisses my stomach—my most hated part of myself. I reach down and try to pull his head away, but he grabs my hands and holds them to my sides while he continues to kiss my stomach.

"There's no part of you I don't want," he says, and I lean back and close my eyes, trying to quell my insecurities and just lose myself in him and his touch. Letting go of my hands, he slides his palms down my hips and to my thighs, gently pushing my legs apart as far as my jeans around my ankles will allow. I feel his lips encompass my clit, flicking his tongue slowly over that tiny sensitive spot before sucking it into his mouth. My entire body lurches from the unexpected shock of pleasure, but he holds me still with his hands and pushes his face between my thighs, running his tongue along my pink flesh, parting my lips. His mouth feels incredible, so warm and wet, and my legs go weak as he licks me, my pussy quivering, aching for more of him.

Standing, he drags his hands up my body and rests them on my neck, lightly squeezing while kissing me long and deep, possessing me, his tongue dancing with mine.

"I'm taking you upstairs," he growls between kisses. "And I don't plan on letting you out for a long time. So if you don't want this, please stop me now."

My breath catches in my throat. Only Lukas would say please in the middle of an insanely sexy sentence and still make it hot as hell. I shake my head. *No. Don't ever stop.*

"Nuh uh," he says. "No nodding or head shakes. Tell me what you want." He runs his thumb across my lower lip, his dark eyes locked on to mine. "I want to hear you say it."

I swallow and try to remember how to make words. "I want you."

He picks me up and carries me past Ray, who squawks at us as Lukas carries me up the stairs then down the hall to his bedroom, laying me down on his king-sized bed. Rock music is coming from hidden speakers, the deep bass sound thumping in time with my heart. To the right of the bed, the flames of an electric fireplace bathe the room in an orange glow.

I lie motionless and soundless on his black comforter, as he pulls off my shoes and the rest of my clothes, then stands at the foot of the bed just looking at me like he's memorizing me. Finally, he backs up a few steps and starts to undress himself, watching me watch him. He moves slowly and deliberately, a private seductive strip tease just for me. I envy his confidence as he peels off his clothes, revealing his perfectly sculpted body, adorned with black tattoos that seem to cover eighty percent of his body. Watching him undress is like watching someone unwrap a beautiful surprise gift, not knowing exactly what's inside but not caring because the journey to get to the reveal is just as special as the gift itself.

His bedroom is magnificent with its cathedral ceiling, wood beams, and massive stained glass windows. Lukas standing naked at the center of it, beneath a huge black metal crucifix on the wall, entices a mix of feelings deep within me. He is dark and light, an angel fallen and lost, sinfully sweet, dirty and damaged from the descent. I want him on me, in me, beside me. I want to breathe him into me and never exhale. I am completely enraptured by him.

He moves slowly toward the bed, his hard cock leading the way, his eyes locked on to mine. Crawling on top of me, he lowers his naked body onto mine and leans up on his arms, looking down at me, wisps of his silky hair falling into my face like a black waterfall.

"Do you think you could love me?" My chest tightens hearing the raw emotion in his voice. Buried in this beautiful erotic man, there still lives an abandoned little boy who believes he's unloved. Unwanted. It breaks my heart in two, not just as a mother, but as the woman who cherishes this man's heart so much already.

I reach up and move his hair to the side, so I can see his eyes more clearly.

"Lukas, I could definitely love you." I swallow hard, afraid to say too much, but even more afraid to not say enough when he needs it. "I feel like I've already loved you, and now my heart's just waking up, remembering how."

"That's exactly how it feels." His voice is low as he slides his hand down my body, between us, between my legs. His fingers glide over my wet lips before one slowly slides into me. He sucks in a breath and kisses my mouth, breathing against my lips.

"Do you trust me?" he asks, his finger swirling around inside me, making me delirious.

"Yes."

"I've never had sex without a condom before. Ever. I want to be inside you. I don't want to keep taking it off and putting another one on to start over. I want to make love to you without any interruptions."

I stare up at him for a few minutes. I didn't know people talked about stuff like this, and to be honest, it's something I hadn't even thought about. Eighteen years of marriage will put you in the dark about these things. But, I know Lukas wouldn't lie to me or do anything to hurt me. I trust him.

"It's okay . . . I won't get pregnant. I'm on birth control."

He nods. "Are you okay with me?"

"Yes."

"Thank you," he whispers and kisses me into sweet oblivion. *He thanked me.*

He moves down my body, kissing my breasts, his tongue circling my nipple, dragging his lip ring over it, making it harden before sucking it into his mouth, flicking his tongue over the sensitive flesh and sending jolts of pleasure down to my core. I squeeze my thighs around his hand, wanting more of everything.

He lifts his head and grins deviously down at me. "I'm gonna let you decide, baby." He bends down and kisses me between my breasts, then drags his tongue up to my throat, gently biting me there.

"Decide?" I repeat.

"I can kiss you everywhere and slowly make you fuckin'

crazy until you beg for me, or I can just bury my cock in you right now and ravish the rest of you after you're done coming all over me."

"Oh," I reply absently, my voice trembling. I almost had an orgasm just hearing him dirty talk while his finger lazily slides in and out of me, lulling me seductively.

"Oh?" he teases, pressing his body hard against mine, his hot, long length resting against my thigh. *Sweet Jesus.*

I wrap my arms around him and slide my hands down his back. "Do the bury thing," I say breathlessly.

Pulling his hand out from between my thighs, he grabs my leg and lifts it up around his waist, while at the same time plunging his cock deep into me in one smooth, hard motion.

I let out a small cry that's a myriad of surprise, pleasure, and pain, and he stills on top of me, unmoving, just holding himself inside me. He feels perfect, like he was made to be right where he is now. I close my eyes and hold my breath, savoring every part of him—how he feels, how he smells, how he tastes, how his breathing sounds. He's incredible. Never have I felt this way, and I probably never will again. Brushing my hair aside with his hand and cupping my cheek, he kisses my face softly.

"Breathe, little doll," he whispers between kisses. "I'm going to make you fly."

He moves in and out of me slowly, making sure I feel every hard inch of him as he spreads and stretches me wider and deeper than I've ever been before. He's long and thick, putting my ex to shame. *Sorry, Paul. Even sorrier, Charlene.*

Everything about him feels so big and powerful; he is solid muscle and has incredible control over his body and movements. Nothing about him is sloppy or awkward. And nothing about him feels twenty-four.

His hips roll in a wide circular motion, grinding his cock into me, rubbing against my clit in perfect rhythm. Sighing with pleasure, I wrap my legs around his waist and slide my hands down his body to grab his muscular ass. He kisses me more deeply, his tongue piercing banging my teeth. I open my eyes to find his dark ones staring back into mine.

"You feel so fuckin' good," he pants, leaning his forehead against mine.

"So do you," I glide my hands up his back, damp with sweat, and grip his wide shoulders.

"You want more?"

I nod and find his lips. "Yes . . ." I purr.

He leans back, grabs my knees and spreads my legs wide, pounding into me, hard and fast.

Holy mother. I feel like he's pummeling me into next week. He slows, tantalizing me, pulling out and using his hand to rub the head of his cock up and down my dripping lips, then slamming deep inside me again. He repeats this insanity until I'm writhing and screaming like a cat in heat. I don't know who I am anymore, and I don't care. All I want is him and everything he wants to give me.

He shakes his head as he drives into me, his sweaty hair flying around his head, and flashes me a sexy smile.

Reaching under me, he pulls me up until I'm on his lap, my legs wrapped around his waist, and his muscled arms around me, holding me close to him. We kiss, slower now, and his hands move down to cup my ass, lifting me up and down on his cock, grinding me against him. It feels amazing, having him buried deep inside me while he kisses me and moves me up and down on him. I hold his face in my hands as we kiss, then slide my hands to the back of his neck, my fingers gripping his hair.

Our bodies find a perfect rhythm, and soon, I feel the ecstasy building inside me. Gripping his hair harder, he moans against my mouth as I start to unravel and explode around him. He holds me and kisses me with turbulent passion, whispering things I can't even understand, as I tremble and shake with orgasm. With a hard thrust and a growl deep in his throat, I feel him come inside me. And he's right; I'm flying. My mind and body revel in how exquisite he feels. Everything else has disappeared. All I can feel, see, hear, and taste is Lukas.

My dark angel.

He lays me gently on my back and turns us on our sides, face-to-face, still connected, our hands slowly caressing each other's bodies, kissing softly. I've never felt so physically and emotionally connected to another person. We lie kissing like this for a long time. He makes love to me again, slow and drowsy, until I am whimpering and quivering against him again, and he whispers my name over and over again as he comes inside me.

I've fallen so hard that my heart has a concussion.

I wake up sometime later in his arms atop his huge bed. Watching him sleep, I'm captivated by how beautiful he is. I don't feel like me anymore, more like I'm just his. I can't remember what it felt like to *not* be his. I want to kiss him, hold him, and love him until time ceases to exist, and then I want to love him some more. I don't want him to ever feel unwanted again. The mere thought of it rips my heart to shreds.

Carefully lifting his arm off me, I climb out of the high bed and tiptoe to the bathroom connected to his bedroom, my legs and lady parts sore from all the bed romping.

I'm surprised by the size of the bathroom with a big jacuzzi tub in one corner and a glass shower in the other. I can't believe someone as young as him lives like this, with so much luxury. He seems unphased by it, though, and not at all spoiled. I freshen up a bit and then realize my cell phone is downstairs with my coat and purse. I grab his shirt off the bedroom floor, pull it over my head, and quietly walk through the house. The glow coming in from the stained glass windows and the dim lights he has placed in various areas of the houses gives me enough light to see where I'm going.

"Hello," Ray says when I reach the bottom of the stairs, scaring the heck out of me.

"Shh . . . go to sleep," I whisper at him.

"I'm taking you upstairs," he mimics in Lukas' voice. *Shit!* This bird not only saw us fooling around in the hallways, he heard us.

"Ray!" I hiss. "No! Bad bird! Stop saying that!" I wonder for how long he remembers phrases, and hope he forgets it by tomorrow.

"Upstairs," he says.

Ignoring the bird, I grab my purse and go back upstairs. Lukas is still sound asleep, the blanket covering him from the waist down. I sit on the floor next to the bed and check my cell phone. I have a text from Macy, saying she's okay and at Shelly's, and a missed call from Tommy. I quickly reply to Macy that I'll see her tomorrow. I feel awful that I missed Tommy's goodnight call and hope he's not upset I didn't answer—something I've never done before. A text comes in as

I'm staring at my phone, and I'm irked to see it's from Paul and not Macy.

> Paul: Where are you?
>
> Me: Out
>
> Paul: Where?
>
> Me: None of your business. Is Tommy ok?
>
> Paul: Yes. He called and u didn't answer.
>
> Me: I know and I'm sorry. I'll call him in the morning.
>
> Paul: Are you home?

What the heck is with his interrogation? Rude.

I look around Lukas' room while I debate answering Paul's annoying messages. I count six different gargoyle statues watching over the bed. I'm not sure if they're cool or creepy.

> Me: No
>
> Paul: Then where are you? It's 2am.
>
> Me: I know what time it is. Why aren't you enjoying the wonders of Charlene?
>
> Paul: She's sleeping.
>
> Me: I'm going to do the same. I'm tired. I'll call Tommy in the morning.
>
> Paul: Where are you sleeping, Ivy?
>
> Me: I'm on a date.
>
> Paul: With who?????
>
> Me: Fuck off

I mute his texts and stuff my phone back into my purse. Who the hell does he think he is?

As soon as I climb up on the bed, Lukas stirs and opens his eyes, squinting at me in the dim light cast from the electric fireplace.

"Ivy? You okay?"

"I was just checking my phone to see if the kids called."

He stretches and sits up. "They okay?"

I nod and scoot closer to him. "Yeah, I missed Tommy's call. I feel bad."

He pulls me into his arms and kisses the top of my head. "I'm sorry. From now on, we'll make sure you have your cell phone with you all the time when you're here, and you can give them my house number. They can call here any time."

"It's okay. I can't be attached to them twenty-four-seven."

"I know . . . but I want you to be relaxed here and not worried, and I want your kids to know where you are."

"You're a sweetheart, you know that?"

He tugs at the hem of the shirt I'm wearing. "Take this off. I wore it on stage. It's probably all sweaty."

I smile but pull the shirt over my head and lay it on the floor next to the bed. "I don't mind wearing your sweaty shirt," I say, smiling.

"You're staying the night, right?" he asks, rolling on top of me.

"If you want me to, then yes."

"Are you kidding? Of course I do. I don't want you to ever leave."

"I can stay the night."

He kisses the tip of my nose. "That'll do for now."

CHAPTER 16

LUKAS

I can now scratch *waking up with the woman of my dreams off my bucket list.*

She's sleeping on her stomach, hugging my pillow, one of her legs bent up. I want to spread her from behind and sink myself into her, but I don't, because I don't want her to think our relationship will only be physical. She's so much more to me than that. But damn, that view is tempting.

Instead, I kiss her cheek, take a shower, and walk to the cafe to get us two vanilla brown sugar lattes and bagels. When I get back to the house, there's a car in my parking lot, which is odd because it's Sunday and we rarely see clients on Sundays. I cross the parking lot, knock on the window of the car, and the guy rolls down his window.

"Can I help you?" I ask him.

He looks from his cell phone to my house then back to me.

"Is this 26 Main?"

"It is. Do you have an appointment?" I ask, hoping Vandal didn't set up an appointment with someone and then forget about it, which he's done before.

"An appointment?" he repeats, confused.

"Yeah, for a tattoo?"

"No, I'm looking for Ivy."

I narrow my eyes at him. "Ivy?"

"Yeah, she's my wife. The GPS software on our phones told me she's here, at this address."

This fucking guy. Fury rages up inside me. No way in hell is he gonna wreck my first weekend with Ivy.

"She's inside sleeping," I say.

He pales. "What? And how the hell do you know that?"

"Because she's in my bed."

Shock contorts his face. "Excuse me?"

"Look, man, I don't know what the hell you're doing here, but let's set some shit straight. First, she's not your wife anymore. You left her and moved in with your girlfriend, remember? Second, you're on my property. My shop is closed today, and I haven't invited you to my home, so in my eyes, you're trespassing."

"What the fuck is my wife doing in your bed?"

"Your wife isn't in my bed. My *girlfriend* is in my bed. And now, I'm going to bring her the latte I just got for her before it gets cold. I want you out of my parking lot."

His eyes darken. "I want to talk to her. She didn't answer her phone last night when our son called."

"That's right, because we were busy. She's going to call him when she wakes up. And, by the way, where is Tommy right now? If it's your weekend to be with him, shouldn't you be with him and not stalking Ivy?"

"Fuck you, pal."

I chew my lip ring and try to control my anger. The last thing I want is Ivy getting all upset about me and this douche-nugget having a fight.

"I'm going inside now," I say calmly. "Get off my property. If you're still here by the time I get inside, I'll call the police and have them come remove you."

I walk away from him, not giving him a chance to say anything else. I'm not happy that this guy is obviously still hung up on Ivy, and he's not dealing with the fact that she's moved on with someone else. Did he really think someone as pretty and sweet as her was gonna stay single, and he could hang on to her while he went out and screwed around?

Not a chance, dude.

"Hands on the wall," Ray squawks when I cross the living room on my way upstairs. *Shit.*

"Ray, you're a pretty bird," I say, trying to divert him back to bird-talk. I forgot he could hear us in the foyer last night, and the last thing I need is him repeating it all back to us.

"I'm a pretty bird," he repeats.

"Yes, you are."

"I want you," he says, mimicking Ivy.

I glare at him in his cage. "Ray, be a pretty bird."

He cocks his little black feathered head at me, pretending to be innocent. But I know better.

"I'm a pretty bird," he says softly.

"Keep it up, bird brain, and you'll end up in a salad."

I climb the stairs and find Ivy sitting up in my bed, holding her cell phone, frowning at the screen. My stomach sinks a little. What if Paul has come to his senses and wants her back? He may be a jerk, but he's shared eighteen years with her, and given her two kids. So far, all I've given her is a tattoo and a night of multiple orgasms.

"Hey," I say, sitting on the bed. "I got us lattes and bagels."

She smiles sleepily at me. "How did you know I was dying for a coffee?" She kisses my cheek as I hand her the latte.

"I know it's your fav." I nod my head at her phone. "Everything okay?"

She shoves her phone into her purse. "Yeah, I called Tommy. He's playing Xbox, said he was alone with Charlene and that his Dad wasn't home. Then I got a text from Paul, asking me where I was."

"What did you tell him?"

"I told him I was with my boyfriend and it was none of his business."

"What did he say?" I ask, wondering if Paul is going to tell her about our altercation in my parking lot.

She shrugs and sips her coffee. "Nothing. He hasn't replied. I don't know what his problem is."

"Obviously, he's jealous, and I don't blame him."

"He can be jealous all he wants. He made his bed, slept with a tramp in it, and now he can stay in it."

I let out a laugh. "Ooh, I like feisty Ivy."

I decide to not tell her that Paul was GPSing her and stalked her right to my house. No sense in getting her upset or nervous, especially when it looks like Paul isn't going to mention it, either. Most likely, he feels like an idiot right about now.

We sit on the floor of my bedroom in front of the fireplace and eat our breakfast, talking a little about the band and my shop. I hope her new questions are coming from interest and not doubt in me.

"What if Paul wants you back?" I finally ask, because I can't get the thought out of my head now. He kept referring to her as his wife, and that just doesn't sit well with me at all.

"He doesn't. Charlene is young and gorgeous."

I tilt my head at her, hating that she believes someone else is better than she is, just because Paul said so. "Ivy, you're young and gorgeous, too. You're beautiful." I kiss her lips. "And sweet." I kiss her again. "And smart." I kiss her longer. "And incredible in bed."

Her cheeks flush, and she looks down at her coffee cup. "Lukas... I'm not."

I lift her chin and force her to look at me. "You're all of those things, Ivy. Trust me."

She shakes her head and touches my hand. "I just don't think of myself like that."

"I know, but I have no problem telling you, so you should keep me around."

Her aqua eyes shimmer as she smiles at me. "I plan to keep you around."

"What if Paul did want you back? If he knows you're moving on, it could wake him up to see what he really had."

She stares at the fire, thinking, and while I want her to be sure, I hate that she's thinking about it. I mean, that's bad, right? If she has to think about it for longer than two seconds?

"Lukas," she finally says. "I don't want to hurt you. Ever."

My heart stops beating. My lungs stop breathing.

"And?" I urge, going mad in the silence.

"And I feel a very intense connection to you. I think you know that."

"And?"

"Lukas, stop being five for a second and let me talk, okay?" she teases.

"Sorry. Talk faster."

She grabs my hand. "I don't want Paul back. I really like what's happening between you and I. It's happening faster than I thought it would... but I love how you make me feel. I love being around you. You make me happy." She looks up into my eyes and smiles. "But..."

"There's a but?"

She moves her fingers up to my wrist, rubbing over the scars that have been there for a long time. "*This* scares me, Lukas. I can't make any guarantees right now, and I don't ever want you to hurt yourself if things didn't work out between us." She swallows hard and continues to rub my wrist. "We have a long road ahead of us, and as much as we may want it to work, we don't know what could happen. I need to know that you're okay, that you wouldn't do something like this… if something happened."

I clench my jaw, hating my past and the demons that haunted me then, and sometimes still do.

She puts her latte off to the side and moves closer to me. "I really didn't want to have this conversation this morning, after we had such a great night," she says.

"No, it's okay. You have a right to know what kind of head case you're sleeping with."

"Lukas, I don't think that at all, but this is serious. It's a red flag."

Ouch.

"Yeah, I guess it is," I admit. "I was young when I did this. I was fourteen. My mother's phone number was in some things I had packed from my great-grandmother. I carried it around with me on a little piece of paper for months before I finally got enough courage to call her. I was pretty miserable at my foster home." I let out a sigh, and she holds my hand tighter. "Anyway, I'm not sure what I was thinking was gonna happen, but I called. When she answered, I told her who I was, and she said, 'I don't want you. Don't ever call me again. I don't want anything to do with you.' And she hung up on me."

"Oh my God, Lukas. I'm so sorry."

"Anyway, I kinda lost it. I was already pretty messed up in

the head, drinking a lot, and just depressed. I wasn't sleeping, and was having a hard time adjusting to being in school after being homeschooled when I was younger—just everything. My friend Finn found me. He lived across the street and just came inside when I didn't answer the door. He called an ambulance, and from what they tell me, I was technically dead for about two minutes."

Ivy squeezes my hand even harder. "Lukas..."

"So, I ended up in the psych ward, of course, and my foster parents were disappointed, to say the least. Then I was in therapy for quite a while, learning how to accept the fact that some people might not want me, but I'm not supposed to kill myself over it. I'm stronger now, Ivy. I'll accept it if you don't want me. I won't try to off myself. I have the shop, and my brother, and Katie, and Gram, and the fucking bird to take care of. I'll be fine."

She throws her arms around me and hugs me so tight I can barely breathe. "I hate that someone hurt you, Lukas."

I hug her back. "It's all right. Shit happens. I'm okay now, really."

She turns her face into my neck, and I feel her tears against my skin. "It's not okay. You're an amazing person. I love your heart so much. I don't ever want you to feel pain like that again."

I love your heart.

"Well, with any luck, I won't ever feel that way again." I pull her away from me so I can see her face. "But I don't want you held hostage over this, Ivy. If you have to leave me someday, then you have to. You can't stay just because you're afraid to hurt me or that I might hurt myself. I wouldn't do that. I just wanted to be sure you were over Paul before we got more involved, because, fuck yeah, it would hurt to lose you."

I wipe the tears off her cheeks with my thumb, and she leans forward and kisses my lips really softly, like she's trying to kiss it all away for me.

"I'm over Paul," she says between kisses. "I'm falling for you pretty fast and hard, though, and it's scary. I wasn't expecting any of this... you, the age difference, the band..."

Leaning back onto the floor and pulling her on top of me, I move her hair over to one shoulder so I can kiss her neck. "None of that matters, Ivy. All that matters is how we treat each other, right?"

"You're right."

"And how we make each other feel." I gently bite her neck, my hands sliding down to her waist.

"Yes."

"And right now, I want to feel you come on my mouth."

I love the little gasp of surprise that she makes. "Lukas—"

I pull my t-shirt up over her head and throw it across the room, liking the fact that she keeps putting my clothes on her body.

"Your shyness is adorable, doll, but you should know it only makes me want to do dirty things to you. You've waited way too long to be fucked and loved the right way." I yank her panties off and throw those, too. "I'm gonna leave the choice up to you again." I kiss her breasts and slide my hands down her body. "You're either gonna sit in that chair over there, and I'm gonna eat you like a Chinese buffet, or you're gonna sit on my face and ride my tongue like a cowgirl."

"Holy shit, Lukas," she whispers.

"Choose or I'll do it for you." I suck her nipple into my mouth and flick my tongue over it, her breath quickening.

"Buffet," she says breathlessly, her nails digging into my shoulders.

LUKAS

I stand and carry her over to the red velvet, antique chair in the corner of my room. "Damn," I tease. "I was hoping to be a pony today." I sit her down in the chair, secretly loving the shocked look on her face as she watches me kneel in front of her and spread her legs.

Sitting back on my heels, I enjoy the view of her spread in front of me, her creamy pale thighs taut, her long hair flowing down her chest, her nipples peeking out. She looks incredibly beautiful and sensual, every part of her waiting for me. I'd love to take a picture of her like this and draw her this way.

"For God's sake, Lukas, don't stare at it," she says, turning eighty shades of red. I slide my finger slowly down her slit, watching as a tiny drop of moisture drips from her. I lean forward and lap it up, and she jumps, grabbing my head.

"Jesus!" she exclaims, her body bucking up toward me.

"You can call me that, baby. We're in my church, after all."

Grabbing her legs, I lift them and rest them on my shoulders, turning my head to lick and kiss her thigh, feeling her muscles quaking.

I lick her lips slowly, my tongue gently sliding between her folds, exploring her sweetness. Spreading her with my hands, I delve into her, swirling my tongue inside her, using my tongue and lip piercings to rub against her sensitive spots, making her quiver against my lips. Pushing one, then two fingers slowly inside her, I drag my tongue up to play with her clit, licking her in circles, slow at first and then faster, as I feel her body pushing against my face. I know she's trying to fight it, but she can't. Sucking her little bud into my mouth, I piston my fingers in and out of her faster, her hands grasping my hair, her hips thrusting against my face, finally letting herself go and giving in to the pleasure. She starts to moan, and I suck her delicate flesh harder, shaking my head, devouring her as her thighs tighten around me. Soon, she's shaking and whimpering, pulling my hair, coming all over my tongue and face, driving me wild for her with her little squeals.

My cock is rock hard in my jeans, and I want to beg her to suck me, but I have a feeling she's not ready for that just yet, especially with her strange mouth-and-fork fetish. Instead, I quickly unbutton my jeans, yank the zipper down, grab my throbbing cock, and thrust it into her as she's still coming.

"Oh my God," she moans, wrapping her legs around my waist. She's so hot and wet around me that I only get a few deep thrusts in before I'm coming inside her, all my control lost.

"Fuck," I gasp, grabbing her neck and pulling her to me for a deep kiss. I literally want to devour this woman with my mouth and my cock.

We kiss long and slow, as our panting subsides and our brains defog. She rubs my back in slow circles and kisses me softly, lovingly, on my lips, face, and neck, as we come down from post-orgasm bliss. It feels like Heaven.

Fuck me; I am so falling for this girl. I'm done. Stick a fork in me.

Ivy told me during one of our epic text conversations over the Christmas holiday that she never gets to relax on weekends because she's always doing laundry, cleaning the house, and taking care of the kids, so I make sure we spend the rest of the day relaxing. I lure her into the shower with me and give her a nice soapy massage, shampoo her hair, and bundle her up in one of the band sweatshirts. Asher had this idea few months ago to print funny hashtags on the sweatshirts and t-shirts for each guy in the band, and mine says #worshipme.

Ivy reads it on the sweatshirt and raises her eyebrow at me. "Do I even want to know what this means?" she asks.

"It's just a joke. Vandal's says #getvandalized, which is way worse."

She giggles. "Definitely. So far, you've been worshipping me . . . soon, I'm going to have to worship you," she says, peeking up at me.

Yes. Now. On your knees.

"Whenever you're ready, doll. The church of Lukas is only for you."

She shakes her head at me. "I can't even. I'm just gonna let that go for now."

We spend the rest of the day relaxing, sitting by the fire in the living room, cuddling, and trying to make Ray forget the bad words he heard by talking about my antiques.

"Is it weird I feel sad that I have to leave?" she asks when it's time for me to drive her home.

"If it is, then we're both weird, because I don't want you to go. Keep my sweatshirt, please. I like how it looks on you."

She smiles at me as she grabs her coat and purse while I find my car keys. "Thank you. I had the best time, really." She looks longingly at me, and I hate that I have to take her home, but Paul is dropping Tommy off at her house soon.

I hug her in the hallway by the door before we leave. "I did, too. I don't want you to go. When can I see you again?"

"Soon . . . let me do some thinking. I have Tommy next weekend."

"You can bring him here. I don't mind at all. I have room

for him. You can both stay. I have an Xbox, and I can get him anything he wants so he has fun here."

"I don't know if I'm ready for that yet."

"I could come to your place," I suggest.

She takes a deep breath. "That's even worse. I don't know how to do this."

"Babe, it's okay. There's no rule book. If you want me in your life, I have to be around your kids, and I want to be. I hope you believe that. I don't want to only see you when Paul has Tommy. That's every other weekend. Don't do that to us."

She nods. "I know . . . you're right. Just let me think about the best way to do this. I promise I will. I don't want to only see you every other weekend. I want more than that."

I lead her out and lock the door behind us. "I hope so."

When I drop her off at her house, I'm worried about Paul confronting her when he brings Tommy home. What if he starts a fight with her?

I grab her arm before she gets out of my car. "Ivy, I have to tell you something."

"Okay . . ."

"Paul was at my house this morning. I found him in the parking lot when I went to get us coffee."

"What?" she shouts. "What was he doing there? Why didn't you tell me?"

Damn. She's pissed.

"He said he used some GPS app to find your phone, and it took him right to my house."

"Shit. Did you talk to him?"

"Yeah, he was in my parking lot. I thought he was a customer or something, but then he said he was looking for you."

"Oh my God. What's wrong with him?"

"Fuck if I know. Anyway, I told him you were inside, so he knows you were with me. He seemed really pissed off, kept calling you his wife. I'm a little worried about him starting with you when he gets here with Tommy."

She lets out an exasperated sigh and stares out the window. "You should have told me," she says pointedly.

"I know. I just didn't want to upset you and ruin our day. He didn't text you about it, so I figured he was embarrassed and didn't want you to know he was stalking you."

"Ugh. Well, I'm sorry he showed up at your place. You shouldn't have to deal with that. But, I want you to tell me things like this from now on."

"All right. Don't be mad."

"I'm not mad at you. I just don't know what's wrong with him. He got what he wanted, so now he needs to leave me alone. This wasn't my choice. It was his."

Her words cut in to me, ramping up my paranoia that he wants her back and may be able to sway her into letting him back in. Sensing this, she turns to me.

"Lukas, being with you is *my* choice. I'm just saying, he's the one that left to begin with. I was happy . . . or I thought I was." She leans across the car and kisses my cheek. "Don't worry. I had an amazing weekend with you. Let's just take things one day at a time, okay? Don't worry about him coming over here. He's not the yelling, fighting type."

No, he's just the stalking type.

"All right. I don't want him on my property again, though. If Vandal catches him creeping around, it's not going to be pretty."

"I'm sure he won't be doing that again."

"Will you call me or text me later? Let me know everything is okay?"

"Yes, of course I will."

I give her a long kiss before letting her go. "I'm crazy about you, Ivy. I really want this." I hug her close to me, burying my face in her hair. She smells like my shampoo, as if she's part of me.

"I do, too," she murmurs. "Your persistence worked."

CHAPTER 17

IVY

My anger at Paul gets worse as I prepare dinner for the kids and wait for him to drop Tommy off. How dare he track me and show up at Lukas' place? Talk about a total invasion of my privacy and just all around juvenile behavior.

"Mom, are you wearing an Ashes & Embers hoodie?" Macy asks, coming into the kitchen.

Oh, crap. I completely forgot that I'm still wearing it and that she would recognize the band logo.

"Yes, I went to their concert last night," I say nonchalantly, hoping she'll get distracted by her cell phone as usual and not zero in on me.

She practically leaps across the room. "Are you kidding me right now? Why didn't you ask me to go? That show was totally sold out! You don't even like that kind of music!"

I take a deep breath, knowing I'm falling deeper into the hole I've dug and just have to come clean.

"Okay, honey, I have to tell you something. You know the tattoo artist, the guy that fixed our shed?"

"Yeah." She nods excitedly. "The hottie with the body."

"His name is Lukas, and he took me to the concert. He's in the band—"

"Holy shit, Mom!" she shrieks. *"Lukas Valentine?* That was him? I thought he looked familiar!"

I take a step back and lean against the kitchen counter. "Yes, that's him. I didn't know he was in the band."

"He's new, Mom! He just plays these amazing solos on their new album. This shit is crazy!"

"Macy, stop swearing and yelling." I rub my temples. Her voice is going straight through my brain and making my head hurt.

She looks at me like I'm crazy and flops dramatically into one of the chairs at the table. "I'm totally freaking out! I mean, what the hell! He's like, twenty, Mom! And he's hot. You don't like hot guys."

I add some pasta to the boiling water, trying not to think about Lukas naked on top of me, with all those muscles and tattoos and long hair.

I definitely like hot guys.

"Macy, he's twenty-four, and of course I like attractive men."

"Yeah, but not like *him*! You like boring old guys like Dad."

Stirring the pasta, I try to think of a decent reply without bashing Paul. "There's more to men than looks, and your father is really not old at all. He's only thirty-seven. Lukas is a nice guy. He's extremely talented. He has his own business, and he's very polite and thoughtful."

She rolls her eyes. "Mom! Get serious! Nobody thinks of those things when they look at someone like him!"

"Well, they should. He's a person, not an object."

"A *sexy* person. I hafta tell Shelly. She's going to freak out."

She whips out her cell phone and starts typing, but I grab it away from her.

"No. This isn't a game, Macy. I don't want you gossiping with your friends about my relationships."

She stares up at me. "Oh, wow. Are you like *serious* with him? Like Dad and Charlene?"

Ugh. What a terrible comparison. I think Paul's interest in Charlene is entirely based on her looks and has nothing to do with what kind of person she is, but I'm definitely not going to tell our daughter that.

I nod. "Yes, I think it could get serious. I need you to be an adult about this, Macy, please. This isn't easy for me, but I really do like him, and I want you and Tommy to meet him and hopefully like him."

Her eyes widen. "Mom? Hello? I did meet him, and I flirted with him right in our back yard."

"I know..."

She chews her lip and looks at me guiltily. "I'm sorry. So awkward. I had no idea. I wouldn't have acted like a hookah with him if I knew you liked him."

"I don't even know what that means, but you shouldn't be acting like that with anyone."

I stir the pasta again and take several deep breaths. I think I'm going to need a Valium to get through the rest of this night.

"Mom, stuff is crazy lately. It's like we're in some reality show or something. First, Dad takes off with the gum scraper, and now, you're dating a rock star. I'm waiting for a camera crew to start following me around."

I suppress a laugh. "Honey, I want things to be normal, or as close as they can be. Lukas is really just a regular guy who happens to be related to a bunch of rock stars who used his talents for a few songs. Being with him isn't going to change me or make anything crazy."

"You're wearing a rock band shirt with the hashtag worshipme, Mom. That's kinda crazy. Just sayin'."

I strain the pasta and put it in a serving dish, visions of Lukas ravishing me up against his church wall playing through my head.

"Macy, please, I really want your support and understanding with this. As you can see, I'm totally out of my element with, him but I really do like him. He makes me happy."

"Well, that's obvious. When Dad was here, you hardly ever smiled. Ever since your tattoo appointments, you've been smiling and dressing nicer, and you seem much happier. If you're happy, I'm happy. I'm totally jelly you have a hot boyfriend and I don't, though," she teases. "It's kinda nice to have a cool mom." She gets up and hugs me. "I love you. I'm glad you're happy now."

I hug her back, hoping my daughter and I will be best friends someday, like I dreamed about when I was only eighteen and pregnant. I wanted her more than anything in the world.

"I love you, too."

She's quiet for a few minutes as she sets the table. "Did you meet Talon?"

"Talon?" I repeat, putting sauce in a bowl.

"Yeah, he's the guitarist. He has longish dirty blonde hair, and he's wicked cute."

Oh. The shirtless guy. "I didn't actually talk to him, but I saw him. I only met briefly with Storm and Vandal."

"Storm! Is he totally swoon-worthy in person?"

"He was very nice. Lukas seems close to him."

"Well, Talon is my favorite. Lukas is the youngest, I think, and then Talon."

We're interrupted by the doorbell, which I finally talked Paul in to using, instead of just walking into the house whenever he felt like it. I didn't feel like he had the right to do that anymore after he left us.

"I'll go get Tommy," Macy offers and disappears, but a few seconds later, she's yelling down the hallway.

"Mom! Dad wants to talk to you!"

Great. I can feel another uncomfortable conversation coming on. I wash my hands and go out into the hall, where Paul is standing with the kids. "Go eat dinner while I talk to your father," I say to them, giving Tommy a quick kiss hello as he walks by me.

"You colored your hair," Paul says when they're gone.

"Is that what you wanted to talk about?"

"No, but it looks really nice."

I cross my arms. "What do you want exactly? I'd like to eat dinner with my kids."

He rubs the back of his head. "What's going on with you?" he asks in a hushed tone.

"Excuse me?"

"You're dating? Spending the night with other men?"

I gape at him. "Are you serious? What business is that of yours? And it's *one* man, not 'other men.'"

"We're still legally married."

"You left me and your kids to move into a condo with some home wrecker, Paul. You filed for divorce a week later. That was months ago, and I've been alone this entire time. I think it's acceptable for me to date."

"She's not a home wrecker."

"She knew you were married. She met your kids and me

several times, and yet she slept with you anyway. Even if you were pig enough to pursue her, she should have stayed away from you, knowing you were married."

He glares at me. "I met your so-called boyfriend. What in the hell are you thinking?"

"I'm thinking he's an amazing man who treats me like a princess and actually cares about me."

"He's a fucking punk kid. He looks like a Goddamn circus act."

I bite my tongue and try not to explode. I am really sick of people judging Lukas just by the way he looks, and not seeing him for the amazing person he is. I didn't know people with body art were so judged by others.

"You don't know him, Paul. He's extremely talented, successful, loyal, and polite. You could take some lessons from him."

He leans in close to me, his breath hot against my face. "I don't want that freak show near my kids."

"You don't get a say in that. You left us for some little whore. You had an affair and lied to us for a year. You have no right to pass judgement on someone else, just because they have tattoos and piercings. He's a good person."

"He's a fucking kid. Are you really that desperate?"

"Are *you*? I think he's older than your girlfriend, just for the record."

He shakes his head and paces the hallway. "I don't know what's gotten into you, Ivy."

"Me? What happened to *you*? You destroyed an eighteen-year marriage. And now you're stalking me? You threw me away. You have no right to follow me around or make comments about who I choose to spend my time with."

"I didn't think you'd do something like this."

"Like what? Find someone to make me happy?"

He stops pacing and stares at me. "What could you possibly have in common with someone like that? He's going to fuck you and get rid of you. You'll probably end up with a disease."

I sigh, bored with his tantrum and lame attempts to turn me away from Lukas. "We get along great and he makes me laugh. We want the same things in life. We both value and want commitment. Most of all, I'm happy, and that's all that matters right now. You're the one who got rid of me."

He edges closer to me and puts his hand on my arm. "I'm sorry I did that, Ivy. I think about it all the time, and I feel like shit about it. I never wanted to hurt you like that."

There was a time I would care about his apology, when it may have meant something to me, but now, I just don't. I'm numb to him now and only feel irritation toward him.

"Well, you did what you did, Paul, and we're both moving on now. I'd like the divorce finalized soon. We need to work out a visitation schedule and figure out what we're going to do with this house. Then we can be free of each other."

He blinks. "Is that what you want?"

"It's what *you* wanted, Paul. I never wanted any of this, but this is where I ended up."

He leans back against the wall and lowers his head. "The thought of that guy touching you is driving me crazy. You've always been just mine. Knowing that kid with long hair and tattoos is crawling all over you makes me feel sick."

I blink back the unwanted tears that threaten to start. "I felt the same way. We were each other's firsts, and were supposed to be each other's lasts. How do you think I felt, knowing you were sleeping with another woman behind my back?" My voice cracks, and I swallow hard. "I heard you telling her you wanted to fuck her. Do you know how much that hurt me?"

He licks his lips and nods slowly, my words sinking in. "I do now."

"Well, good. You deserve it."

He meets my eyes, and I see regret and sadness there, but it's too late. A few months ago, I would have taken this opportunity to try to make him see how much I love him and what we had together. I would have asked him to come back, and tried to start over fresh. I would have begged him to leave Charlene, and I would have forgiven him.

But not any longer, because now, my heart belongs to a man who's woken up way too many new desires in me. I want to see his hair falling into his deep, emotional eyes. I want to feel that hard, inked skin against mine. I want to be held like a doll one moment and taken up against a wall the next. I want to hear more beautiful music from him, and to see more of his incredible art. But most of all, I want to be the keeper of his damaged heart.

"You should go," I say, straightening my spine. "I want to spend some time with the kids."

I turn and leave him in the hall, and hear the click of the door by the time I reach the kitchen to enjoy dinner with my kids.

Lukas: I had the best night with you. I miss you.

Me: So did I, and I miss you, too. So much. Xo

Lukas: How did your night go?

Me: It was interesting. I told Macy about you. She was shocked, but I think she's ok with it. She loves the band, especially Talon. :-)

Lukas: Oh, hell no. He'd be all over her.

Me: Yes, let's keep them apart please.

Lukas: How was everything else?

I know he's hinting at how it went with Paul, and he wants to know if anything has changed.

Me: Paul came in when he dropped Tommy off. He was freaking out about me being with you. You were right, he's jealous. He's the only man I've ever been with before, so he's having a hard time dealing that I was with you.

Lukas: Tuff shit. He let you go.

Me: I know. That's pretty much what I said.

Lukas: I'm proud of you. I know this is hard on you.

Me: It is. I feel a little beat up.

Lukas: I wish I could hug you and make you feel better

Me: I do, too. I could use it right now. You give the best hugs.

He doesn't reply, so I check on the kids, change into my pajamas, and snuggle up in bed to read for a while, hoping it will take my mind off everything so I can get a good night's sleep. As I'm climbing into bed, my phone buzzes.

Lukas: What are you doing?

Me: Just sitting in bed reading. I thought you fell asleep. :)

Lukas: Come to your front door.

Me: What?

Lukas: Just do it ;)

Oh my God! He's here?

I throw on my robe and quietly go downstairs. When I

open the front door, I step outside to find him standing there, smiling.

"Lukas! You're crazy!"

He pulls me to him and hugs me tight. "Hey, if my girl needs a hug, she gets a hug."

"You. Are. The. Best," I say, winding my arms around his waist and squeezing him.

Putting a hand under my chin, he lifts my head up to face him. "You okay, baby doll?"

"I am now. You're so sweet. And I'm so scared." I start to cry, and I really don't even know why. I just feel totally overwhelmed by my feelings for him. Everything feels so intense and so perfect.

"Hey, hey, hey. Everything's all right," he whispers. "I'm here, and I'm not going anywhere. I'll take care of you, Ivy." He kisses my lips softly. "I think that's what you need, someone to take care of you for a while."

My heart bursts as I bury my face in his warm chest. He's the stuff women dream about, and he's right here, on my steps, hugging me. And he's real—not a dream, not a book, not a movie. *And he's mine.*

CHAPTER 18

IVY

"Oh my God, Mom, do you think any of the guys from the band will be there?" Macy asks as we stop at a traffic light.

Shaking my head, I turn the radio down. "No. We're going to his house so you two can meet him and get to know him. None of the guys will be there."

"Can I talk to the bird?" Tommy quips from the back seat. "Will he talk back to me?"

I smile at him in the rear-view mirror. "Yes, you can talk to Ray, and he'll probably talk back." I pray that Ray doesn't say anything inappropriate.

Macy turns the radio back up. "I can't believe we're going to Lukas Valentine's house. This is epic. Dad had a major episode when I told him. Charlene's a fan. Did you know that?"

"What?" I ask. "You told him?"

The car behind me blasts their horn at me to move. "Mom, it's not gonna get any greener. Go," Macy says, rolling her eyes.

I step on the gas and grip the wheel, trying to get my sudden anxiety attack under control. My mind is racing in a million different directions. I'm nervous enough bringing the kids over to Lukas' house for the first time, but knowing Macy told Paul, and that the home wrecker is a fan of Ashes & Embers, is just adding to my anxiety.

"Honey, I'd rather you didn't tell your father what I was doing."

"I'm sorry. I was just excited. He got really mad, though, when Charlene said she went to one of their concerts last year."

"Well, let's try not to add to the stress of the situation, okay?"

"I wasn't trying to. They fight all the time anyway."

"Who does?" I ask, turning into Lukas' parking lot.

"Dad and Charlene. Every time I'm on the phone with Dad, she's whining in the background, and the few times I've visited, she's like, the face of misery." She looks out the window and then at me. "Why are we stopped?"

I smile at her. "This is where Lukas lives."

I watch her face light up like only a crazy excited teenager's can. "What? You're dating a guy who lives in an old stone church? Mom, for real, I totally want to be you."

"You can live in church?" Tommy asks as we get out of the car.

I take his hand. "Yes. It's not a church any more, but it was a very long time ago. Now, it's been turned into a house."

He stares up at the building as we get closer to the door. "Do I have to be quiet? And pray?" he asks.

I smile down at him and squeeze his hand. "Well, you shouldn't yell, since it's his house, but you don't have to whisper, and you don't have to pray."

"I'm gonna pray he hooks me up with Talon," Macy jokes.

I don't know why I'm always surprised when Macy talks

about guys, because I was actually only a few months older than she is now when I became pregnant with her. Was I really that young when I was having sex, thinking I was in love? I felt so old and mature at the time. No wonder my parents were worried sick. I cannot even imagine Macy being pregnant and getting married any time in the near future. I shudder at the thought of it.

Lukas answers the door with a big smile and gives me a quick kiss on the cheek, and I'm grateful that he's being conservative with the affection in front of my kids. He looks extra hot and cute today, wearing a black beanie on his head, his long hair poking out, a white t-shirt, faded jeans, and my favorite black and white Converse.

"Hey," he says, shaking Tommy's hand. "I'm Lukas."

Tommy literally beams at him. "I'm Tommy! Your house is so cool!"

Lukas laughs. "Well, thanks, Buddy. Come on in."

"Holy shit," Macy gasps, gaping around the house as we move into the living room. "This place is incredible."

"Thanks," Lukas says. "Make yourselves at home."

Tommy makes a beeline for the birdcage. "Wow!" he yells. "Look! He's really real!"

Ray tilts his head and flaps his wings. "I'm a pretty bird," he says.

Tommy looks over at us, his eyes wide and his mouth open. "Wow! He really does talk!"

"I want you," Ray says next, and Lukas and I look at each other and try not to laugh.

Tommy jumps up and down. "He wants me!"

Macy stands next to her brother and looks at us, crossing her arms with a teasing smile on her face. "What an interesting thing for a bird to say," she says.

I grab both of their hands and pull them away from the incriminating bird. "Okay, let's leave the bird alone so he doesn't get scared. He's probably not used to lots of people, right, Lukas?"

Lukas nods quickly. "That's right. He gets a little crazy around crowds."

I sit on the couch and watch as Lukas shows the kids around his house, answering Tommy's endless questions about the antiques and statues and Macy's fawning over the band. He's patient and sweet with them both, and I can tell they genuinely like him. He wins them over even more by bringing them into the kitchen and letting them build their own mini pizzas to bake with various toppings and dough he made earlier. My mind wanders as I watch them together, going to places that maybe it shouldn't be going yet, but I can't help thinking that Lukas will make a great stepfather.

With every week that goes by, I'm growing more attached to him and falling more in love with him, wanting more of him and more with him. And now, my fears of the kids not liking him have pretty much been obliterated.

He catches me watching him with the kids and winks at me from across the room. I want to smother him with happy kisses but hold myself back, not wanting to be too kissy and touchy in front of the kids. I'm not sure how Paul and Charlene behave in front of them, but I don't want them feeling awkward around us.

After dinner, I help Lukas clean up the kitchen while the kids go hang out in the living room.

"They're great kids," he says, pulling me into his arms for a quick hug. "They both have great personalities."

"Thank you. They really like you. I can tell."

He grins. "They must take after their mother."

I cross the room to the doorway and look out at them in the living room, seeing Tommy sitting on the floor playing a video game and Macy curled up on the couch reading one of Lukas' art books.

He comes up and wraps his arms around me from behind, leaning his head against mine. "See? They're happy here, Ivy. Macy's reading, not sitting on her phone texting. And your son just made an amazing pizza."

I nod and relax back against his muscular body. "You're right."

He gently turns me around to face him. "I'm babysitting Katie tomorrow night, and I have her all day on Sunday. Why don't you and Tommy come over tomorrow for dinner, stay overnight, and then spend the day with us on Sunday? I have two guest rooms, so they'll each have their own rooms. It'll be fun. Katie's adorable. You'll love her."

I hesitate to answer, not because I don't want to, but because it feels like another big step in the staircase of this relationship. Tommy and I both spending the night with Lukas, and meeting a child in the family, which is serious to me. It means we're becoming more involved in each other's lives and families, and other people's feelings are at stake.

His forehead creases as he studies my face. "What's worrying you?" he asks softly.

"Getting the kids more involved . . . it's a big step."

"I know that, and I wouldn't ask you to do it if I wasn't

completely serious about you and wanting to be part of your life. I don't hurt people." He squeezes my waist. "And I definitely wouldn't be wanting to spend time with your kids unless I was sure this was going in the right direction."

"I know that. I do." I close my eyes and take a deep breath. "All right . . . we'll stay tomorrow night. I think Tommy will like that. He seems really comfortable with you."

He looks over my shoulder at the kids in the living room. "I like him, too. This is what I want."

"And what's that?"

He looks down into my eyes and smiles. "You, the kids . . . All of it."

My heartbeats start to quicken as his words sink in. "You're sure?"

"I'm positive. No doubts, baby. This is what I've always dreamed of."

"Okay then. Let's have a sleepover tomorrow and see how we do with two little kids running around and a bird repeating everything we say."

Laughing, he hugs me tighter. "That sounds awesome to me."

CHAPTER 19

IVY

After spending a few hours with Lukas and two little kids, I begin to think he should be running a day care and not a tattoo parlor. He's absolutely amazing with kids. His five-year-old niece, Katie, is the sweetest little girl and adores her uncle. We snuggle on the couch with her and Tommy, watching a few Disney movies, and then Lukas helps them make their own ice cream sundaes. At bedtime, I take Tommy to his guest room, while Lukas takes care of Katie.

"Did you have fun tonight?" I ask Tommy, tucking him into the huge king-sized bed that he looks dwarfed in.

"I did, Mommy. Lukas is fun, and Katie is, too."

"I'm glad."

"Can we come back again?"

I kiss his forehead. "Yes, we definitely will. We'll probably be spending a lot more time with Lukas. How do you feel about that?"

A big smile spreads across his face. "And Ray, too?"

"Yes, and Ray, too."

"Mommy, are you going to marry Lukas?"

"I don't know, sweetie. We like each other very much, though."

"So, you're like best friends for now?" he asks.

I smile and nod. "Yes, for now, we're best friends."

"Can we get a puppy?"

A puppy? Where did that come from? "We'll talk about it, okay?

"Okay. Good night, Mommy."

"Nighty night." I kiss his cheek and go out into the hall, stopping at the doorway to the other guest room to watch Lukas with Katie. He's sitting on the edge of her bed, reading her a story, impersonating the voices. She's surrounded by stuffed toys, and the dark maroon bed set has been replaced with a pink one with cartoon kittens on it. My heart smiles, realizing that he changed the sheets and comforter just for her. After a few minutes, her eyelids slowly close, and he kisses her softly, arranges her stuffed toys around her, and meets me at the doorway.

"You're amazing," I whisper.

"She's adorable, isn't she?"

"She is, and so are you."

He takes my hand and leads me to his bedroom, closing the door halfway. Kicking off his shoes, he glances back toward the door. "We'll hafta leave that open in case one of the little ones needs us. I know it's going to be hard, but you're gonna have to try to keep your moans of ecstasy down a few decibels." He pulls his t-shirt off, then the beanie hat, and reaches for me.

"Moans of ecstasy?" I repeat, knowing I'm blushing.

Capturing my mouth with this, he walks us closer to the bed, pulling my shirt off as we move.

LUKAS

"Maybe we shouldn't fool around with the kids down the hall . . ." I whisper as he unhooks my bra.

"No, no, no . . ." His voice is low as he pulls my bra off and gently cups my breasts in his hands. "We are *not* going to be those parents who won't have sex just because the kids are down the hall. We're just going to be really quiet."

"Do you know how hard that is?"

"I know exactly how hard it is," he teases, pressing his body against mine.

Giggling, I nuzzle into his neck. "You're so bad."

He gently pushes me down on the bed and quickly pulls off my shoes and pants.

"Get under the covers," he whispers, pulling the comforter and sheet back. "I want us to be covered in case one of the kids wanders in."

"Good idea!" I whisper back, crawling under the sheets while he takes his jeans off and climbs into the bed next to me. We lie on our sides face-to-face, and I push his hair out of his eyes. "Thank you for having us over. I love Katie. She's so sweet and well-behaved. Tommy loves her, too."

He rests his hand on my hip. "She really likes you guys, too. I love that kid. She's my little princess."

I kiss his lips softly, allowing my heart to tumble further over the feeble wall trying to protect it.

"I'm falling for you pretty hard," I whisper, playing with his hair. He pulls me on top of him and gathers my hair in his hand, pulling it to the side.

His eyes seek out mine in the dim room. "Ivy . . . me, too. So fucking hard."

My heart surges, and I close my eyes, capturing his words and locking them away. His hand caresses my cheek.

"Baby, this can be our life. You know that, right? We can be forever."

Forever. I used to believe in forever, until it ended. Maybe there's no such thing as forever, and what most people really mean is, as long as it's easy. Forever seems to be measured in good moments, but ends with the bad.

Staring down into his dark eyes, I know without a doubt that, to Lukas, forever is infinite. I can *feel* it.

His hands slide down my body. "If you let me . . . I can give you so much, Ivy. Mentally and physically." He kisses my mouth, biting my bottom lip before pulling away, tugging my soft flesh. I gasp and press myself against his hard cock beneath me. "I want to drag you into my world and never let you go."

"I want that, too, Lukas. Please, don't think I don't."

Bowing my head down, I kiss his lips, softly at first, then deeper, my tongue finally mingling with his. His warm hands slowly creep up my sides, over my shoulders, and down my arms until his hands meet mine. Clasping our fingers together, he raises our hands above our heads against the bed's headboard, stretching us out.

"I want you to fuck me just like this . . . without using your hands," he says, his voice low.

"Lukas . . ." Warmth spreads through my body, firing up between my thighs. His dirty talk shocks and excites me, always making me wet instantly. Kneeling up slightly, I position myself over his hard cock and rotate my hips, grinding down on him until I've got his moist head at my entrance, and slowly move down onto him, taking him into me.

"That's perfect," he whispers, his voice hoarse with desire, his fingers tightening around mine. "I love your body. Let it love me back."

His words snuff my insecurities of feeling less than attractive on top, a position I've never been fond of—until now. Seeing him under me, his hair fanned out around his head, those sultry eyes half-closed, and his inked arms stretched over his head, muscles taut, quickens my pulse. He buries his face between my breasts, running his tongue over the soft curves as I slowly ride him, his tongue ring flicking over my nipples and sending electric shocks through me.

His hips rotate against mine, inviting my body to move in unison with his in slow languid circles, pressing up into me as I arch down to meet his subtle thrusts.

"Kiss me." His voice pulls me from the erotic delirium I had slipped into, but only for a brief moment. I've never been commanded or restrained—even for fun—during sex before and could never understand the appeal when I saw it in movies. But having my hands held, not being able to touch him, and being told to kiss him in that sexy raspy voice is a true aphrodisiac. My body liquefies, melting into him, my mouth crashing down on his, opening to let his tongue slip in. My fingers curl tighter around his.

His thumbs trace small circles against my palms as we make love, and somehow, that ignites an even deeper ache in me. He's always in the moment with me, never losing himself in his own head and body. This simple touch, his fingers gliding over my palms, is so sensual to me, the way his thumbs move in rhythm with his hips, that I completely lose myself, moaning his name against his lips as I shudder on top of him.

"Don't stop . . ." Still clasping my hands in his, he pushes me up until I'm sitting straight up on top of him. "I want to watch you." My hands are released, and his slides up to cup my breasts.

My pussy clenches around him as another jolt of ecstasy courses through me, but the little voices edge into my brain. *You probably look fat. You have stretch marks. Get off and hide under him!*

Arching up, his strong arms go around me, pulling me tighter against him, rocking himself into me. "You're gorgeous," he groans, pulling my head back by my hair, his lips on my neck, sucking and softly biting. Then, gently, he's pushing me back, bending me backward until my thighs are spread wider over him, my breasts pointing up as he grips my waist, moving me back and forth on his hard shaft. I become so mesmerized watching him, the way his arm and thigh muscles flex, the droplets of sweat dripping down his chest, glistening over the tattoo of the dragon that almost appears alive on his flesh as he moves, that I almost become paralyzed, unable to move. He's beautiful. He is living art. He's everything I never knew I wanted. And want him, I do.

He grins wolfishly and yanks me up against his chest in one quick, strong movement, cupping his hand against the back of my neck. "Your eyes kill me, Ivy," he whispers, thrusting upwards inside me so deep that I suck in a breath. "I don't think I'm ever gonna let you go."

Gripping his shoulders as we move faster and harder against each other, I kiss his waiting lips. "I don't think I want you to," I tease.

Grasping my face in his hands, he kisses me deeply, his cock smoldering deep inside me with a final surge.

CHAPTER 20

IVY

A couples date.
  A fun dinner at my house with my long-time best friend and her husband shouldn't be causing me stress. We've done it at least a hundred times.

But not with me dating a younger guy.

Setting the dining room table, while Lukas prepares lasagna and chicken parmesan in my kitchen, I glance at Lindsay. She's nibbling on a breadstick a little too intently, practically drooling over Lukas as he moves around my kitchen.

"My God, Ivy" she whispers. "You hit the jackpot."

"What are you talking about?" I ask her.

"Him. He's sexy as hell, and he even cooks. He's like a god. I want one."

"Lindsay . . . this isn't a strip club. Have some class," Sam warns.

She takes a long sip of her wine, continuing to eye Lukas like a piece of meat. If she wasn't my best friend, I'd be annoyed, but she's harmless so I just playfully smack her arm and take a seat across from them at the table.

"Last week, we all had dinner at that new place. It's kinda overrated. The food wasn't that great," Sam says, trying to divert his wife's attention.

"The new place in town? I went there with some guy at work a while back. It was mobbed," I reply.

"It was mobbed the night we went, too. We had to wait forever for a table big enough for all of us," Lindsay adds.

"For all of you?" I repeat.

"Yeah . . . you know . . . all of us," she says awkwardly.

'All of us' used to be Paul and I, Lindsay and Sam, and two other couples that we've been friends with since our early twenties.

"Paul and Charlene were there?" I ask, my chest tightening. Why would they want to be with them and not me? They're *my* friends.

"Nice going," Sam says, nudging Lindsay, who smiles weakly at me.

"I'm sorry, Ivy. We thought it would be awkward, inviting you and Lukas, too."

"I don't understand why you'd invite Paul over me, though."

"I'm still friends with Paul," Sam says. "We golf together, with the other guys. Lukas doesn't exactly fit into our group." He leans closer to me, lowering his voice, like we're talking about something taboo.

"So?" I shoot back. "He still eats dinner."

They blink at me, and I continue, my annoyance growing. "So now you guys hang out with Paul and Charlene? *She* fits in? She's younger than Lukas."

Lindsay touches my arm. "Don't get upset. It doesn't matter. You hated those group dinners, anyway."

That's true, but I still hate that Charlene is now hanging out with *my* friends.

"It just feels kind-of like betrayal to me," I say. "We've been friends forever, all of us."

Lindsay attempts to soothe me. "Ivy, it's just because he's . . . different. He's not going to want to sit around with these guys and talk about boring business meetings and golf. Don't worry about it. Have fun and enjoy him. It's not like you're gonna marry the guy."

"I know, but I would still like to keep my friends," I mutter.

"We're still your friends. We love you," Lindsay says. "Everyone thinks Paul is a douche for what he did to you. We're on your side. That's why we're here."

I shake my head at them. "I didn't know we had to pick sides. What are we, twelve?"

"Stop being so dramatic, Ivy. You're happy. That's all that matters. He's exactly what you needed to get out of the slump you were in."

Shaking my head at her, I go to the kitchen to help Lukas with the serving dishes. I still feel strange when Lukas comes to the house, and I can't wait until the divorce details are finalized, so I can sell this house and move away from the lingering memories here.

Lukas is unusually quiet over dinner, which is delicious as always. I wait until Lindsay and Sam leave and I have Tommy settled in bed before I approach him about his sudden distance.

"Are you okay?" I ask him when I come back downstairs and find him sitting at the table in the dim kitchen. I wonder if he feels weird being in this house, but since I'm still living here, he has to come here if he wants to see me when I have the kids.

He spins a quarter around on the table. "I heard what you said," he says.

I look at him, confused. "What did I say?"

"When Lindsay said, 'it's not like you're gonna marry the guy', you agreed with her."

Shit. I did.

"Lukas, you saw how they are. I don't want to get into my feelings with them about you. As you can see, my friends seem to be Team Paul."

He scowls at me and turns his stare back to his quarter. "They don't even know me. I'm not the one who fucked someone behind your back and left you and your kids. But he's the acceptable one?"

"They're idiots. And you're right. They have no idea how amazing you are. It's their loss."

He spins the quarter some more and eyes me. "Did you mean that?"

"Mean what?"

"That you wouldn't marry me."

I feel trapped by this loaded question. We've never talked marriage. We've talked love and soul mates. We've talked about commitment. We've talked about our amazing sensual connection. But marriage?

Now that he's brought it up, my mind and heart are going round and round like a Ferris wheel.

"I'm not even legally divorced yet. How can I seriously think about marriage again?" I say defensively, which probably isn't the best answer, but now it's out there.

He raises an eyebrow at me. "We're sleeping together, and you're still legally married."

"We've never talked about anything like marriage, though," I say, nervously. Could he actually want to marry me?

He shakes his hair and stands up, shoving his quarter in his pocket. "I wouldn't be dating you if I didn't want it to eventually lead to that," he says. "But now, I want to know if you think that way, too." He stands in front of me and backs me up against the kitchen island.

"Yes," I answer with no hesitation.

He leans down into me and kisses my neck. "Yes, what?"

My eyes flutter closed, and I lean into his kisses. "Yes, I would marry you." I run my hands up his muscled arms as the butterflies manifest in my stomach again.

"Is this a proposal?" I ask.

He pulls away a little. "Hell no," he says, and my hopes quickly dash. Why did he even bring it up then? Disappointment seeps through me, my brief flash of hope distinguished quickly.

"When I propose to you," he says, lifting me up and carrying me over to the kitchen table, sitting me down on top of it. "It's going to be romantic, and not in this house, of all places."

"Oh," I say as he pulls my shirt off. *In the middle of the kitchen!*

"Where are the kids?" he whispers.

"Tommy is asleep, and Macy is staying at a friend's house."

He unhooks my bra and places it on the table next to me. "Good, because I'm going to fuck your still legally-married-ass on your soon-to-be-ex-husband's table, and hopefully ram some sense into you."

He unbuttons my jeans and pulls them and my panties down. I open my mouth to protest, but he puts his finger over my lips.

"Shh . . . I have another question," he says. I watch as he pulls his shirt off. Seeing him half-naked in my kitchen makes him look even more sexy, because I know he's so out of place here. "I want to know if you're going to say yes first," he continues, unbuttoning his jeans.

"To what?" I'm so enthralled with watching him undress that I can't remember what he asked me.

"When I propose. I don't want to go through all that, get my hopes up, and have you say no. So I'm going to cheat and ask for your answer first."

Hot damn, he's adorable. "I already said yes," I say breathlessly as he kisses my breasts, leaning me back against the table. "I would say yes a thousand times."

"Once is enough." His kisses move back up to my neck, then to my lips. "What's your ring size?"

I smile against his lips. "The same as my shoe," I tease.

He grins impishly and picks my shoe up off the floor. "Six?" he says, and I nod, rubbing my foot up his leg.

"That will make my life easier, for when I want to buy you shoes and rings."

He scoops me up into his arms. "I have a better idea for this room, though." He sits me down on one of the breakfast stools.

"There's something I've been wanting from you for a while now," he says, moving my hair away from my face and staring down into my eyes. His cock is huge and hard, level with my face while I'm sitting on the low stool, and I know what he wants.

"What's that?" I ask softly, reaching up to stroke him. He sucks in a breath and closes his eyes for a few moments as I run my fingers along the length of him.

"Your mouth . . . on me," he says. "You can't use a fork for this one, Ivy. I'm sorry."

I try not to laugh, but I can't help it.

"Can you do that for me, or is it too hard for you with your weird mouth aversion?"

"That question is so full of innuendoes," I tease, continuing to stroke him.

"I know, and none of them were even intentional."

Okay, so I'm strange. I hate things coming at my face and going in my mouth. Plus, I have a bad gag reflex. But this guy . . . how can I say no to him?

"If I say no, is it a deal breaker for the marriage proposal?"

He caresses my cheek and opens his eyes to meet mine. "No. I'm going to marry you no matter what."

I can't deny him what he wants. He's too sweet, too giving. I slowly suck him into my mouth. He's big; there's no way I'm even getting half of him in my mouth, but I hope it's enough. I run my tongue over his head and wrap my fingers around his shaft, as I suck him as far as I can into my mouth, all while he watches me, his eyes filled with lust, his hand on the back of my neck.

"That feels amazing," he whispers.

I move him in and out of my mouth, fisting him with my hands, and his breath quickens, his chiseled ab muscles flexing near my face.

Suddenly, he pulls out of my mouth, picks me up, and lays me on the kitchen table, on my stomach. Pulling me up into the doggy style position, while he stands at the edge of the table, he grabs my hips and slides into me from behind. *Oh my God. On my kitchen table. That Paul's mother gave us!*

He reaches around and rubs my clit in perfect timing with his thrusts, and it's not long before I can't take anymore.

"Lukas . . ." I moan lowly, giving in to the cascade of

pleasure that flows over me, arching my back against him, taking him deeper.

"That's my girl," he whispers, running his hand down my spine, and I feel him jetting inside me. "I love you so much."

My mind spins in the midst of orgasm. It's the first time he's ever said those words, and the fact that it just came out of him naturally when he felt it, and he didn't make some sort of event out of it, means the world to me. I don't care that he said it while he was making love to me on the kitchen table. All that matters is that he said it, and I know with all my heart that he meant it.

I love him, too. Without a doubt.

"I feel really weird having sex with you here, in this house," I say as we're getting dressed.

"I'm not a big fan of it, either." He zips his jeans up. "It feels way fucking awkward."

"I'm sorry. We've been talking to the lawyers and trying to figure out what to do with the house. I can't really afford to live here alone much longer."

He hands me my shirt. "You could move in with me."

Pulling the shirt over my head, I look at him like he's got five heads. "What? With you?"

"Yeah, why not?"

"Lukas, I've got the kids."

"So? I have two extra bedrooms. There are three bathrooms."

"It's on top of a tattoo studio. It was a church."

He frowns. "Why does that matter? That's where I work. I own the building and everything in it. Do you know how bad I've always wanted a unique place like that? Me finding it when Vandal and I were looking for a place for the shop was a friggen' miracle."

"I know . . . and it's a beautiful place. But there's no yard for Tommy to play in."

"There's a park right across the street we can take him to."

"There's also a cemetery right next door."

He shrugs. "So? It's not spooky at all. It's grounding. Where there's life, there's death. We can't hide him from it, Ivy."

"Don't you have half-naked women in that place?" I ask him, churning the pros and cons in my head.

"Ivy, I have customers that come in to get tattoos. They don't come in naked. It's not a sex club."

"I don't know," I say skeptically. "I'm not sure if it's a good place for a child to be."

"The bedrooms are huge, so is the living room. Tommy can teach Ray new words. There's a finished basement you haven't even seen, with another bathroom, and it could either be a playroom or another bedroom down there."

"You have gargoyle statues everywhere. It's a bit creepy for a little boy."

He pulls me against his chest, wrapping his arms around me. "Is that what you think?" he asks.

I lean my chin against his chest and look up at him. "A little bit, yes."

"Do you want to know why I collect gargoyles?"

"Of course. I want to know everything about you."

He weaves his fingers through my hair as he talks, making my scalp tingle. "When I was really young, I had nightmares.

I've always had problems sleeping, like insomnia, nightmares, that sort of thing. My great-grandfather gave me an old statue of a gargoyle and put it on my dresser, and he told me it would protect me while I was sleeping, so I've collected them over the years and keep them in the bedrooms."

Whenever Lukas talks about his past, I want to crawl inside him and find the little boy who still lives there and hug him. His childhood, although sad, has truly made him the wonderful man he is today. I've never met a person with so much depth, who is so in tune with who they are and where they came from.

I wind my arms around his neck and pull his head down to me. "You are an amazing person," I tell him. "Being with you is like reading a book I can't put down, and every page gets better and better."

He kisses my nose. "Think about moving in with me. I would love to have you and the kids there."

"Are we really talking about marriage and living together?" Things are happening so fast, but everything feels so *right* with him.

"Yes, Ivy, we are."

I let out a deep breath and stare up at him, thinking.

"What?" he asks me. "You have doubts? About me? Still? We've been dating for months. "

I chew my lip and contemplate my answer. "No, not you really. You're just young. It's a lot all at once . . . marriage and two kids all of a sudden."

"You and this fucking age stuff, Ivy." He shakes his head slowly. "You need to get over it. I'm not a kid. I grew up a lot faster than most guys my age. I know what I want. I've wanted to have my own family for a long time. I *want* to be married. I can take care of you. I have money and a successful career. I don't fuck around. I love kids, and I love *you*. I can't change my age. What do you want to do? Wait until I'm thirty? Thirty-five?"

"No, no, of course not. I want you now. I'm just worried . . . I'll be forty when you're twenty-eight."

"So? You don't look or act thirty-six. You're cute, you've got a great body, and you're fun. You actually look closer to my age than you think. You have a warped perception of yourself, and you're stuck on numbers. We get along great, and we want the same things . . . our ages aren't going to change that. Let it go. I've gone slow with you like you asked, but at this rate, I'll be old and gray myself before you finally just accept our age difference."

I try to pull away from him, but he holds on to me tightly.

"No running away." It's a soft command, but I know he's serious. "Let me be a man, Ivy. You gotta take me as I am or not at all. I'm always gonna be younger than you. Sorry, but it's true. I'm always gonna have tattoos. I'm always gonna be an artist. I'll probably always have long hair." He runs his hands up my arms and squeezes my shoulders. "And I'm always going to want what I want. I want to be married, and I want it to be with you. I know myself. I'm not going to change. I'm not going to take off with some young chick. Accept that I know myself. Your heart will always be safe with me."

I let out a breath. "You always say the right thing."

"They're not just words, doll. It's all real. You just hafta let yourself accept it."

God, this man, where did he come from?

CHAPTER 21

IVY

B*zzz*
  Bzzz

I sit up in bed, my brain foggy with sleep, and reach for my cell phone on the nightstand. Lukas' name is lit up on the screen. I squint at the blue neon numbers on my digital click—two-thirty A.M.

Grabbing the phone, I swipe my finger across the screen, wondering why he would be calling so late.

"Lukas?"

"Ivy . . ." His voice pitches and cracks. "I need you . . ." He takes a deep shuddering breath, and my heart drops to my stomach.

He's crying.

"What's wrong? Where are you?" I throw the covers off and turn on the bedside lamp, grabbing my clothes off the chair in the corner.

His breathing is heavy and congested, muffling the phone. "At the hospital . . . there was an accident . . ." He sniffs and chokes. "Oh my God, Ivy . . ." He whimpers my name, agony stripping his voice of its usual deep rasp.

Cold fear rips through me as goosebumps break out on my flesh. "Are you all right? I'll leave now . . ." I yank my jeans on, cradling the phone against my shoulder.

"It's Vandal . . . he was in an accident. Katie's gone . . . Ivy, she's gone . . ." He sobs into the phone. I freeze, horrified, and grab onto the dresser to steady myself. *Katie . . . Oh, dear God, no.*

"Sweetie, I'm on my way there. Okay? I'll be there as fast as I can." I fight back the tears that well up in my eyes and try to keep my voice level. "I'll be right there."

He doesn't say goodbye, but I hear a thump, as if he just dropped the phone.

I finish dressing as quickly as I can and run to Macy's room.

"Macy, wake up." I shake her gently.

"Mom? What's wrong?" She wakes quickly, and her eyes go wide with worry as she focuses on me in the dark room.

"Vandal's been in an accident. I need to go to the hospital. You have to stay here with Tommy, all right? Don't leave this house until I come back home."

She sits up. "Is he okay? Is Lukas okay?"

"I don't know . . . Lukas is okay, but I need to be there for him." I can't tell my daughter that little Katie is gone. How can that even be true? I can't wrap my head around it. Just a few weeks ago we all spent the weekend at Lukas' house while he babysat for Vandal. Macy painted Katie's nails bright pink with tiny white hearts, and she was so excited. My God, how can this be happening? She's just a little girl. I cover my mouth with my hand and turn away from my daughter.

"Mom?"

Forcing the tears back, I shake my head. "I need to go. I'll call you, but please stay here with your brother."

She nods somberly. "I will. I promise."

As I get into my car, I realize I don't even know which hospital Lukas is at, but there's only one big hospital nearby, so that's the one I head toward. Hot tears stream down my face as I drive, blurring the road. I'm speeding, but I don't care; I have to get to him. *Maybe I misunderstood him.* He was crying and not speaking coherently. I must have heard him incorrectly. Katie has to be fine.

When I reach the hospital, the visitor's lot is practically empty, but I see Lukas' Corvette near the main entrance and pull my car in next to it. I'm almost to the glass doors of the hospital foyer when I see him sitting on a bench a few feet away, doubled over, with his head in his hands, rocking back and forth. I run to him and drop to my knees on the icy lawn in front of him, wrapping my arms around him.

"I got here as fast as I could," I say softly, stroking his back as his entire body trembles.

He clings to me, leaning his head on my shoulder. "Oh, God, Ivy . . . I can't . . ." He swallows hard.

My heart aches and shatters for him, his beautiful soul so broken. "Tell me what I can do for you." I kiss his wet cheek and hug him to me tighter. "We'll get through this together. I promise."

He lifts his head and shakes it slowly, his eyes dark and glazed, seeing things I can't see. "Katie's gone . . . Vandal's hurt pretty bad." A deep sob robs him of his breath, and he chokes, wiping his face with the back of his hand. "They were in a head-on collision. He had a girl in the car with him, but she's didn't make it . . . neither did the person in the other car." His eyes finally meet mine. "It's a fucking nightmare. He's a mess, but he doesn't know yet . . . about Katie." His body shudders again saying her name.

Oh God.

I take his hands in mine. "Is anyone else here? Your family?"

"They're on their way. I couldn't see Vandal yet . . . I need a minute. . . and then I need to go back in . . . they want me to answer questions . . . about them. I just had to get some air."

I take some tissues out of my bag and wipe his face like I do to Tommy. I feel so helpless. What can I possibly say or do to comfort him?

"Can I call anyone, or get you anything?" I can't hold back my tears anymore.

He takes the tissue from me and blows his nose. "Please, just stay with me."

"Of course. I'm not going anywhere." I brush his hair out of his face and caress his cheek. "I love you. I'll do anything for you."

He grabs me and pulls me to him so tight that he squeezes the breath out of me. "I love you, too." Taking my hand in his, he stands and pulls me with him. "I need to go inside and take care of this. My brother needs me."

Lukas transforms the moment he steps foot in the hospital. He's calm, composed, in control. I stand by his side, silently supportive, his hand never letting go of mine as he meets with police officers and doctors. I'm amazed at the amount of information he has about his brother and niece—their birth dates, blood types, medical histories, Katie's mother's name and number, the name of Vandal's girlfriend. All memorized.

His cousins from the band begin to arrive, and there is chaos in the waiting room as they find out their niece has tragically died. Storm and Evie huddle in a corner and cry. Mikah is pacing, yelling, *"What the fuck did he do this time?"* while Talon trails after him trying to calm him down. Asher arrives with a gorgeous older woman I assume to be Aria, Lukas' aunt, who I haven't met in person yet. They approach us, teary-eyed, and Lukas fills them in with what little he knows.

"I'm going to call our manager and lawyer," Asher says. "Have they let you see Vandal at all yet? Is he talking?"

Lukas shakes his head. "Not yet. I think he's still unconscious. No one will give me a fucking straight answer, except to say that he's going to be all right, but he's banged up good. Apparently, he wasn't wearing a seatbelt and was thrown from the car."

Asher winces. "This will gut him and send him right over the fucking edge. We have to make sure the doctors let one of us tell him about Katie. If he hears this from a stranger, he's liable to strangle someone."

"I'm not leaving until I can be with him," Lukas says.

"I'm staying here with you, Lukas," Aria says, dabbing her eyes. "We'll tell him together. I'm not leaving you boys to deal with all this alone. Ronnie is on his way here, too."

I wish I wasn't meeting Lukas' family in the midst of a family tragedy. For weeks, we've been talking about getting together with his aunt, uncle, and Gram for dinner, but haven't been able to find a good time. Now, here I am meeting them during a horrific time. I wonder if I should leave them alone to talk, but he holds on to my hand so tightly that it hurts. I refuse to let go. He can crush the bones in my fingers if it makes him feel better. I'm not letting go of him.

Time drags as we all wait in a large private lounge that the nurses moved us into, and soon, the sun is coming up. Lukas and I napped for a short time earlier, leaning against each other on a small couch.

"You should go home and be with the kids," he says softly. "I'll stay here and keep you updated."

"I don't want to leave you—"

He kisses my lips quickly. "I'll be okay. I can't thank you enough for being here this long. He'll be awake soon, and we're going to have to deal with that. I promise I'll call you as soon as I know anything more."

"Do you want me to bring you something before I leave? Coffee? I could go get you guys some breakfast?"

"I can't eat anything, but thank you, babe." He holds my coat out so I can slip into it, and then wraps his arms around me. I hug him tightly, wishing I could steal all his pain away from him.

"If you need or want anything, you call me." I comb my fingers through his rumpled hair. "I mean it. I don't mind sitting here with you all day."

"I know, and that means so much to me. You have no idea. The next few days are going to be even harder. I can't . . ." His voice catches, and he bows his head down, taking a quick breath. "I can't believe she's gone."

I hold his head against mine, my hands wrapping around to clasp behind his neck. "I know, sweetheart. I'm so sorry. I know how much you loved her. I did, too."

He lifts his head to meet my eyes, biting his lip. "You should go now. Text me when you get home so I know you're okay."

When I get in my car I find another tiny black feather on

my car seat. Picking it up, I put it in my pocket so I can put it with the others I've found that are in a tiny velvet pouch in my nightstand. I drive home in a total daze, emotionally and mentally exhausted. I debate turning around and going right back to stay with Lukas, but wonder if maybe, as much as he needed me there, that he also needs to be alone with his brother, too. My heart aches, thinking of Vandal and poor little Katie, and the other victims of the crash. What a horrible reminder of how precious and fragile life is.

I steel myself for the hard road ahead. Seeing Lukas crumble, and then become a rock for his family, exposed layers of him I haven't seen before. He proved himself someone to be counted on in an emergency, with a level head and quick thinking, but inside, he was falling apart, his heart breaking for his little princess, as he called her. I worry that hiding and suppressing his own emotions will take a toll on Lukas emotionally and spark up his past depression.

I have to admit to myself that Lukas was right. He's mature beyond his years, and he's more of a man than I could ever hope to have in my and my children's lives.

CHAPTER 22

LUKAS

I battled intense grief at a very young age. It nearly consumed me and almost turned me into a dark shadow slithering throughout my young life. Since losing Katie, I can feel those demons whispering to me again, luring me back into their fold, but I refuse to let them drag me back down into that dark hole. I have to try to focus on the positives in my life. And while those demons definitely have their gnarly claws in my brother right now, I know he has to fight them on his own. I've helped him as much as I can the past few months, and now, I have to sit back and hope he finds his way out on the other side of his grief. If I continue to let it all eat at me, I risk losing everything I've worked so hard for.

Easier said than done, to watch someone you love be hurt, while hurting themselves even more in the process. Even harder when they don't accept your help.

"I'm going to propose," I tell Finn once he's settled in my tattoo chair and under my gun, so he can't freak out too badly at the news.

"Wow," he says. "I'm flattered, dude, but I don't like you in that way."

I punch his leg. "To Ivy, fool."

He twitches his arm, almost causing me to gouge his artwork right out of his flesh. "Lukas, are you kidding me? Fucking marriage?"

I lean my elbow on his arm. "Sit still. And yes."

"Dude. Why."

I frown up at him. "Because I love her."

"You can love her and not, like, legalize that shit, bro." He shoves his shades up on his head, pushing his long hair back, and stares at me like I've lost my mind.

"I *want* to legalize it. I really love her and the kids. Her divorce is finally final, too. It took forever."

His face twists into a smirk. "Fucking divorce! Do you really want to be second, man? The second husband? The stepfather? That shit sucks."

Turning to my worktable, I shake my head at him. "I don't care about all that. We love each other. We're good together. She makes me feel safe."

"Safe? Is she a ninja? Safe from what?"

I don't know why I ever bother to talk to Finn about my relationship. He's had a string of one-night stands since he was fourteen, and has zero concept of commitment or love. I keep hoping that, one day, he'll meet the right chick and fall in love, and experience it like the rest of the world, but so far, no dice.

Turning back to him, I hold his arm down and continue his sleeve. "I mean content. That kind of safe. Like, I know she won't hurt me or blow my friends. I can trust her."

"Speaking of blowjobs, where's the chick that used to work at the front desk?"

Dana worked here for a little while and seemed to think

that offering sexual favors to our customers was part of her job description.

"I fired her."

"Well, shit. That new babe working the front now is even hotter, though. I gotta get me a piece of that."

I freeze and glare at him. "That's my younger cousin, Rayne, asshole. Don't you go near her."

"What the fuck, cockblocker."

Sighing, I try to divert his attention. "Anyway, I'm going to propose this weekend, I think. I need something happy in my life now. I just have to organize something really cool."

He tilts his head. "You could jump out of a plane together and propose in mid-air."

"No."

"You could tie the ring around your dick and tell her to blow you, and when she gets down there, kabam!"

"No."

"You could send her on a treasure hunt. Like, give her clues that she has to solve, and at the end, there you are. With the rock. Boom."

I nod slowly, wondering how crazy I am for even considering any idea that comes out of Finn's head.

"Hmmm . . . that's actually not a bad idea. I'll think about that one."

"The plane and the blowjob sounds much cooler to me, man."

Rayne pokes her head around the curtain, and I wave her in. "What's up?" I ask.

"I was going to order lunch. Do you want anything from the café?"

"Just my usual latte, thanks. Get Finnster one, too, and take some money out of the register."

She turns on her heel, but Finn stops her. "Hey, baby, wait a sec. If I was gonna propose to you, would you rather jump out of a plane with me and get the ring mid-air, or find it tied around my dick?"

I laugh as she curls her lip at him. "Um, neither?"

Finn frowns at her. "What? I'm not good enough for you?"

I watch in horror as she smiles shyly at him. "I'm only nineteen. I don't even want to think about marriage until I'm like forty."

"Yes!" he yells. "Perfect answer. You are the woman of my dreams." He winks at her, and I hold back from punching him, even though I really want to pummel his face for flirting with my sweetheart of a cousin. "Now, you hafta marry me" he says. "When you're forty, of course."

I point to the door. "Rayne. Out. Get lunch. Don't provoke him."

She giggles and skips out, leaving me to glare at my best friend. "Dude. Don't even think about it. She's off limits. Period," I warn.

He stretches his arm out, and I start the design on the top of his hand that will extend down his fingers. "Why? She's legal. And she's fucking hot."

"Are you dim? Do you know who she is?"

"Your hot cousin? What else is there to know?"

"She's the little sister of like everyone in Ashes & Embers. Storm and Asher would kill you if you went near her. Not to mention ruin your career."

He lets out a low whistle. "Fuck. I didn't realize she was related to all them."

"Yeah. So forget it. She can't be one of your playthings."

He shrugs and grins. "So, how old is your future stepdaughter?"

CHAPTER 23

LUKAS

Most people think that a marriage proposal is all about the woman and making it special for her—and it is *(calm down, chicks)*—but I think a lot of guys want it to be meaningful for themselves, too. They just don't want to admit it because they think they're too cool. Me? I got no problems admitting I want this night to be memorable for both of us. But, yeah, I really wanna blow her fucking mind and obliterate any memories that she once had a first husband.

Finn was kinda right; I hate that someone married my girl before I found her.

I couldn't have asked for a more perfect night for my plan. The air is warm, but not humid. Placing the last flameless candle on the table, I take a step back and look at the balcony I've transformed. I decided to not use real candles, so I could leave everything set up while we go to dinner and not have to worry about burning the house down. I've shoved the love seat to the far side and laid a huge faux fur rug in the middle of the balcony floor. The electric fireplace is lit in the corner, with the heat option turned off, and earlier today, I strung new tiny purple lights around the edges of the balcony. It looks magical, exactly as I envisioned it.

I pick her up at her house and take her out to dinner to the nicest restaurant in the area. She looks beautiful wearing a little black dress that shows off her curves perfectly, and I love that she has no clue how sexy she looks. I notice that she's wearing the amethyst I gave her a few weeks ago, dangling from her neck on a delicate white gold chain. Before Ivy, I never bought a girl many gifts, but I love to surprise her with them. Giving her gifts has become a sort of addiction for me. Sometimes, it's cute things like stuffed toys, or maybe something I've made for her, and other times, it's expensive like jewelry. The best part is seeing her face light up, how her eyes go wide like saucers, and then she jumps up and down excitedly before tackling me with kisses. She's the reason I wake up smiling every day, my own sunny anchor keeping my world grounded. Without her, I'm not sure how I would have been able to get through Katie's death. Ivy held me when I needed to cry, listened when I needed to talk, spent hours with me looking at photographs reminiscing, and pulled me back up when I started to slip too far into grief.

On the drive back to my house after dinner, we hold hands but don't talk much. I'm a little lost in my own head, worried that maybe what I've planned isn't good enough and is just too simple. I thought about a thousand proposal ideas, some insane like Finn's suggestions, some over the top and just cheesy, but I finally decided that romantic is the way to go. What better place than where we had our first real deep moment—on my balcony? I hope she feels the same way.

"Tonight's the night," Ray squawks when we enter the house, and I want to smack him. He must have heard me on the phone earlier with Finn.

Ivy laughs at him as she takes her coat off. "What's he talking about now?"

I throw the cover over his cage, hoping he'll shut up and go to sleep, and shrug nonchalantly. "He's been watching too much television again. I keep forgetting to turn it off when I go down to the shop in the mornings."

Grabbing her hand, I lead her upstairs, and I actually feel shaky, like I'm gonna skitz out from nervousness.

"Wow, it looks even more beautiful here tonight!" she marvels when she sees how I've got it decorated. "I love the new lights you added. When did you do all this?"

"Let's sit." I guide her to the white rug and gently pull her down on the floor with me. She takes off her black high heels and tucks her feet under her, eyeing me suspiciously.

"Are you okay?" she finally asks. "You look a little pale." She reaches toward me and puts her palm on my forehead.

"Ivy . . . I love ya, babe, but don't do the mom stuff right now. I'm fine." I reach beside the fireplace and grab my violin. "I have a surprise for you, and I'm a little nervous. That's all."

"Oh!" she exclaims excitedly. "You're going to play for me? *Finally?*"

I grin and nod at her. "I wrote a song just for you. No singing, though. Just an instrumental. I'm sorry it took so long."

She claps her hands like a little kid, a big smile spreading across her face. "Lukas! I'm so excited."

She's been begging me to play for her since she heard me play at the club, but I've been writing her a special melody over the past few months and didn't want her to hear it until it was perfect.

I close my eyes and start to play. The melody is slow, deep, and emotional. It's everything she makes me feel, and I'm grateful I'm talented enough to play with true emotion, to make her feel it with me.

Her eyes don't leave me as I play, and she sways as she listens, her eyes glimmering with tears. She loves it; I can feel it pouring out of her. She loves *me*. She has become my world, my best friend, my lover, my biggest fan, my queen. I've played the violin and piano in front of all sorts of crowds, ranging from metal concerts to classical plays to open mic night at the café, but playing this for her means more to me than any other audience I've ever been in front of. I want her to be proud of me and feel equal standing next to me as my wife. I won't ever be some big fucking executive in a corner office wearing a tailored suit, but I know for damn sure that I'll be someone she and the kids will be proud of.

"I loved it," she whispers when I'm finished playing, her voice hoarse. "It was so incredibly beautiful . . . and moving. I have goosebumps." She sniffles and wipes at her eyes. "You're amazing."

"I'm glad you like it. It's called Fierce."

She nods, smiling knowingly at me, remembering. "You *do* love me that way, just like I asked you to," she murmurs.

"I do, Ivy. More than you could ever know."

Moving closer to her, I take her face in my hands, kissing her deeply, wanting to possess every part of her.

"I love you the same," she says breathlessly.

"I was hoping you'd say that. Close your eyes, little doll."

A nervous smile touches her lips, and her eyes close. I take her hand and gently slide the diamond ring onto her finger. After weeks of searching, I found it at an antique shop, and it's perfect for her—for us. A two-carat heart-shaped diamond set in rose gold with tiny diamonds and floral etchings down the side, it's delicate and feminine, just like her.

"Open your eyes." I whisper.

Her eyes flutter open, but she doesn't look at her hand. Instead, she locks her eyes on to mine. "I know what you just did," she says, choking up. "And I'm not going to look at it yet. First, I'm going to tell you how precious you are to me, and I love you with everything that I am. My soul recognized yours that day we first met, and I just couldn't deny it, even though I tried. I love you more than I ever thought possible."

She stills my heart in the way that only she can. "I had a big speech memorized, but you just made me forget it," I say, taking a deep breath. "So, I'm gonna just say what I feel now. You're everything to me. You're the stability and safety I need, and the only one I would trust my heart with. You can make all my dreams come true, and I want to make yours come true, if you let me. I promise I will always cherish you and your kids."

We kiss before she finally looks down at her hand, her eyes widening and her mouth falling open. "My God, Lukas, it's beautiful." She covers her mouth as she stares at it. "Wow. Holy moly, I love it," she turns her hand, making the diamond sparkle. "I don't even know what to say. Thank you so much."

I smile at her and take her hand in mine, lifting it to my lips for a kiss, my eyes not leaving hers.

"You don't thank me for an engagement ring, baby. You say yes. Or no. But, hopefully yes."

"Yes. It's still yes. It will always be yes."

"Good." I lean closer and kiss her softly. "Welcome to your happily ever after."

She grabs my shirt and pulls me against her. "God, Lukas, I don't know how you do it, but somehow you always manage to take my breath away." She presses her soft lips to mine again and then pulls away, grinning impishly at me. "This is kinda funny, but I have a special gift for you tonight, too."

I lean back against the love seat and stretch my legs out in front of me. "Does it entail you getting naked soon? Because I'm about to rip that dress off you." Emotional closeness with her always mutates into an intense need to have wild sex with her, and tonight is no different. I want her clothes off like yesterday.

She laughs and smiles seductively at me. "You get that, too, but first . . . this." She digs into her purse and hands me a small box.

I take it in my hand and slowly turn it over. It's a very small box, like a ring box, and it's made of oak. I've never seen such a tiny box made of real wood before. "It's wild. I love it."

She lets out an exasperated sigh. "Lukas! That's just the box! Open it."

"I love the box, though. It's handmade. I can tell."

"I know that. I found it just for you, for what's *inside*. Now open it."

Inside the box, nestled in purple velvet is a black metal ring with a tiny teal gem that's the exact color of her eyes. I suck in a breath, and my heartbeat quickens. No one has ever given me such a meaningful gift. My fingers shake as I try to take the ring out of its velvet bed, but I can't even grab it. She leans forward and takes it out of the box for me.

"Looks like we've had the same thing on our minds lately," she says softly. "I wanted to give you a symbol of my love for you, a promise that I'm going to be here with you forever." She slips it onto my right hand. "We'll leave that finger open for your wedding band." She nods toward my left hand.

"I'm never gonna take it off. Ever." I pull her onto my lap and slide my hand up her thigh, under her tight skirt, and squeeze her ass. "I can't say the same about this dress. You look

LUKAS

hot as hell in this thing, but it's totally in the way of me making love to my future wife."

I grab the front of her dress and rip the fabric apart, splitting it at the v of her cleavage all the way down to her belly button. Black lace remains, cradling her breasts. I slip my finger under the fabric of her bra between her breasts and pull her closer to me.

"Did you think I was kidding?" I nip at her lip and give the thin fabric a quick yank, tearing it in two. My hands roam up to caress her breasts, and I suck a nipple into my mouth, flicking my tongue over the hardening bud. She gasps and grabs onto my shoulders, her nails digging through the fabric of my shirt. The quick panic that overcomes her when I let myself loose on her turns me on like fucking mad. Most times, I like to treat her sweet and go slow with her, but other times, like now, going slow just isn't enough to tame the beast that likes to come out and play.

I slide my tongue over her soft mound and encircle her nipple with my tongue, while my hand delves between her legs, disappearing under her skirt and pushing the thin fabric of her panties aside to feel her wetness.

"You know I love you more than anything in this world, right?" I slip my finger between her soft wet lips, and she lets out a tiny whimper.

She nods, which she does when she's so turned on that she can't speak.

"Remember all those times you said I was too young for you?" I slip a second finger into her and twist them both inside her, spreading her.

She nods and reaches between us to unbutton my shirt.

"That was bullshit, wasn't it?" I taunt, wanting to hear her talk dirty to me. Nothing gets me going like when she does that.

Her hands touch my chest, and she leans her head against mine.

"Say it," I coax, fingering her deeper and kissing her breasts.

"It was bullshit," she whispers, spreading her legs a little bit more.

"Tell me why... I wanna hear you say it."

She kisses my lips hungrily as I finger her. "I love it all... your tattoos and your long hair and your hard body. I love your music and how sexy and wild you look on stage. I love knowing you're mine. I love how you fuck me and how wet you make me. You drive me wild." My thumb finds her clit and rubs it languidly, while my fingers thrust deeper inside her. "And I love how sweet and caring you are. You're perfect."

My heart swoons, and my cock grows harder. "I kinda love having an older chick that sits in a big office, wearing a pretty little suit and librarian glasses, that comes home to let me fuck her brains out in a church."

She reaches between my legs and rubs my cock through my jeans. "I want you..." She sighs. "I can't wait to be your wife."

Fuck. I love how that sounds. *My wife.*

I love how she's sweet and sexy just for me.

"I want you to do me one favor," I say, watching her crawl down my body to kneel at my feet and pull my shoes and pants off.

"Anything."

"Please, don't ever refer to me as your second husband. I hate it. It makes my heart scream."

Her hand encircles my hard cock and slowly glides up and down my shaft.

"I promise. In my heart you'll always be the only one," she

says, before lowering her lips down over my cock. I lean back and gather her hair in my hand, gently pulling it away from her face so I can watch her. I know it makes her uncomfortable to be so visible, but I've learned that if I don't push her a little, she'll let her insecurities take over, and she'll hide from me. It's a shame Paul never made her feel sexy and wanted, but I'm going to spend the rest of my life doing just that.

Watching her suck me turns me into an animal, because she sucks me like her life depends on it. The way she moves her tongue over my flesh, grips my shaft in her hand, and breathes so deeply, drags me so far into her that I can barely think. With her, it goes way beyond just a blowjob and getting off. She fucking cherishes every inch of me with her mouth and hands, building me up slow and seductively, then taking me deeper and faster into her sweet mouth. The world could explode while she's blowing me, and I wouldn't even blink. It doesn't take long before I'm shooting my load down her throat. She swallows everything I give her then slowly laps my cock like it's a decadent treat and doesn't want to waste one drop.

"There are so many ways I want to fuck you right now," I say, caressing her cheek. "But since tonight is special, I'm going to just lay you out on that fluffy rug and do you nice and slow." She blinks up at me like a sleepy kitten. "Would you like that?"

"Yes," she breathes. "I would love that tonight."

I remove what's left of her dress and lingerie, and she sprawls out on the white rug for me, waiting for me. Wanting me. *Loving me.*

"I like that the only thing you have on is your ring." I like how it glistens on her finger like a little star.

"I love it. I love *you*, Lukas."

I lower myself between her legs and slide into my forever.

CHAPTER 24

LUKAS

I'm woken up by my cell phone ringing and vibrating. I turn over and glance at the clock on my nightstand to see it's one A.M. Grabbing my phone, I look at the screen and see Macy's name and number flashing across it.

"Hey, kiddo," I say.

"Lukas . . . did I wake you?" she asks, her voice louder than usual.

"A little bit. What's wrong? Do you know what time it is?"

She giggles into the phone. "Um, late?"

I sit up, shaking the sleep out of my head. "Are you drunk?"

"Maybe a little?" She giggles some more.

I run my hand through my hair and rub my eyes. "Where are you? Are you okay?"

"I'm at a party, and the asshole I came with took off with some bimbo and left me here. I have no ride home."

"Shit. Did you call your mom?"

"We had a fight this morning. She didn't want me to come to the party, but I came anyway. I can't call her now, or she'll freak out, and I can't call my dad. You know what a jerk he can be."

I blow out a frustrated breath. "Fine, I'll come get you and you can crash here, but your mom stops by in the mornings sometimes so we can have coffee together. She's going to see you here."

"That's fine. I'll deal with it then. She won't yell as much if we're at your place. Please, just don't tell her about the drinking part, okay?"

"Fine, but you're going to tell her yourself tomorrow. I'm not gonna keep secrets from your mother."

"You're the best! Thank you. Lemme give you the address of where I am."

I throw on some clothes and drive half an hour to pick her up at some house in the ghetto. Drunk kids are stumbling all over the front lawn, reminding me of my own party episodes back in the day. Ivy would freak if she knew Macy was hanging out here.

"Who the hell is this kid that left you here?" I ask her when she gets in the car. "And don't puke in my 'Vette."

"He's just some asshole."

I pull the car back out into the street and head for home. "Macy, you can't just be running off to parties with guys, and getting drunk. You could get yourself in a lot of trouble. This is a bad neighborhood."

She rolls her eyes at me. "Seriously? Are you going to lecture me?"

I glance over at her and shake my head. "Yes, I am. Don't do stupid shit."

She goes into hysterics. "Don't do stupid shit," she repeats. "You would make the best dad, Lukas. Really."

"Thanks, kiddo. I'm fucking exhausted. I worked all day, ya

know. Next time you need a ride, call me earlier."

"Okay."

"How much did you have to drink?"

"A few beers and some shots of Jack Daniels."

"Listen to me, Macy. I know you're going to college soon, and it's gonna be party central, but I want you to keep your head together, okay? Don't drink and do drugs. Trust me. I did that shit when I was your age, and it's only fun for like a week. Then it sucks ass."

"Duly noted."

"I'm serious."

"Okay, okay. My head hurts. Stop talking."

"It'll hurt worse tomorrow."

"Oh, joy."

When we get to my house, she stumbles directly to Ray's cage. "Macy, don't get him started, please," I say, not in the mood to hear Ray babbling all night. "He knows he's supposed to be quiet at night."

"But I love him!"

"I'm a pretty bird," Ray says.

"Yes, you are! You're amazing."

"I love you."

She sways and grabs onto his cage. "I love you, too, Ray. You'd make such a great boyfriend if you weren't a bird."

"You're so hawt," Ray squawks back. *Jesus Christ.* I have to stop fooling around with Ivy downstairs.

Macy starts to giggle and almost knocks his cage over. "I love this fucking bird," she says.

I grab her arm and gently tug her away. "Come on. It's late. We don't need to have drunk conversations with the bird."

"Whatever," she snaps, pulling her arm away from me.

I get her some water and aspirin from the kitchen, and

hand them to her when I return to the living room, where she's staring intently at one of my drawings on the wall. "Drink some water and take this. Are you sure you don't want to call your mom?"

"Yes. She's just gonna yell at me and my head will explode. She thinks I'm staying at Shelly's."

"Come on, then. I'll set you up in the guest room, and we'll deal with this tomorrow. It's almost three A.M. I need to get some sleep, and you should, too."

She follows me upstairs to the guest room, babbling, "Oh my God, all these stairs. Why do you have so many stairs?"

"All the sheets are clean," I say, ignoring the drunken talk. This is exactly why I never liked dating girls my age or younger. Most of them party and act like idiots, and I have no tolerance for it at all. "Do you need something to sleep in?"

She looks around the room. "Your house is amazing. Look at the size of that bed. I want to live here."

"Yeah, I'm working on that with your mom. I want us all to live here, but she doesn't think it's a good place for your brother to grow up."

"Mom is so lame sometimes. This would be a great place to grow up. You have tons of cool stuff."

"Thanks," I reply absently. "You didn't answer me. Do you need something to sleep in?"

She looks down at the skinny jeans and blouse she's wearing. "Yeah, that would be great if you have something. All I have is what I'm wearing."

"I'll be right back."

I find her a t-shirt and a pair of sweat shorts to sleep in from my room. "Here ya go," I say, walking back into the guest room, just as she comes out of the adjoining bathroom wearing nothing but her bra and panties.

"Whoa!" I say, putting my hands up and looking away. "Where are your clothes?"

She strolls up to me and touches my chest. "I don't think I need them."

"What the hell? What's going on?" I take a step away from her, still not looking at her.

She rubs her hand across my chest. "What do you want to go on, Lukas?"

I grab her hand and glare into her eyes. "Stop it. Why are you acting like this? Did you take something?" I push the clothes against her chest and scan the room for any pill bottles. "Put these on, please. Stop playing games."

She takes a step back and turns around slowly in front of me, showing off the black push-up bra and thong she's wearing. "Don't you like me?"

I quickly avert my eyes to the floor. "Get dressed. *Now*. Of course I like you. You're like family to me. You know that. But I don't like you like this at all."

I wonder if she really did sneak some pills to be making her act like this, because she's never behaved like this before with me, not since the day I fixed the shed and she blatantly flirted with me before she knew who I was. Since then, she's always treated me as her mom's boyfriend, coming to me for help or advice, and I've always considered her as my future stepdaughter. I've never once thought of her in any other way, especially sexually.

She puts her hands on my chest again, goes on her tiptoes, and presses her lips against mine, before I have a chance to back away from her again. "We could be together, you know. We're closer in age than you and my mother are."

"Macy, don't even go there. What the hell is wrong with you? I love your mother."

She slides her hand down and squeezes my cock. "Well, maybe you could love me, too."

I grab her hands and hold them tightly away from me. "Do *not* touch me. Ever." I hiss at her. "You're drunk."

"And you're hot. Come on, Lukas, have some fun." She giggles, trying to lean her body against mine.

I push her away from me, disgusted. "Go to bed. I don't know what the fuck is wrong with you, but you better stop. I don't think of you that way and I never will."

I want to catch her as she stumbles to the floor but I keep my distance from her.

"You're a fucking rock star. Don't tell me you don't want to nail everything in sight, including me."

My hands clench at my sides. "Nothing could be further from the truth. Go to bed."

I storm out of the room and go to my own, closing and locking the door behind me. What the fuck was that about? I sit on the bed, feeling sick to my stomach. I would never touch her. I love Ivy more than anything and would never cheat on her, especially with her own daughter. The thought of it makes me sick. I have no idea why she's suddenly acting mental.

I should call Ivy right now and tell her Macy is here and how she's acting, so she can come get her, but then she'll get all upset and race over here. She'll have to wake up Tommy and bring him with her, and it will be total chaos. I don't want to do that to her at three-thirty in the morning.

Stretching out on my bed, I resign myself to the fact that I'm not going to be able to get much sleep, knowing my fiancée's daughter is down the hall and just fucking manhandled me like a stripper trying to get an extra twenty bucks. Nothing good is going to come of this. I can feel it.

CHAPTER 25

IVY

I drop Tommy off at my parents' house early Sunday morning, because they want to take him to a matinee and dinner. On the way back home, I decide to bring Lukas our favorite lattes and bagels. More and more, I am leaning toward the idea of moving in with him. We haven't set a date for the wedding yet, but we both want it to happen within the next year, so we're going to have to figure out living arrangements soon.

When he answers the door, he looks surprised and disheveled, wearing old faded jeans and nothing else.

"Hey! You're earlier than you usually are." He lets me in and gives me a quick kiss.

"You look exhausted," I say, concerned. "Do you feel okay?"

He runs his hands through his hair and glances toward the stairs. "Yeah, I just have a bad headache. I'm not really awake yet."

Handing him his latte, I go to the kitchen and get him some aspirin.

"Thanks, love," he says when I return, swallowing the two pills I hand him. "I didn't get much sleep. We need to talk."

Other than during the time of Vandal's accident, I've never seen Lukas look so out of sorts and distraught.

"Can I do anything for you?" I ask him, feeling his head for a fever, the mom in me coming out again. I try not to baby him, but sometimes, I can't stop myself.

Grabbing my hand, he smiles and kisses it. "No, I'm fine. I just feel bad that you stopped by and I feel like crap."

"You're allowed to have bad days. I just wanted to see you. My parents called last night and asked if I'd bring Tommy by for the day, so now I have the entire day free. You could go back to bed. I'll lie next to you and read until you feel better."

"Whatever," Ray squawks from his corner, in what sounds like my daughter's voice.

I laugh. "Wow, is he mimicking Macy? That's her trademark word."

Lukas looks uneasily at the bird. "Yeah, maybe. He may have heard it on the TV."

We move into the living room and sit on the couch, and he looks positively green, rubbing his eyes with the heels of his hands.

"Are you sure you're okay?" I ask him, worried.

"I'm fine, baby. It's just a migraine. I had a bad night."

"I didn't get much sleep myself. I still haven't heard from Macy after our fight last night," I say, sipping my coffee. "She stayed at Shelly's house and didn't even text or call me. She knows how much that upsets me, to not hear from her. I worried all night."

"She'll be okay. It's just growing pains. You know, trying to be an adult when she's still a kid."

LUKAS

"I know. I just hate fighting with her, and I don't like her going to parties and drinking."

"We'll have a talk with her when she calms down, but I have to talk you about—"

Movement from the top of the stairs catches my eye, and I have to do a double take. My daughter is standing there with nothing but a towel on, her hair and makeup a mess, and she came from the direction of Lukas' bedroom.

"Mom, what are you doing here?"

I'm too stunned to speak. I jump up, spilling my coffee, and look from him to her. He stands quickly, his eyes wild with panic.

"Ivy, this isn't what it looks like. This is what I wanted to talk to you about."

Macy stands at the top of the stairs, glaring down at me. "I still have nothing to say to you," she says to me angrily, then turns to Lukas. "Are you coming back up?"

Bile rises up to my mouth, and I choke it back before I vomit all over his living room floor. "What the hell is going on here?" I demand, my voice cracking.

He grabs my shoulders. "Ivy, I swear I didn't touch her. She was drunk—"

"Why is she here? Did she sleep here? With you?" My brain starts to derail as everything Paul did to me comes crashing back into my mind and my heart. *It's happening again.*

"Ivy, no. She called me in the middle of the night from a party. She didn't have a ride, so I went to get her and brought her here so we wouldn't have to get you upset."

"Why the hell is she naked and in your room?" I practically shriek.

He glares up at her, still standing at the top of the stairs. "I don't know! She slept in the guest room. I don't know what the fuck she's doing. She's been acting crazy since I picked her up."

I look up at my daughter, who's smirking at us. "Is that true, Macy?"

She shrugs. "Yeah, he picked me up, but then some stuff happened."

Oh my God. My head is spinning and my stomach is turning. *This can't be happening. This can't be happening.* I look at Lukas, shirtless and exhausted looking, his hair a mess, with a smudge of lipstick at the corner of his lips. My heart pounds harder and faster in my chest as I stare up at my daughter, holding a towel against her. They definitely look like they've been up all night doing God knows what. I can't believe I was this stupid, to trust someone like him.

"You're disgusting," I seethe at him. "How could you do something like this with my daughter? You have lipstick on your face."

His hand flies up and touches his mouth. "She tried to kiss me. I pushed her away from me. I swear, Ivy, I didn't touch her."

Disgusted, I head for the door, and he slams into me from behind, spinning me around.

"Look at me, Ivy. Look into my eyes, and you'll see I'm telling you the truth. You know I would never do something like that. Are you crazy? I love you."

I sob and shake my head. "I *am* looking at you. You're a mess this morning. You look like you've been going at it all night, and I know what that looks like very well."

"Ivy, please." He holds my arms, his fingers digging into me. "I would never do something like that. Fucking ever. I'm just tired. She woke me up in the middle of the night. I had to drive a fucking hour back and forth to get her. I put her in the guest room, but she was drunk and acting crazy, coming on to me. I think she may have taken something, or maybe someone slipped her something. She wasn't acting herself at all, and she still isn't. I pushed her away and locked myself in my bedroom. I didn't touch her."

"She came on to you?" I repeat incredulously. "For God's sake, Lukas, she's just a kid, and she looks up to you. She would never do something like that."

His eyes are wild, tears forming in the corners of his bloodshot eyes. "Ivy, I swear to you, I'm telling the truth. *You know me.* You know I could never do that to you, or her, or our family. What we have is everything to me."

I slam my hands into his chest and push him away. "I have to get out of here. I'm going to be sick. I can't look at either one of you."

I rip the diamond ring off my finger and hurl it at him. It bounces off his bare chest, and he watches it skid across the floor, stunned.

"No. Please, don't do that." He grabs the ring off the floor and comes back after me. "Please, put this back on. Don't do this to us. Please," he pleads.

I shake my head in total confusion, my insides trembling uncontrollably. I just want to get away from him as fast as I can. This is just like Paul, only this time, I actually caught him. *With my daughter.*

I swallow hard over the lump in my throat. "You did this to us, Lukas, and I have no idea why! I will never marry another cheater," I cry, shaking my head, my heart breaking. I can't take my eyes off that smudge of lipstick on his face. *Pink Explosion,* it's called, and it's Macy's favorite. "I can't believe you did this to me. I trusted you!"

Throwing the door open, I run towards my car.

"Ivy!" He chases after me and catches up to me just as I slam my car door and lock it.

"Ivy, please, you have to believe me." He bangs on my window, but I speed out of his parking lot, sobbing uncontrollably, leaving him standing there, barefoot and shirtless.

As I drive home I can't get the sight of my daughter half-naked out of my mind, smirking at me like she won. Has she been after him this entire time, just pretending she was happy for me? Could she be that conniving? My cell phone starts to blow up in my purse with missed calls and texts from Lukas. I contemplate throwing it out the window at the intersection, but instead I turn it off, not wanting to hear or see another word from him right now. I can't handle any more lies, deception, and broken promises.

Everyone was right, after all. He played me for a fool.

And my own daughter fell under his spell and betrayed me.

I can't trust anyone.

Lukas was wrong. There is no happily ever after.

CHAPTER 26

LUKAS

I run back into my house, slamming the door behind me, and fly up the stairs, taking them two at a time. I find her in the guest room, dressed and sitting on the bed.

"What the fuck did you just do?" I yell in her face.

She looks up at me, her eyes wide. "I'm sorry. I don't remember what happened last night." She stands up and grabs her leather bag and phone.

"The hell you fucking don't!"

"Whatever, Lukas. Thanks for the ride." She tries to push past me, but I grab her arm.

"Where the fuck do you think you're going? You're gonna tell me what the hell you just did and why."

Fear settles in her eyes, and I loosen my grip on her arm, but don't let her go.

"Why did you take off your clothes and sneak over to my room? You set that whole thing up."

"Let me go," she says, her voice shaking. "And stop yelling at me. You're not my father."

"You're fucking lucky I'm not. No daughter of mine would

ever do something like that. Did your father put you up to this?"

"No," she says, looking down at her feet. "I don't know what you're talking about. I can't remember anything other than touching you."

Fury takes over, and I see red. "Why are you doing this, Macy? I thought we were friends. I thought you cared about your mother. Do you see what you just did?"

"I do. I guess this just happened." She shrugs.

"This didn't just happen. You did this shit on purpose, and I want you to tell me why right fucking now."

"Leave me alone! I just want to go home," she yells back, and I remind myself that she's only eighteen. She's also obviously messed up or on something, but I need her to help me get Ivy to see that nothing happened between us.

I take a deep breath and try to calm myself before I do or say something that I can't fix. "Macy, please, just tell me what's going on, all right? I promise I'll calm down, and I won't be mad at you anymore. Just tell the truth so I can fix this with your mother, okay?"

"I don't remember anything," she says. "I remember that asshole leaving me at the party and you coming to get me, and us kissing."

I grab her shoulders and shake her. "I did *not* kiss you. *You* tried to kiss me. I pushed you away, and you know it. Why are you doing this?"

Suddenly, Vandal is standing in the doorway, looking from Macy to me. "Dude, I've been ringing your bell for ten minutes and heard you screaming from the lot. What the fuck is going on?"

I throw my hands up in the air. "I don't know. She set me up to make it look like I slept with her, and Ivy believes her."

Vandal narrows his eyes at her. "The fuck did you do?"

"I didn't do anything." She cowers away from him and looks toward the door. "Stop looking at me."

"You're lying. It's all over your face," he accuses, towering over her, and she cringes back from his menacing look.

"Leave me alone," she says.

He backs her into a corner, his six-foot-four frame building a wall in front of her. "If you did something to hurt my brother, I'll make you regret it, little girl. Trust me."

"Vandal, she's just a kid," I remind him.

He stares her down. "She's eighteen, old enough to know better and old enough to deal with the repercussions of fucking with people's lives."

She starts to shake at Vandal's threat. "I just want to go home. I don't remember what happened."

"I can make you remember." He puts his hand to her throat, barely touching her, but I can see she's petrified. And she should be. Vandal is a psychopath and not someone to be fucked with. I don't think he'd really hurt her, but since Katie died, he's been even more mentally unbalanced than usual.

"Vandal . . ." I warn.

"You wanna go a round with me?" he says to her, his voice dark and nasty, like I imagine Satan would probably sound like. "You want to play games? I'll show you what that's really like, baby, and you'll need a wheelchair to get out of here."

Holy shit. My brother is off the rails. "Vandal, stop. Just call her a cab and get her out of here."

"No. She's going to remember. Aren't you, Macy?"

She cringes against the wall, tears streaming down her face.

"Talk. Now," he commands, his huge frame towering over her. "You want to know what it's like to fuck with a man? I'll show you if you don't fucking spill it right now."

"Vandal!" I yell, grabbing his shoulder. "Enough. Let her go. She's family."

He glares at her. "Family doesn't hurt each other." He pulls out his wallet and throws a fifty at her. "Get the fuck out of here and get a cab."

I watch as she picks up the cash and runs downstairs, the door slamming, shaking the house as she leaves.

Vandal turns to me, his eyes still dark and wild like an animal. "You look like shit, man. Did you—?"

I stop him dead. "No. Absolutely not. She called me, drunk from a party. I went and got her, and brought her back here. She was acting weird and kept trying to touch me. I pushed her away and slept alone in my room. I would never touch her. She's the daughter of the woman I love. She's family to me. You're a father, Van. Could you do something like that?"

He stares out the window, his jaw muscles twitching. "I *was* a father. And I think I could pretty much do anything."

I grimace at my bad choice of words. "I'm sorry. I'm not thinking…"

He crosses the room and slaps my back. "Don't worry about it. What are you going to do now?"

Good question. "Well, obviously, I have to somehow get her to admit that she set this up and get Ivy to believe me." I pull all the sheets off the bed and throw them in a pile on the floor, wanting all traces of her gone. "She threw my ring at me, Van. It fucking gutted me."

He leans against the doorframe and crosses huge arms, his jet black hair flowing down his chest. His looks freak me out most of the time, so I can only imagine the fear Macy felt at being his target.

"I think the jealous ex had something to do with this, fiddles."

Smirking at his sarcastic nickname, I nod in agreement. "I think so, too. That guy fucking hates me and can't stand that we're together. I think, when he found out we got engaged, it threw him over the edge."

"Want me to go talk to him?"

Vandal's method of talking scares me. "Not yet. I need to talk to Ivy, and Macy again when she calms down."

He cracks his knuckles. "Just say the word, bro, and I'll fuck his shit up."

"You really like to hurt people, don't you?"

An evil grin crosses his face. "Not all people, but yes, I enjoy a good amount of pain infliction in any form I can give it."

I'm glad that gene skipped me.

After Vandal leaves, I take a quick shower and drive over to Ivy's house, but I take another hit to the gut when I see Paul's car in the driveway. Already, this asshole is here trying to move in on her. I can't believe it.

I bang on the door in a fury until she opens the door, teary-eyed and red-faced.

"What are you doing here?" she asks, not letting me in.

"What the hell is he doing here?" I shoot back.

Paul appears behind Ivy in the doorway. "Where the hell is my daughter?" he demands.

I can't believe this shit. I'm engaged to her. I've fucked her on the kitchen table. Now, I'm standing outside their door like a stranger while they block the doorway. Together. "She left my house over an hour ago. My brother gave her money for a cab."

Paul pushes Ivy out of the way. "You slept with my daughter then sent her home in a fucking cab?"

I lose my shit. "Can we all stop this charade? I didn't sleep with her, and you fucking know it. What the hell is going on? I know you did this, Paul. You did something to Macy to make her lie like this about me."

Ivy ramps up, shock all over her face. "Lukas! He would never do anything like that to one of our kids!" she says, defending him. *Him. Not me.*

"Neither would I! You know how much I love your kids."

Paul gets back in my face, and my fists clench, wanting to punch him right in his smug face. "Looks like you loved one a little too much. You're not their father, and Macy is a pretty girl. You took advantage of her when she was vulnerable. You're lucky I don't call the cops," Paul threatens.

"No one is calling the cops!" Ivy cries, putting a hand on my chest and her other hand on his. "Lukas, please, just leave."

Leave. She wants me to leave. And he's still here.

I shake my head, my breathing heavy, feeling everything slip away from me. "I need to talk to you. Alone. Please, Ivy."

She peers up at Paul. "Give me a minute," she says to him, and I don't understand why he's here, why she's not telling him to leave. He sneers at me from behind her back and walks away, into her house. *Their house.*

I try to put my arms around her, but she backs away from me and crosses her arms. "Ivy, I don't know what's going on here. I didn't touch Macy in any way, other than to push her off me. Why are you believing all this crap? What is he doing to you? What kind of warped circle of hell is this?"

Her eyes are red and puffy as she looks up at me. "Macy

would never lie to me about something like this, Lukas. She knows how much I love you. I think she was drunk and maybe flirted with you, and you just got caught up in the moment."

Her words are like a knife in my chest, stopping my heart for a moment.

"What? You think I'm that weak? I have women throwing themselves at me all the time, Ivy. Adult women, not drunk teenagers who have no idea what they're doing. Do you honestly think I'd risk what we have for a quick fuck with a drunk kid, who's also the daughter of my fiancée?"

Tears stream down her face. "She was in your room. I saw her come out."

"She must have snuck in there when I went downstairs to answer the door. She was *not* in my room, not even for a second."

"But why would she do that? She's never been a devious person, or a liar. Not ever."

My heart falls into my stomach. "And I am? You believe I could do that?"

She shakes her head and puts her hand over my heart. "No, I'm having a hard time believing that, too. Unless this has all been an act, the past few months with you."

"For *what*? What would I gain from it?"

"I don't know," she cries. "I don't know what to believe."

I run my hand through my hair and do a quick circle, wishing she would let me inside, and that asshole would leave.

I hold her face in my hands and force her to look at me. "Ivy, I think Paul put her up to this. He's messing with your head, trying to break us up. He knew exactly what to do to make you doubt me. He knows how scared you are of getting hurt again, after what he did to you. He set this all up. I know it."

She shakes her head wildly back and forth. "He wouldn't use one our kids to do that."

I put my arms around her, ignoring her protests and squirming. "I think he would. I think he *did*." I kiss the top of her head and smooth her hair down. "Please, you have to trust me, Ivy. I love you. I love the kids. I would never hurt any of you. I don't want to lose you."

Her face presses into my chest, and her arms finally circle my waist.

"I love you, too. I just don't know what to believe. This looks really bad. Even you have to admit that. I'm so confused."

I force her to look up at me. "Believe *me*. Please. You know my heart better than anyone."

Her big watery eyes stare up into mine, deep pools of sad blue, filled with doubt.

She slowly pulls away, taking pieces of my heart with her. "Just give me some time to figure this out. I have to talk to Macy alone."

"Don't make me leave. Get rid of him, and let's figure this out together."

"He's leaving soon. Lukas, just go home. Give me some time to think and straighten this out."

"I want you to put your ring back on. I have it with me."

She shakes her head and steps back away from me towards the door. "No." She sniffles and wipes at her eyes, her makeup running down her cheeks. "I can't do that, not until I figure this out. I'm sorry."

My vision blurs as stabbing pain fills my chest, squeezing my heart. "You don't know what you're doing, Ivy. You're killing us. You're killing *me*."

CHAPTER 27

IVY

A lifetime of days passes by. Days wasted, spent doubting myself, doubting my daughter, doubting Lukas. With every day that passes, I can feel the damage being done, not sure if I can fix it. Not sure if any of us can fix it.

Lukas's persistence to try to fix this mess puts his initial persistence of asking me out to shame. He calls every night and sends more text messages than I can count every day. He's sent roses. He's written letters. He's sent poetry and drawings. I ignored it all, and then it stopped. I think a part of me died when I realized that he had finally given up. And if he is in fact telling the truth, then I deserve every bit of pain I feel for breaking the most precious heart in the world.

I feel sick. Sick to my stomach. Sick in my head. Sick in my heart. Torn between two people I love more than anything and thought I could trust.

With my own eyes, I saw my daughter walk out of my fiancée's bedroom, naked, with nothing but a towel on. I cannot get that image out of my head. I just see it over and over and over again, unstopping. She didn't deny they had been together. She asked him if he was coming back upstairs. *Right in front of me.*

Macy may not be perfect, but she's never been a liar, not even as a little girl. She would tell the truth and just deal with the repercussions of her actions, knowing she might get punished or grounded. But she still would admit whatever she had done.

I know she was mad at me when I tried to keep her from going to the party with her new boyfriend. Any eighteen year old would be mad at their parent for not letting them go to a party and pulling the "my house rules" card. Did I push her too far? Could she have been mad enough that she would try to get back at me by fooling around with Lukas, or pretending that she did? I can't even fathom my daughter doing that to me. And how did she know I would be there? That was a last minute decision on my part, to surprise Lukas with coffee. Did she think that quickly and set up a scheme that fast? I can't picture her doing that. Not at all. Unless I just don't know her as well as I think I do.

But Lukas . . . my sweet Lukas with his dark, sensual side. Would he touch my daughter? I've known from the start that she had a crush on him. Did that ever go away? Or did I make it worse, having them spend time together, trying to integrate him into our family? Could that have fostered her feelings for him, and she just pretended to be okay with it all, just so she could get closer to him? Macy is beautiful, with a perfect body. Any man would be taken with her, and have a hard time saying no to her if she offered herself to him and made herself available. If she was drunk and flirting with him, was she able to press the right buttons to get him to go over the edge with her?

Nausea overwhelms me as I try to force myself to envision

that scenario—Lukas touching her, taking her into his bedroom, kissing her, and touching her. *No. I can't see it.* Lukas doesn't do quickies. Lukas is a lover in every sense of the word. He can't do meaningless sex. Unless something has been building between them for a while now, and I was blind to it . . .

Could he have grown bored with me? Maybe Macy, being young, sexy, and carefree was more appealing to him. Like Charlene was to Paul. Macy is so into the band; she would love that lifestyle with him, and fit into it as the young beautiful girlfriend of the rock star. Not like me, the older, boring mom that sits on the balcony with him and drinks lattes.

You're what I want. The stability and safety I need. The only one I would trust my heart with. You can make all my dreams come true.

Those words he said when he put the ring on my finger echo over and over in my mind, acting as the north star of my lost heart and soul right now. He meant them with every part of himself. I know that without a doubt. I felt it straight into my bones. The little boy in the attic, playing with antiques, teaching himself beautiful music, believing he was protected by gargoyles, grew into a man who wanted one thing: someone to love him enough to never leave him.

I *am* that person. He believes in that. He trusted in that. I promised that to him. And in return, he offered me everything I want and need, and then some. He gave me the fairytale I dreamed about.

He would never risk that. Never.

Would he?

My heart screams no, but then I have to turn to the other side of this coin and face a horrible fact. My own daughter lied to me and set out to hurt me.

Macy has been staying with Shelley for almost a month when she finally shows up at the house again, and when she does, she's in a new car. I walk out to the driveway in a state of shock.

"Where did you get this?" I demand, looking over the shiny new red sports car in the driveway.

"Daddy bought it for me. He didn't want me driving my piece of crap car to college. He said it wasn't safe."

"Really? Is that all?" Of course. It's all clear now. Tremors of rage course through me.

"Yes."

She walks toward the house, and I follow her inside, hot on her heels.

"Macy, sit down. We're going to talk."

She turns and rolls her eyes at me. "Mom, I'm tired. I've been sleeping on Shelly's couch for weeks, waiting for things to diffuse."

"Diffuse?" I repeat. "Sit down right now. This isn't over."

Throwing her purse onto the couch in a huff, she sits and stares at the floor. "Mom, I'm sorry about Lukas."

"Are you, Macy? Really?" I try to keep my voice as level as I can, when all I really want to do is blow up.

"Yes, of course I am. I didn't mean for it to happen . . . it just did."

I sit next to her and try to remain calm. "Tell me what happened. All of it."

"What? That's sick, Mom."

"I want you to tell me. Now. If you don't, I'm going to have that car towed right out of the driveway."

Her eyes shoot daggers at me. "You can't do that."

"Watch me."

She squirms, playing with the wrist strap on her phone. "I went to the party with Brent, even though you told me I couldn't go. I was mad at you. I'm eighteen. You can't tell me what to do."

"As long as you live under my roof, you follow my rules. We went over that. Continue, please."

She sighs. "I had a few drinks, and he was being a total jerk to me. There were a lot of kids at the party, but no one from my school. There were a lot of college girls there, and I found him fooling around with one. We had a big fight, and he took off with her and left me there. I had no way to get home, and I didn't want to call you and hear the 'I told you so', so I called Lukas to come and get me. He wanted me to tell you what happened, but I said no, I'd call you in the morning."

"Then what? Were you drunk?"

"Yes. Not like fall on my face drunk, but I was a little messed up. He said I could sleep in his guest room. When we got there, he offered me some clothes to sleep in, and I took off my clothes and kissed him."

My blood goes cold. "Why? Why would you do something like that?"

She shrugs. "Because he's hot. And I was mad at you."

"Then what happened?"

"We kissed some more, and then we did it. I fell asleep in his bed and woke up when I heard you downstairs."

"You did it?" I repeat.

"Yeah, I was still pretty messed up and tired, though, and can't remember everything that happened."

"So he took you into his bedroom?"

"Yeah." Uncertainty starts to edge into her voice.

"Macy, this is serious."

"I know."

"And you slept in there?"

"Yes. I woke when he got up to get the door when you showed up, and I was mad that you interrupted us." Her voice wobbles and she continues to play with her phone strap. "That's what happened."

"You're lying."

She swallows hard and takes a deep shaky breath. "I am not."

"You are, Macy, and you're going to tell me why. But first, I'm going to tell you how I know you're lying. I know because I believe Lukas. I've sat here for weeks, mulling this over and over in my mind and in my heart, because I trust *both* of you. I love *both* of you." I try to fight back the tears, but I can't hold them in. "You're my little girl. Everything I've done since I got pregnant at eighteen has been for you, to give you a good life, to make sure you would always be happy, and I never would have thought you could do something like this to me. To anyone, for that matter."

She starts to shake and tears roll down her cheeks. "Mom . . . I'm so sorry."

I put my hand on her leg. "It's terrible to have to try to choose between two people you love and figure out which one would hurt you, to try to figure out which one would lie to you, and I hate to say this, honey, because it hurts me so much . . . but I don't believe a word you're saying. I believe Lukas, because I know how much our relationship means to him and how badly he wanted something real. He would never throw it away, and he would never lie to me or hurt me, because I know how much he loves me."

My daughter blinks up at me, her face reddening, tears streaming down her face. "But for some reason, you decided to set out to hurt me, to wreck my life and take away my happiness, and I couldn't for the life of me figure out why you would do something so horrible." I swallow, and she bites her lip, refusing to look at me again. "At first, I thought you still had a crush on him. I know what that can feel like. But now, I know what the real reason is, and it's sitting in our driveway. Isn't it?"

She tries to stand, but I grab her hand. "Isn't it, Macy?" I demand.

Her voice is barely a whisper. "Yes," she admits.

My heart almost stops beating. "Why would you do such a thing?"

She starts to cry, her shoulders shaking. "I'm so sorry, Mom. I didn't want to."

"Then why did you do it? Just tell me the truth."

"Daddy said he'd buy me a car if I broke up you and Lukas. He said to make sure I made it look like he slept with me. At first I said no, but he kept bringing it up every time I talked to him. He was obsessed with it, and kept trying to twist my head all up with new ideas of what I could do. He showed me pictures of the car he would get for me. I told him I didn't want to, but then that night when Lukas let me stay at his house, it all just kinda happened. I really didn't think you would fall for it, but everything kinda worked out perfect."

Worked out perfect. My daughter thinks hurting people is perfect, and her father talked her into it, bribing her with a new car.

That bastard. I'm so furious that my hands are shaking. I want to smash his face in.

Macy's voice breaks through my anger. "Mom, I'm sorry. I didn't think it would be this bad."

"I don't know who I'm more disappointed in," I say quietly. "You or your father. What he asked you to do is disgusting, and I can't believe you would go along with it. For a *car.*"

"Mom..."

I put my hand up, angry tears falling down my face. "What you did was unforgivable and so incredibly devious. Lukas is a good man. He would do anything for you and Tommy."

She wipes her face with her hand. "I know that. I love you guys together, Mom. Me and Tommy both do. He's a better dad to us than Dad ever was."

"Then how could you do that to him?" I practically scream. "And to me?"

"I don't know!" she wails. "Daddy kept saying it was the best thing to do. He said Lukas isn't who he pretends to be, that he's just a young guy taking advantage of a lonely older woman, and that he would hurt you, too. He said I'd be helping you in the long run."

"Do you really believe that?"

She shakes her head and sniffles, wiping her eyes with her fingers. "No. I just really wanted the car, Mom. Mine was a piece of junk! All my friends have new cars."

The mindset of a teenager—they can justify anything, just because they want it.

"So you hurt two people who love you over a car? For God's sake, Macy, Lukas probably would have lent you the money for one if he knew you needed a new car. He's just that nice."

"You're right," she says, nodding. "I'm sorry. I didn't know it would hurt you so much. I wasn't expecting Lukas and his psycho brother to go crazy on me."

"Is it true that you touched him?" I silently pray this part isn't true. "He said you put your hands on him."

She squirms uneasily. "Yes, I grabbed him and I kissed him."

Nausea bubbles up in my stomach. "I am so sickened by you right now, Macy. I can't even put it into words."

"This isn't all my fault, Mom! He could have tried harder to push me away if he really wanted to. He's much bigger than me."

I jump up off the couch, my limit reached. "That's *it*. You need to leave, right now. Pack up some things and go to your father's house. I can't have you living here."

Shock and fear touches her face, her mouth falling open. "Mom! You can't kick me out!"

"Yes, I can. You can stay at your father's until college starts. I can't believe you would hurt me like this. I have no idea who you are, but you are definitely not the daughter I raised."

"Okay, it was all my fault," she admits, as if it's somehow going to make things better. "I totally provoked him. Are you happy now? He pushed me away and kept saying he loves you. Okay? I told you everything. Can I just stay here, please? I don't want to live with Dad and fucking Charlene!"

I shake my head furiously.

"Absolutely not. Take your new car and go stay with them, and think about the horrible things you've done out of greed. I didn't raise you to behave this way, and I can't be around you right now. You're right. You're eighteen. You're an adult. Go be one at your father's house until I can forgive you for this. Or go live with one of your friends."

It tears my heart out to watch her cry as she runs to her

room and returns a few minutes later with an overstuffed duffel bag, just like her father did not long ago.

She stops at the front door and turns to me again, her face red, her makeup smeared all over her face. "Can I please just stay here? Mom?" Her voice cracks. "Don't make me leave. I promise I'll apologize to Lukas. Nothing like this will ever happen again. I won't ever talk to him again if you want."

I hold my ground, clenching my jaw. "No. I love you, Macy, but what you did is horrible beyond words. I'm going to need some time to get over this." I turn away from her and hear the door open and close, and seconds later her shiny new car is pulling out of the driveway.

I fall onto the couch and burst into tears, hating Paul for once again ripping away everything I love and destroying my life.

"I'm going out for lunch," I tell my assistant, breezing past her desk. "I'll be back in about an hour."

She nods at me, so immersed in her work that she doesn't look up from her computer screen, and I make a mental note to find out when she's due for her next review.

I walk to the park a few blocks away from my office and sit on a bench under a huge willow tree, the crisp late summer air helping to clear my head. I haven't been sleeping much at all, and I feel like it's catching up to me, giving me brain fog and making me cranky. When I called Lukas the night I had it out with Macy, I wasn't expecting him to tell me he needed some time to think before he could let me back into his life. Sleepless nights and endless days have plagued me since.

Stupidly, I thought that, once I apologized for doubting him, he would welcome me back with open arms. He's not like other people, though. He may be incredibly loving and have a huge heart, but I learned the hard way that he gives that part of himself to very few, and second chances are rare when it comes to him.

With Lukas, it's all or nothing, and I didn't give him my all. I thought I did, but when it came to proving it, I failed miserably. I shouldn't have pushed him away and shut him out the way I did. I should have talked to him and worked it out together. So much for me being the supposed mature one of the relationship.

"Can I sit?"

I look up, but he's already taken the liberty to sit on the bench next to me.

"Asher?" I glance around to see if anyone else is with him. *Like Lukas.* But he's alone. "What are you doing here?"

He chews the toothpick hanging out of his mouth. "Meeting a friend. You?"

"I'm on my lunch break. My office isn't too far from here."

"It's a nice day to get out."

"Yeah. It is."

He nods and studies me. "Did you know Lukas was born with a hole in his heart?"

My head snaps to face him, shocked by his sudden statement. "What?" My voice quivers, and I swallow the lump that instantly forms in my throat. "No . . . he never told me that."

"I'm not surprised. He doesn't like to talk about it. It's why his mother gave him up. She was afraid he'd need too much care."

I don't bother to brush the tear that creeps down my cheek. My heart races, and I'm suddenly stricken with fear that he's sick, or dying.

Asher continues in his melodic voice. "I find it ironic that someone with such a huge heart has a hole in his own, and that the people who should love him keep falling through it."

"I *do* love him," I say defensively. "More than anything. You don't understand."

He pulls the toothpick out of his mouth. "Oh, trust me. I do."

"I still want to marry him. I've tried to talk to him, I apologized for what happened. He's all I want."

Another man comes along and sits on the bench next to Asher. He's tall and broad, wearing a worn black leather jacket, black motorcycle boots, and dark sunglasses. His head is shaved but covered in tattoos.

"Hey, man, how's things?" Asher asks him.

His friend laughs. "I'm dying. How do you think I'm doing?"

Asher nods slowly, staring off across the park. "We're all dying. Some of us just faster than others."

I want to get up and leave, but I feel riveted to this bench.

"How's your other half?" the friend asks.

Asher hands him a small bottle, of what, I don't know. "She's sleeping," he replies.

"I wish I could fucking sleep," the friend says.

"Me, too," I mutter in agreement.

Asher turns his attention back to me. "What do you think is worse, Ivy? Not trusting the person you gave your heart to, or giving your heart to someone and them not trusting you?"

The friend sighs loudly. "Here we go . . ."

Asher kicks him in the shin. "Shut the fuck up."

He turns back to me. "Well?" he asks softly.

I try to answer him honestly. "I think both scenarios are equally upsetting," I reply, wondering what the heck is happening on this park bench with these two. Did they arrange this?

He leans back against the bench. "Indeed, they are."

We sit in silence, watching the birds and squirrels scavenge for food around us. A tiny black feather drifts from above and lands on my leg. I pick it up and hold it gently between my fingers, admiring its soft downy fuzz.

"You know what they say?" Asher asks, standing up.

"About what?"

"A lost feather means an angel is near."

I stare at the feather and think of all the little black feathers I've found in random places over the past few months. Are they a sign? Of what? He leans down and kisses the top of my head, an affectionate gesture that surprises me. "You need to go fill that hole in his heart, okay? You're family now."

His friend stands up and stretches. "Nice meeting you." He nods his chin at me.

"You, too . . ." I say, not having a clue who he is. Maybe another brother or cousin? He looks like he could be part of the band, but he definitely wasn't there the night I saw them at the club. I tuck the feather into my jacket pocket so I can put it with the others in my nightstand.

"One more thing before I go," Asher says. "He's going to need your help with something. If you could do it with him, it would mean a lot, and I think it would be good for both of you."

I look up at him and frown, confused by all of his strange vagueness. "Help with what? Is he okay?"

"He's okay, sweetness. Just be there for him."

"All right . . . I will." I'll do anything to make things right with Lukas again.

He smiles at me. "You guys are gonna be okay. Set a wedding date soon, so I can make some plans."

Before I can answer, he and his friend have left and are walking down the pathway to the park exit. I watch them until I can't see them anymore, wondering where they're going and if it was a coincidence that Asher found me here. What are the chances of that?

CHAPTER 28

IVY

Me: Can I come over tonight? I really want to see you. And talk. I have so much I need to say to you.

Lukas: No

My heart drops.

Lukas: Come now. My last appt is leaving in ten mins. I don't want to wait.

Shit. I can't tell if this is good or bad.

I tell my manager I have an appointment, and leave the office in a hurry, heading straight to Lukas' house. I don't have to pick up Tommy from school, because Paul is picking him up to take him for the weekend, which I'm not happy about after the stunt he pulled with Macy. What if he tries another maneuver like that and uses Tommy to hurt me next? We don't speak to each other at all since the incident with Macy, so all communication is done via our lawyers. I honestly don't even want him to have joint custody, but my lawyer says that will be a hard fight to win, even after how he manipulated Macy. The lawyer is also afraid provoking Paul will make him drag Lukas into the situation and try to make him look like a bad influence around Tommy, and that's the last thing I want. So for now, I have to let things be.

My hands are shaking with nervousness when I get to Lukas' house and ring the bell. It's been a month since we've seen each other, but it feels like so much longer. Despite Asher's riddling comments, what if Lukas just doesn't want me anymore? I can't even blame him if that's the case after the way I treated him.

When he opens the door and lets me in, he looks different, somehow older, as if he's aged in just a few weeks. He also looks bigger and more muscular, meaning he's been hitting the gym more than his norm, probably using it to work out his frustrations and anger. He's even more attractive to me now, if that's even possible.

Without a word he quickly pulls me into a tight hug in the middle of his front foyer. I wrap my arms around him, so scared that this could be our goodbye. I breathe him into me, missing him, his scent, and his embrace.

"We have to talk," he whispers.

I nod. "Yes. We do."

We move into the living room and sit on the big couch together, where he holds my hand but seems to be struggling for words, so I take the lead.

"Lukas, I can't tell you how sorry I am. I know I hurt you, and I can't apologize for that enough. I just didn't know who to believe. I love and trusted you both. Trying to figure out which one of you wasn't telling the truth was so hard for me. She's my daughter…"

He stares past my face as he listens to me, the pain still evident in his dark eyes.

"You were right," I continue. "Paul bribed Macy with a new car. She planned the entire thing. I just didn't think she was capable of such a thing."

He finally speaks, his voice despondent, lacking the sexy, teasing rasp that I grew to love so much. "I already knew that, Ivy. The problem is, you didn't believe me. You were so quick to think I could do something like that. Like you don't know me at all."

An emotional vice clenches my heart. My God, I've hurt him so badly, and I swore to him I never would.

I take a slow steady breath in an effort to calm my quaking nerves. "I can only apologize and try to start new. I'm so sorry. She's my daughter, Lukas. You don't know how torn I was, not knowing who to believe. She's never lied to me before."

His eyes switch up to meet mine, and they're filled with sad defiance. "Neither have I."

I squeeze his hand tighter. "I know you haven't. It just looked so bad, her coming out of your room with no clothes on. You had her lipstick on your face. What was I supposed to think?"

"You threw my ring at me. You threw *me* away." He takes a deep breath. "You broke my fucking heart."

My heart pounds with fear against my ribs. "I didn't mean that. I was scared and confused, and I acted irrationally. All the shit that Paul did to me just bubbled up to the surface. I know I was wrong and I should have given you a chance to explain better, but I just had a total meltdown."

"I've been scared and confused my entire life, Ivy. Until I met you, and then everything felt right to me. But then, you went and tore my heart out. You wouldn't even listen to me.

You made me talk to you out on your front steps, while your ex was inside, and then you made me leave while he stayed."

I cringe at that memory. Why did I do that? He has every right to be furious with me for that, and I deserve it.

"You're right," I agree. "That was awful of me to do, and I can see that so clearly now." How could I have been so blind? "But, that day, I just couldn't get my head together."

"I've had a rough time dealing with all of this—losing Katie, losing you, Vandal and his problems with his new chick. I can't fix everyone, especially when I'm broken myself. It's been really hard for me to keep it together during this, without you."

"Lukas, you don't have to fix anyone. Vandal can take care of himself. He's stronger than you think. And we can fix us, together. Give me the chance to prove to you how much I love you, and I won't ever let you down again."

Saying nothing, he stares at the wall for a few minutes. I know he's thinking, because that's what he does. He *thinks*. But every second that ticks by scares me, not knowing what he's going to say or do.

"I can forgive you, because I know how torn you were. I had a hard time believing Macy could do something like that myself, and I actually witnessed it. So, yeah, I get it." He rubs my hand slowly with his thumb as he talks. "But, in the future, you have to trust me. There can be no gray area. I can't . . . I *won't* be with someone who doesn't trust me completely. I need you on my side, no matter what, just like I would be for you. No fucking questions or doubts. If you can't give me that as my wife, then this will never work."

"You're right. You shouldn't accept any less. And I promise you I'll never doubt you again."

He brushes his hand across my cheek and locks his eyes onto mine. "I hope not, Ivy. It would be a deal breaker if it happened again. I'm in this forever. You have my heart, and I want yours. Unconditionally. I'm willing to move past this and put it behind us, because I know how confused you were with your daughter being involved, but I don't ever want to go through something like this again."

"I don't, either. I don't ever want to be apart from you again," I whisper. "I love you, and I miss you so much. These past few weeks have been horrible. I hate myself for hurting you..." My wall collapses and the tears break free, making me choke.

He pulls me against his chest, holding the back of my head with his hand, and presses his lips to the top of my head.

"I love you, too, Ivy. And I hate to do this to you right now, because the timing couldn't be fucking worse. But, I need to talk to you about something. So much happened while we were apart," he swallows hard. "And if you can't do this with me, I understand."

I sit up and stare into his face, and I can see he's tortured, dealing with some sort of struggle I know nothing about. Whatever it is, I should have been here helping him through it and not off by myself trying to figure out if he had cheated on me.

"You're scaring me," I say, remembering what Asher told me about his heart. "Are you sick?"

"No, I'm fine. I'm exhausted, though, from trying to figure out how to do this and not lose you all over again. It's why I needed some time to think this all through, and I'm sorry for my part in that."

I grip his hand. "Tell me. Please."

He licks his lips nervously. "It changes a lot, Ivy."

Fear ripples through my body, but I nod assuredly. "It's

okay. I love you. I still want to marry you. That hasn't changed. Nothing could change that."

"I want that, too, but it's a little more complicated now." He takes a deep breath. "I have to know if we can get through this together, so I can make a decision. So we can *both* make a decision."

I can't follow where he's going with this conversation. "I'm confused," I admit. "Did something happen?"

He shuts his eyes for a long moment. "Yes."

"You're really scaring me."

"Rio came by last week."

I tilt my head at him, not sure who that is. "Rio?" I repeat.

"She's a friend of mine, but I was also involved with her before I met you."

Oh, no. My heart pounds, knowing that what he's going to tell me is going to change our lives forever.

"Okay," I say, slowly remembering. "You told me about her during one of my first tattoo appointments. You had just broken up with her."

He nods. "Yes, that's her."

"What about her?"

"She's pregnant. Due very soon, actually."

My heart seizes. "Oh." Is all I can manage to say. *Another woman is having his baby.*

He touches my chin and lifts my head to stare into my eyes. "It's not my baby, Ivy."

"Wh- what do you mean?" I ask, my voice shaking.

"It's Vandal's."

My mouth falls open in shock. "He was with her?"

"Yup. Apparently before, during, and after me. He stopped when he met Tabi."

I cover my mouth with my hand, knowing how much the

fact that two people betraying him at the same time must be tearing him up inside. "I'm so sorry, Lukas. I can't believe your brother would do that to you..."

He lets out a little laugh. "I'm not surprised. Vandal takes what he wants. And to be honest, that part doesn't bother me. I wasn't in love with her."

I'm not sure what's going on and what about this could have him so upset. "How does this affect us, though? I'm confused."

He's quiet for a moment. "Rio is in no position to have a baby. She's in a band, traveling and partying a lot, and she told me just doesn't have it in her to take care of a baby. She's not ready. Vandal doesn't know."

"She didn't tell him?"

"No, and she doesn't want to. He'll come unglued, Ivy. She and I both know that. Hell, everyone knows that. He'll freak the fuck out if he knows she's pregnant so soon after losing Katie. It will tear him apart. He's still a mess from everything that happened to him."

"You don't think it would make him happy? To have another child in his life? Maybe it will make him better? A new beginning?" I suggest hopefully.

He chews his lip ring. "No. It won't. I know him, Ivy. He'll resent the baby for being alive while Katie is dead."

"Lukas, that's a terrible thing to say. You don't know that-"

"I *do*, Ivy. Trust me. He isn't wired right. Rio refuses to let him be involved, she's afraid of what he'll do to her, or the baby, or to himself. And as much as I love my brother, I have to admit I think she's right. It's way too soon for him."

I shake my head, not wanting to believe this about any parent. "But it's his baby. He has a right to know."

"Rio wants to put the baby up for adoption. She's been

telling everyone she doesn't know who the father is," he sits up and leans his elbows on his knees. "You have no idea what it's like to not be wanted by your parents, Ivy. I lived that. So did Vandal. I don't want this baby to grow up like that. That's my niece or nephew she's got, and I can't let that go."

I gently rub his back and he turns to look back at me, his hair falling into his face, giving me just a glimpse of his anguished expression. This is completely tearing him apart.

"I can't let her adopt that baby out to strangers, Ivy. I'll never be able to live with that, knowing my brother's kid, a part of *my* family, is out there somewhere. Not knowing if they're okay, or if they're loved. I just can't let it happen."

My hand freezes on his back. I can't understand where he's going with all of this. I don't want the baby to end up in a bad place either, but what can we do about it? It's Rio's baby, it has to be her decision.

"Lukas, what are you going to do? If it's not your baby, you don't have any rights. You're only the uncle."

"*We* know that, Ivy. But no one else has to."

My heart jumps for the hundredth time today as what he's eluding to slowly sinks into me. "What do you mean?" *Does he want to raise the baby with Rio?*

"I want to let everyone believe the baby is mine. And I want to adopt it, and raise it with you. Rio is willing to sign over her rights, and agree to a private adoption, to let us adopt the baby together. I talked to Gram and Asher about it, we talked to a lawyer, and had papers drawn up. Rio is in total agreement; she thinks it's the best thing for the baby. She trusts me. I just need to know if you can do this with me, because I don't want to lose you."

This is the last thing I ever expected. My brain ricochets around in my head, trying to recover from the stress of the past few weeks with Lukas, Macy and Paul, and now this unexpected shock on top of that. Could I raise someone else's baby? Under the guise that it's my husband's and another woman's? I've always hoped I could have one more child, but I've never considered any kind of adoption. Or such a bizarre scenario.

He turns and takes both of my hands in his. "Ivy, I know this is a lot to take in and I'm asking you for a lot at the worst possible time. Even though we just had a huge misunderstanding with Macy, I still have nothing but faith in you and I. And I know it's going to be hard for you to raise a baby, with everyone around us thinking it's mine and someone else's, and you don't deserve that. At all. But you're a great mother. We can give that baby a great life. I know we'll love her. Or him."

"Lukas..." What twenty-four-year-old man wants to raise a baby that's not his? And take on that kind of lifetime responsibility, without hesitation? *Only Lukas.*

"I can't let my brother's baby be given away. It's just not right. I can't let him lose two kids, even though he doesn't even know one exists. *I'll know.* And I can't let it happen. I loved Katie so much, and this baby is her half brother or sister. Family means so much to me. I just can't let Rio allow someone else raise that baby and never know if it's okay. I'm afraid I'll never get it out of my fucking head."

He waits for me to answer but I just can't even put a coherent sentence together. My mind and my heart are whirling around with everything he's asking of me. *Adopting a baby. Raising another baby. That isn't mine. Or his. That belongs to his psychotic brother...*

"I *can* do this without you, Ivy. But I'd much rather do it *with* you, as a couple. And that's not the reason why I want you back. I love you and I want to spend my life with you. The timing of this is just so bad, but I have to make a decision soon. Even if you don't think you can be a part of this, I still want us to be together. We'll find a way to make it all work, so I can adopt the baby and still have a relationship with you. I'm not going to let you go. I'll make this work."

"This is a lot to take in," I finally say, letting out a deep breath. "Do you plan to tell him someday?"

"Honestly? I don't know. Maybe someday, if he ever calms down."

"If he finds out, he could hate you, Lukas. He could try to fight all this, and take the baby away. He's the biological father. I have no idea what kind of mess that could be."

"I don't think that will ever happen, Ivy. The only people that know are Rio, us, Asher, and Gram. No one else will ever know."

Years of watching Days of Our Lives makes me believe that everyone will find out eventually and it will turn into an epic fight with an innocent child being stuck right in the middle. That's the last thing I would ever want to happen.

"I think what you want to do is very caring and noble, Lukas, but someday, this could get really messy. A lot of hearts could get broken. Relationships destroyed."

He chews his lip ring and nods. "I know that. But the alternative is even worse. At least to me. If someday it happens, then we'll have to deal with it. But at least the baby will be safe, and in his or her own family."

"Are you sure it's not your baby? Is it possible?" As much as I don't want another woman to have his baby, it seems like it would be way easier to deal with than the dark cloud of Vandal hanging over our heads.

He shakes his head. "I only actually slept with her twice,

and I used protection. She said she and Vandal were together a lot while they were both drunk and there was a time when the condom ripped. She wasn't with anyone else."

I remember being eighteen and pregnant, scared out of my mind--not knowing if Paul would stay by my side, and dealing with my parents disappointment in me. My entire world changed when I got pregnant, and the only thing I was sure about was that I wanted my baby to be safe and loved. My parents tried to talk me into adoption, but I couldn't bear the thought of giving my baby away, not ever knowing what happened to her. And while I'm very disappointed in Macy right now, I wouldn't change a thing. I understand what Lukas is feeling. His love for family is so deep. His need to take care of people has been ingrained in him since he was a little boy. To try to sway him from his intense beliefs to raise this baby would destroy him, and go against the very traits in him I respect the most.

I prayed for unconditional love, and I have that with him. Of course I'll give it back to him.

"Okay..." I say slowly, exhaling deeply. "If this is what you want, then yes. We'll do this together, and hope for the very best for all of us."

He blinks at me, absorbing my words, holding my hand tighter in his. "Really? You love me enough to do this?"

"Lukas, I love you more than enough to do this. I want you to be happy, and have peace in your heart. That's the most important thing to me. If I can stand by your side and give you that, then I'm going to do it. No matter what."

Before I can say anything else, his lips are on mine, kissing me long and deep "God, I love you. And I've missed you so much," he says between kisses. "I love you, Ivy. I promise I'll never hurt you. I'm going to make all our dreams come true."

He reaches into his pocket and pulls out my engagement ring. "Can we try this again?" He asks, the sexy teasing rasp back in his voice. "You know how persistent I can be, I'll propose to you every day if I have to."

"I totally believe you will," I laugh softly. "Let's make this the last time."

He slides the ring back onto my finger and pulls me into him, covering my mouth with his, taking me to that magical place again that only exists with him. Soon we're frantically pulling each other's clothes off, never breaking our kiss. As we make love on his living room floor with the light shining down on us from his stained glass windows, I know without a doubt that everything is going to be okay, as long as we have each other.

EPILOGUE

LUKAS

My wife. I watch her from across the room as she carries Hope from person to person so they can give her a birthday kiss. Hope giggles and waves her little chubby hands around as each person hugs and kisses her. Gram's house has been turned into a party extravaganza for Hope's first birthday, with balloons and everything unicorn-themed you can imagine, including a unicorn-shaped cake with a glittery horn Macy and Tommy helped me bake and decorate that came out awesome. Thankfully, lots of love and patience brought our little family back together. It's going to take us a while to fully trust and forgive Macy, but we're getting there, slowly, but surely.

I didn't think I could love Ivy more, but I do. Every day, I love her more intensely. She's everything I've ever dreamed of, hoped for, and desired. Like fine wine, she's getting better with age.

And she's mine.

. . .

My daughter.

I smile as my wife hands Hope over to Vandal for a kiss, and the baby promptly grabs a fistful of his hair in her tiny hand. His girlfriend, Tabi, kisses his cheek, and he laughs before handing the baby back to Ivy. I can still see the flash of pain in his eyes, even though he tries hard to hide it.

But I see it clear as day.

Hope's the most adorable baby I've ever met. She hardly ever cries or fusses. She's always smiling and laughing. Having her has brought Ivy and me even closer together, strengthening our bond. She's our little angel, and she's definitely Daddy's little girl.

I don't care that she's not really mine. I love her like she is.

Rio and I were right; Vandal isn't ready for another baby so soon after losing Katie. It would have torn him up inside and sent him into a mental tailspin if he found out she was pregnant with his baby. He's trying hard to get his life together, but he's still got a ways to go. Tabi confided in Ivy a few weeks ago that any time she's mentioned having a family, Vandal shuts down. That just proves to me that I did the right thing in keeping his daughter safe for him.

Ivy approaches me with a very happy, cake-faced baby in her arms, and leans in to give me a big kiss. "We love you," she says softly. "Thank you for today."

Wrapping my arm around her waist, I pull her closer, that electric feeling pulsing through me like it always does when she's near.

"I love my girls," I kiss the top of her head and Hope stretches her arms out to me, wanting me to hold her, which of course I can't resist. She wraps her chubby arms around my neck and leans her cheek against mine, something she does often that melts my heart every single time. Ivy plucks a tiny black feather from Hope's dress and smiles.

"I find Ray's feather's everywhere," she says. "Even when we were apart, I found one."

I wink at her. "Maybe that's so you wouldn't forget me."

"As if I ever could?"

"Don't forget Macy's babysitting tonight. I think we should start practicing making our baby."

"You're sure?" She whispers, peeking up at me with blushed cheeks. I know Ivy loves Hope as if she were her own, just like I do. But even though we've never actually said it, I know how bad we both want an "us" baby; a part of both of us that was planned for together, wished for together, experienced every part of together.

"I'm positive," I catch her lips with mine. "I need a baby with you to make my life complete. Then all my wishes will have come true."

Ivy

Not long ago, I wished on a shooting star in a dark parking lot with a man that captured my heart and soul the moment our eyes met.

I wished for one thing: for all *his* dreams to come true.

And within that, all mine came true, too.

Thank you for reading Lukas! I hope you enjoyed it and continue to read the rest of the series. They are all standalones, with no cliffhangers.

Don't miss Torn, which is book one in my bestselling spin off series. You'll find out a lot about Asher in Torn!

Join my Facebook reader group! Its a fun, safe, drama-free, female-only group where I interact with readers daily:

Join the Carian Cole Groupies

SNEAK PEEK OF TALON

ASHES & EMBERS BOOK 4

TALON - CHAPTER ONE

TALON

"Harder...harder..." she moans, arching up beneath me, her fake nails digging into my ass. Her eyes close and her mouth falls open as I pump into her harder. She has so much makeup on, she looks like she face-planted into a bag of Skittles.

"Oh, my God...yes...deeper..." she begs, but I can't go harder or deeper, even with my notorious eleven inches. I've maxed out my level of hardness and depth.

"Faster..." she pants just as I pull out and roll away from her, snapping the condom off before tossing it carelessly onto the faded carpet.

"What the hell? Why did you stop?" She bolts up to glare at me. "I wasn't done."

Yawning, I cross my arms under my head and close my eyes. "Well, I was." Seriously, I can't get past her face now. I just can't fuck Skittle-face.

"You didn't even get off."

I don't bother to open my eyes. "Did you hear me saying

wetter? Tighter? No. It was as deep and hard as it was gonna get. And then your face happened. Sorry."

I open an eye when I hear her rummaging around the cheap motel room for her clothes. "You're an asshole! It's just dirty talk. I didn't actually mean it."

Great, a rainbow-faced, lying groupie. Just what I wanted. *Not*. She looked much hotter backstage. Now…not so much.

"It doesn't work for me." I shrug casually.

She yanks her clothes on in a huff, grabs her bag and high-heeled leather boots, but she doesn't bother to put them on as she storms toward the door barefoot.

"Hey…" I say, stopping her. "Do you wanna grab a bite to eat, maybe?"

"Seriously? No. I came here for sex, not dinner. Some fucking cock star you are! Loser!" She slams the door so hard the ugly painting above the bed tilts. Damn. I was hoping it would fall off the wall and land on my head, putting me out of my misery.

No such luck.

Rolling over, I close my eyes, eager to sleep off the dull ache in my head from partying after the concert earlier. However, the bed smells strange and the sheets are rough and scratchy against my skin. Somehow, I've turned into a person who can only sleep on Egyptian cotton sheets. I'm not sure if that makes me a spoiled brat or just a guy who appreciates the finer things money can buy.

Since I won't be getting any sleep in this dump, I get dressed, tie my long hair back, grab my wallet, cell, and smokes, while laughing at the irony of it all. When I was younger, I believed if I ever reached famous rock-star status I would be as happy as a pig in shit. But here I am, goal achieved, and the only thing that really makes me happy is clean, soft sheets that smell like lavender. And to top it off, my years of sexual escapades have earned me the hashtag of #Cockstar on social media. I kind of wish my guitar-playing skills were more notable than my dick skills.

Pitiful.

ACKNOWLEDGMENTS

TO EVERYONE who has read my books, *Thank You!* You have helped my dreams come true!

I am continually overwhelmed and blown away with the amount of support I have received by so many people. It would be impossible to thank you all individually, but please know that you are all wonderful and I appreciate every single one of you so much—more than words could ever say. So just know that if you've talked to me, pimped me, beta read for me, helped me, attended a take over, or just left me a fun message or picture—I love you and you have made a huge difference in my life.

And, of course, thank you Eddie for loving me and giving me the perfect writing place of my dreams. I appreciate you more and more every day. xo

ALSO BY CARIAN COLE

ASHES & EMBERS ROCK STAR ROMANCE SERIES:

Storm - Ashes & Embers book 1

Vandal - Ashes & Embers book 2

Lukas - Ashes & Embers book 3

Talon - Ashes & Embers book 4

Loving Storm (sequel) - Ashes & Embers book 5

ALL TORN UP SERIES (Ashes & Embers Spin Off Series, Contemporary Romance):

Torn - All Torn Up book 1

Tied - All Torn Up book 2

STANDALONE BOOKS:

No Tomorrow

ABOUT THE AUTHOR

Carian Cole has a passion for the bad boys, those covered in tattoos, sexy smirks, ripped jeans, fast cars, motorcycles and of course, the sweet girls who try to tame them and win their hearts.

Born and raised a Jersey girl, Carian now resides in beautiful New Hampshire with her husband and their multitude of furry pets. She spends most of her time writing, reading, and vacuuming.

Stalk me!
www.cariancolewrites.com
carrie@cariancole.com

CPSIA information can be obtained
at www.ICGtesting.com
Printed in the USA
FSHW012114140819
61070FS